ALL THOSE WHO WANDER

ALL THOSE WHO WANDER

A NOVEL

Kiran Manral

AMARYLLIS

An imprint of Manjul Publishing House Pvt. Ltd.
•C-16, Sector 3, Noida, Uttar Pradesh 201301 – India
Website: www.manjulindia.com
Registered Office:
•10, Nishat Colony, Bhopal 462 003 – India

All Those Who Wander by Kiran Manral

This edition first published in India in 2023

ISBN 978-93-5543-256-8

Cover design: Drawater by Mishta Roy
Cover image: Caju Gomes from Unsplash

Printed and bound in India by Manipal Technologies Limited, Manipal

'Not all those who wander are lost.'

J. R. R. Tolkien

Contents

1	The Open Window	1
2	On the Other Side	21
3	Good Morning. Or Good Night.	51
4	The Heavens Tipped Over	62
5	The New Girl	72
6	The Clouds Fell Down	82
7	Drowned In	98
8	Swimming in the Tears of a Cloud	106
9	When It All Drained Away	116
10	Because Tomorrow is Here and Yesterday Too	124
11	Recalibrating Oneself and One's Selves	134
12	Jumping Across the Pond	141
13	The Escape Back to the Present	155
14	Where Worlds Collide and Recoil	166
15	If It Were Only Just a Dream	174
16	They Waited, Ghosts of the Past	184

17 And the Mirror Cracked 195
18 To Let Go, To Never Return 207
19 What Lay Beyond 223
20 Who Are You, Ana? 230
21 Where Do You Go To (My Lovely)? 248
22 And in the Beginning is the End 257

Acknowledgements 271

1

The Open Window

'The past beats inside me like a second heart.'

—John Banville, *The Sea*

A THUNDERCLAP RENT THE SKY THE SAME TIME THE PYRE WAS lit on the television. It was not the time the actual pyre was lit, mind you. The pyre had already been lit earlier, cremation done, mourners dispersed. This was a re-telecast. Not everyone would remember the unseasonable thunderclap in the city that night or the sudden drizzle that followed. It happened in the place and time where Nayna lived, this Nayna, the one watching this Dyanora television with its rabbit-eared antenna, in this city, in this country, in this time, in this universe. Outside the window the sky flickered for the briefest moment, like a portal to another dimension had been peeled open roughly and then closed again. Not lightning, that was of this earth. The flickering came from something far beyond it. This Nayna, here, did not notice it. She was glued to the television screen, which also flickered at that exact same moment, a flickering that brought for a moment the buzz of static to the screen.

The prime minister of the country had been assassinated, shot dead by her personal bodyguards while walking across from her home to her office, where a television channel was waiting to interview her. She had around thirty bullets shot at her point blank. A pogrom had swept through the country, a pogrom so horrific that decades later the victims would find no closure. The country was now in state mourning. Maa and Pappa had exchanged cross words again this morning, and it had ended with Pappa saying he did not want to stay home with such a daayan and stomping out of the house. He had slammed the door with such force that the television went grainy and Nayna had to get up to adjust the antenna.

'Are you really a daayan?' Nayna asked. Maa smacked her across the face in reply. It stung. Maa did that often, and was sometimes contrite. This time she wasn't, not even when the blood pooled in Nayna's cheek and turned blue-black after a while, creating a Rorschach blot all its own.

'He thinks I'm a daayan. I should really drink his blood.' She had laughed in that strange way she sometimes did, with her laughter reaching a high-pitched crescendo that made the peeling, faded walls ring. It frightened Nayna when Maa laughed like this. Perhaps Pappa was right, Maa really was a daayan. But then she would be her loving Maa again, the moment would pass, like all such uncomfortable moments did, trembling beneath the veil of conscious acknowledgement, buried within the subconscious only to resurrect itself, years later, when Nayna would seek Maa out in the distant recesses of her memories. Nayna didn't realise that yet. It upset Nayna to think of her mother drinking up her father's blood in quite the nonchalant manner she would drink a glass of Rooh Afza or Rasna. What upset Nayna more was that she wouldn't quite put it past Maa to do so. Pappa would notice the bruise on her cheek in the evening and not comment on it. The bruise would be soothed by a thin layer of Boroline. Nayna had learnt to apply it immediately so it healed quickly. Pappa had taught her that when the slapping and hitting became a regular occurrence, but had never told Maa off for hitting Nayna. Parents hit children. Nayna swore to herself she would never *ever* hit her child when she had one.

Outside, unseasonal droplets began pitter-pattering on the tin cover that shaded their balcony from the sun. There was no sun right now, of course, only the unseen light of the night sky and dead stars sending them love from billions of years ago. Light that leaked from behind the clouds, edging them with the orange blue of the distant nebulas they came from. Something or someone had opened the portal that enclosed this earth, and passed into this time, this place, in that brief flickering that no one noticed.

'It's raining, Maa.'

'An omen,' Maa grumbled. 'Why else would there be thunder in November?'

'Just a drizzle, Maa,' Nayna replied.

'No, it is an omen. She sent in the army into a place of worship.'

'It was sunny when they lit the pyre,' Nayna replied with the practicality of youth that knew all the answers. The gun carriage bearing the assassinated prime minister's body was escorted by a guard of 175 soldiers over a three-and-a-half hour journey from Teen Murti Bhavan to the banks of the Yamuna, where her older son lit the pyre. Her younger son had died a few years ago in a plane crash. They had said she'd been curiously dry-eyed at the funeral. Four days of violence had preceded this cremation. Though Nayna was vaguely aware of some unrest, the real horror of what had happened would unfold later, much later, for decades later the dead and the living would cry out for justice and reparation.

The day it happened, there had been nothing on the television or radio until the night. Old Bosco uncle, retired professor of philosophy, University of Mumbai, on the ground floor of B wing, heard the news on the BBC radio and had been yelling it throughout the day from his balcony at whoever was passing by. He was half crack everyone said, no one paid him much heed. He could rightfully be called 'Doctor', he told Nayna once. He was a Ph.D., and Nayna had laughed at him saying, only those who studied medicine were doctors and a Ph.D. meant a phone directory. He had laughed back and nodded, saying his Ph.D. was not worth the paper it was printed on, and wouldn't even fetch him anything in *raddi* money.

He stopped yelling about the prime minister being shot when his grandson gently escorted him back into the house with the promise of tea with bread and strawberry jam. They realised he had been right when Salma Sultan announced the death of the prime minister on the 9 pm Doordarshan news on October 31, with her characteristic gravitas and immaculate diction. Nayna couldn't remember whether the iconic newsreader had her trademark rose tucked behind her ear the night she read out the news. Perhaps she had not. It would have been disrespectful, and Salma Sultan was always so proper, so graceful, so elegant. Maa could have been a newsreader. She was beautiful, with her limpid grey eyes, strong brows, lips like a bow and an oval face framed by thick, wavy, black hair, hair up in a bun or down her hips in a long plait. Nayna had inherited all of her, her grey eyes, milky skin, hair black as night. Maa spoke beautifully, liltingly, correctly, softly. But when Pappa was around, her voice grew and grew.

Banshees! Should she ask Maa if she was a banshee and if banshee was different from daayan. Banshees could be Irish daayans, Celtic daayans. Maa could be an Indian banshee, she had the unearthly beauty that daayans were supposed to have. Nayna had read that some banshees wailed in such a high pitch they shattered glass. Maa flung glass and cup, plate and pan. Pappa swept the shards.

It was the first cremation Nayna ever saw on television. Death was beautiful, the final pause to whatever restlessness life demanded of a person. There was a stilled beauty in the face of the deceased prime minister, her sternness so evident in life dissipated with death. Years later, there would be a human bomb that would take the life of the son lighting her pyre right now. Death followed, miasmal and fetid, waiting, biding its time.

Maa was now shelling peas. They plopped into the small bowl. She believed in omens, Nayna did not. In all the wisdom of her eight years she believed in coincidences. Omens gave Maa solace, but Nayna was neither wise enough to understand omens, nor old enough to need their solace. Maa finished shelling the peas and took the bowl into the kitchen. She was wearing a night dress that was affectionately termed 'nighty'—voluminous gowns with huge prints meant to camouflage the stains and discolorations incurred in the course of daily domestic tasks.

The tinny voices on television droned on about the dignitaries present at the funeral, the grief of the nation enforced by a state mourning that would turn the national broadcaster into a cyclopean oracle broadcasting only mournful dirge-like religious songs through the week. Nayna quickly lost interest and turned back to the comic book she was reading. The image on the screen flickered and then it began snowing down the screen, flakes of static that shimmered, creating shadowy faces of evil doppelgangers waiting to smash through the screens and emerge crawling, intent on sucking unwary souls into their ghastly dimension. She closed her eyes for a moment, then looked at them without flinching. The images on the screen returned to normal.

Pappa always told her she had an overactive imagination. So did Maa. She didn't have an overactive imagination. She just saw things no one else did, and now she kept quiet about them. They didn't startle or scare her anymore. When she was younger, she assumed everyone else could see them too. One day when she was very young, she told her mother about the lady in blue who was waving at them from across the road, her head bent at an awkward angle. Her mother burst into hysterical sobs and took her to the nearest temple immediately. She gathered from the hushed conversation between her father and mother that night that a young lady in a blue salwar kameez had been knocked down by a speeding bus on the street a week ago. Her neck had been broken by the impact. Nayna hadn't known about it. When she saw the lady the next time and the time after that, and then again, she smiled and waved at her, stepping behind her mother to do so.

Nayna was an expert at adjusting the antenna, which basically meant she turned it all around until the image on the screen came back. Some days, it wouldn't clear up at all, especially on rainy days and they were resigned to watching the television through hissing static. The faces within came back most times she did this. At others, disembodied voices spoke with shimmering otherworldly bodies. Once in a while, the channel went off completely, and the screen was a world where nothing existed and everything did. It was perhaps Nayna's earliest introduction to the thrumming Greyness. She knew what to expect when she eventually went there.

Nayna had passed the Doordarshan tower at Worli often enough to know that television channels came out of its tip, their city's own miniature version of the Eiffel Tower—tall, unornamental and triangular, a matter-of-fact pylon of steel and stairways with no concession or pretension to being decorative, lancing the flat city landscape. She wondered who climbed the Doordarshan tower to keep it in working order, how the city might look spread out beneath it, especially at night, with all the lights twinkling from Colaba's edge to the mouth of the river at Mahim that cut off the island from the mainland, and beyond, far beyond, in the distant suburbs where Nayna lived with her parents and the ghosts of her unborn siblings.

Maa insisted she listen to the English and Hindi news every day. 'It will help you with your diction. Sit still for half an hour and just listen to how they speak, how they modulate their voices and enunciate certain words.' Maa was acutely conscious of the crassness of Bambaiya Hindi, and worried that Nayna would pick up this unsavoury variant… one that was far removed from the crisp perfection of the language spoken in the genteel town in North India she was born and bred in. And so Nayna sat still and listened to the news, but her mind wandered and so did her eyes, which went unbidden to the window of A-302 across the divide of the quadrangle between the staff quarters that masqueraded as a play area. The drizzle had stopped. The window, as always, was closed and unlit in a building, where come evening, all other windows were lit up by tube lights or the gold glow of bulbs. No one lived in that house. No one had for years. Until recently.

At first, it seemed like a light was switched on and off for the briefest second, a blue-white flame licked the glass panes. The house shuddered with the impact, wrenching itself back to absolute darkness. The window remained closed. No other lights were switched on in the room it shuttered, no movement denoted any form of life within, but Nayna knew. There always was someone who had entered the house when it crackled with incandescence and then went dark. She went to the balcony and began calmly unclipping clothes from the clothesline, regardless of the fact that all of them were not quite dry, and looked at the window opposite, willing it to open. It remained impassive. She picked the pile of clothes and turned to go into the house when, like a sudden gap-toothed smile in a face, the window opened wide. Ana was back, and waving. Nayna waved back. No one in the colony, all those homes teeming with lives, noticed them waving at each other.

She had first noticed Ana standing at that dark window many months ago. Of course, she didn't know her name back then. It was January perhaps. The early morning was still grey and Nayna had been dawdling in the balcony, waiting for Crow to come for his biscuit. It was Parle-G biscuits that Crow liked; it scoffed at offers of other biscuits, even the cream ones. Cream biscuits were precious, they were treats for when she had been good or scored well in class tests. But this was a nice crow; Maa believed it was her late father slipping through a gap between the living world and the dead to have conversations with his favourite grandchild. Pappa thought perhaps the crow could be his mother, a sour-faced harridan. When she died, all the mourners were dry-eyed.

Crow was just Crow to Nayna, not her deceased maternal grandfather or paternal grandmother. 'A raven,' as Crow had never tired of correcting her, most offended at being called a crow. 'From the Corvid family. Crows are the lesser cousins. I'm a raven,' he repeated, looking away in a huff, then looking back, settling a single beady eye on her, tilting his head at an angle. 'Have you not read your Poe, child?'

She'd picked up a copy of Edgar Allen Poe from the school library. Her raven wasn't scary like the raven in Poe, she concluded. Perhaps he was just a posh crow.

He did look like what a raven was supposed to look like though. Not for him the mottled mix of charcoal and black. Much as the night that dropped like a stone over the planet during winter, untempered by even a sliver of moonlight, he was dark and wide-winged. Eyes chipped marbles, beak sharp as a knife.

'Someone's come across a great distance to meet you,' Crow told her that morning, delicately flicking biscuit crumbs off his beak with a wing.

'To meet me? Who? Where?'

Crow inclined his head graciously to the flat opposite. It was rare that someone came to meet her. People generally came to meet her father or her mother. She was incidental.

'She will meet you in the evening perhaps when you go down to the park, after you finish playing. Wait for her.'

She. Her. Nayna peered at the flat opposite. Perhaps a family had moved in, and there was a young girl there who also wanted a best friend. She didn't have a best friend, the slot lying vacant since Sheeba Nambiar's father was transferred back to their native town of Kottayam. The window had been closed every single day she had stood in the balcony and looked across the quadrangle, at the building opposite, peering into homes, making up stories to amuse herself about the lives being led by the denizens within.

'That damned crow,' her mother had muttered as she hastily got tiffin and lunch boxes ready for her husband and daughter, a chore done with no enthusiasm and minimal effort.

'He's not a crow, he's a raven.'

'Whatever it is, don't waste your time, you have to get ready for school.'

She was a scolding mother. 'That's just how she is,' Crow had told her once when she'd told him about how she felt unloved by her mother. 'Some are hugging mothers and some are scolding mothers as a wise person once said.'

Nayna envied other children whose mothers hugged them unabashedly and grabbed their hands when they crossed the road. Her mother hated touching and being touched. Nayna could never quite understand why she was so prickly. When she was in a rare good mood, Nayna would rest her head on her mother's lap and Maa would stroke her hair distractedly for a moment or two before pushing her off roughly. Nayna lived off those few moments of tenderness for months.

Right now the raven was telling her that someone in the flat opposite had come from really far away to meet Nayna. His voice, as always, was heavy and ponderous, each word pronounced right. To an ear that could not understand him, he was cawing a cacophony.

'She has something to tell you.'

'What?'

'Speak full sentences, child. She knows you from a long time ago.'

'How long ago?'

'Very many long times ago,' the raven replied, looking her in the eye with his beady one. 'And from many long times ahead too.'

Sometimes Crow didn't make sense, and it didn't make sense to argue with him. She would just nod. That seemed to suffice. He inclined his head, as he normally did when he was leaving. She inclined hers in return.

'When will you be back, Crow?'

'Sooner or later,' he replied. He didn't object to being called Crow now. Crow was easier than Raven, and frankly it didn't matter. In the realms he flew to, beyond the layers of what Nayna understood as the world, he was called something completely different, a confluence of consonants that would be far beyond Nayna's limited human vocal abilities.

Crow opened his wings, wings so broad they blotted out the sky, did a few trial flaps and then flew away, swiftly merging into the soot of the still escaping night. Nayna waited, looking at the window opposite. Nothing. More nothing. Then a sharp flash of light coloured the shut home an iridescent blue and white, making the windows shudder, and then it was gone. The sun rose, casting feeble pale pink rays through the smog of the city before falling on the window, which was now suddenly flung open. A woman stuck her head out from the darkness within, gasping for breath. She stood, uncertain, framed by wood and light, ethereal and fragile, the wind blowing in from the distant sea ruffling her hair like an uncertain lover, anxious about taking liberties not yet permitted. She lifted her head and looked directly across the quadrangle to the flat above. Directly at Nayna.

'Look, Maa,' Nayna had called. 'There's someone in the empty flat opposite.'

Maa looked out from where she was at the dining table, with cursory curiosity. She couldn't see anyone, anything, and had no inclination to come out into the balcony to peer closer.

'Go, get ready or you'll be late for school again. Where is your father, he's been in the toilet for over an hour. Probably constipated again. Tight-fisted even with his shit.'

Nayna didn't move, she was too busy watching the woman standing in the window opposite. She smiled and raised a hesitant hand in greeting. The lady smiled back just as the first rays of the morning sun fell on her face, lighting her up in a golden blaze.

She was beautiful, Nayna could make that out despite the distance separating the two wings. A little taller than Nayna's mother, which made her taller than average. She stood straight at the window. It was an assertiveness that Nayna was not accustomed to in the women around her. Her shoulders did not hunch with the unspoken indoctrination that most women of the previous generation had received and internalised, that of not occupying space, of not being visible. She was wearing what seemed like a black vest. No women Nayna knew wore vests, and definitely not black vests. In Nayna's world, men wore white vests under shirts to office and back home when the office shirts were put into the washing, the shoes and socks taken off, the carapace of what made them working men now discarded, the mantle of the householder pulled on. At home, vests were worn over brightly patterned lungis or blue striped shorts that went down to their knees, bestowing upon those who wore them the curious indignity of chicken legs and paunchy torsos. The women wore sarees, prized Garden Vareli printed georgettes for outings, regular nylon and cotton sarees bought at the market for daily wear and a few precious trousseau silks for weddings, family events and temple visits. At night though, all the aunties in the society wore nightgowns with puffed sleeves and floral prints with colours so garish, they could cause retinal damage. They topped these with dupattas for added modesty and saree petticoats beneath when they went down to the gate or the park to drag recalcitrant offspring back home after the sun had set. None of them wore only a vest over trousers. Nayna was fascinated.

'Crow told me someone had come to meet me from very far away, someone who knows me,' she told her mother.

'You and your crow, both full mad,' her mother replied, hassled by the morning chores, pushing Nayna into the bathroom.

By the evening though, after a long day at school, Nayna had forgotten all about the lady at the window. The sun went down early these days and by five-thirty p.m. dusk had checked in.

Her friends had gone up to their flats as the lights came on. Nayna's home was still dark, as Maa had gone to pick up some vegetables and groceries. She had been alone on the swing, listening to the long creak the swing emitted at each move, when the lady from A-302 walked straight to the park and settled herself on a bench opposite the swings, looking at Nayna with a faint smile on her face. She was wearing the same black vest and loose pyjamas from the morning. Her hair was now in a careless top knot with tendrils tumbling down from where they would not be contained. She had wrapped what seemed like a dupatta around her upper half, a dupatta that Nayna had seen earlier hanging on Mhatre Kaku's clothesline. She was strangely familiar in a way film actresses seem familiar, the known face of someone you have never met in the flesh before, but know intimately, having seen up close countless times.

'Hello, Nayna,' she had said. 'I'm Nayna.'

'Wow,' replied Nayna. 'We have the same name!'

'No one ever calls me Nayna though, except my mother, and she's dead. Call me Ana. That's what everyone calls me now.'

'Okay, Ana,' Nayna had replied, confused about whether she should add an 'Aunty', but Ana was quite different from the ladies who commanded that sobriquet. At eight, everyone above the age of twenty was automatically fast-tracked to being an aunty or an uncle, and it was considered an impudence to not address anyone by this tacked-on relationship.

'How do you know my name? And why did Crow tell me you had come to meet me from far away? And where did you come from? Will you live here now?'

Ana laughed. 'So many questions.'

It became a regular occurrence, these conversations on the bench with the lady from A-302 after all the other children had gone home after play, conversations no one noticed or remarked upon, strangely enough. The area where the swings were lay between two blocks at an awkward angle, so that no one could quite see the benches from their windows. Nor who was sitting on those benches.

Ana would come and go over the next few months. She would come one random day and disappear the next. Sometimes she would stay for a couple of days and chat with Nayna in the park, after the other kids had run off home. She was always dressed in the strangest of clothes: a loose dress with only straps holding it up, a pair of shorts with a vest, a t-shirt that fell to her knees. It was like nothing anyone Nayna knew wore at home. Ana was nothing like anyone Nayna knew. She knew everything about Nayna's home and parents, she paid attention when Nayna spoke. No grown-up ever did, caught up as they were with the busyness and importance of being grown-up.

Now, after waiting a bit for Ana to come to the window, Nayna went back to the enticement of the television set where a studied male voice droned out the news in Hindi. His voice stopped, and the crisply dulcet tones of Salma Sultan's voice filled the little room. She was pretty, Salma Sultan, like a film star. When she grew up, Nayna told herself, she would cut her hair in exactly the same style. Parveen Babi bangs on either side of her forehead, with a rose tucked behind her ear, and floral print chiffon sarees gracefully wrapped around her shoulders, a pearl necklace and a lipstick bright red or pink. Her hair though was too unruly to behave like Salma Sultan's did. Her hair was like she was. Not well-behaved. In a world that defined women by how they confined their hair, she often wondered why Maa let her and her hair run wild.

Her paternal grandmother had been horrified seeing Nayna running out of home to play, her hair untied, on one of her occasional visits to Bombay during the winter months when the chill of the North acted on her arthritis.

'Mandira,' she had called out to her daughter-in-law in a tone laden with reproach. 'No girl from a decent home goes out with her hair open. But then, what will the girl learn when you yourself don't keep your hair tied up at all times?'

Her mother said nothing in reply but yanked Nayna's hair harder than usual while combing it into two plaits for school the next morning. And in the evening, she sat Nayna down in front of her grandmother and slowly, deliberately untied Nayna's hair from the red ribbons. Nayna's grandmother had pursed her lips disapprovingly and said nothing.

As Nayna's hair grew longer and longer, spilling to her waist, all her mother would do was pull on a rubber band to hold it off her face, except when she went to school because school strictly insisted on two plaits tied with red ribbons and not rubber bands. Her mother had glorious hair too, it went down to her hips and when she combed it out after washing it, it was a black cloud that followed her from room to room as she moved, before she tired of it and rolled it into the careless bun at the nape of her neck, from which it all escaped despite the pins.

Maa was calling her.

'Naynaaaa.' The vowel at the end of the name echoing in the still air, her voice dripping with weariness and an exhaustion that went beyond the bodily, sunk from the bone into the soul. 'Haven't you brought the clothes in yet?'

'Bringing, Maa,' she replied, stretching out her little hands with their tiny fingers to the line fixed outside the ledge where wire and wood nailed to the frame held the clothes hung out to dry.

There was one last piece of clothing outside the window and her hand couldn't quite reach it, so she stood on her toes and leaned out at a slight angle to extend her reach and it was then that she saw her. There she was, Ana, at the window. She raised a hand and waved at Nayna. Nayna waved back.

'Maa,' she yelled. 'Ana is back.'

Her mother yelled back from the kitchen, 'Let her be back, just get the clothes inside before they get wet.'

Nayna quickly unclipped the clothes from the line and brought them in, dumping them on the bed. She then folded those that were dry as neatly as she could manage, spreading the ones not quite dry on the bed and on the side table. Her pink and white checked cotton dress that she wore every other day down to play even though it was now above her knees with gaps where the buttons met as her torso lengthened and broadened, her mother's faded petticoat and nightgown, its print now an amorphous sludge of muted colours, one of her father's white office shirts, made a peculiar blue white with the whitening agent her mother used liberally in the mistaken assumption that it made the shirts look cleaner, its collar shiny and threadbare with wear. She would need to take these clothes to the dhobi at the end of the lane the next day after she returned from school. She helped her mother, she did, she was a good girl. Her mother told her that often, that she was a good girl. Her father told her that too, so did the nuns at school and her teachers. She'd always been a good girl. She wondered what made someone a bad girl.

Was Ana a bad girl, she wondered? She was different definitely, totally different from all the women in the complex. She dressed like she didn't care who was looking at her. Most people seemed to look through her, like she didn't exist. Ana came and went as she pleased. She didn't speak to anyone else in the complex, and no one spoke to her. People walked past her without acknowledging her, and she acknowledged no one. Nayna was the only one she smiled at, spoke with. Ana didn't have a mother, a father, a husband or children – she was alone. Women weren't supposed to live alone, even Nayna knew that at eight. Women were supposed to be attached to families, who were the *suraksha kavach* that kept women protected from the predators of the world. The fathers, the brothers, the husbands, the sons, they were all the outer ring that kept the women within, away from the claws of all that sought to pillage them given half a chance. Ana was attached to nothing and no one. It made her interesting. She sparkled like she was hiding fairy lights beneath her clothes. She sought Nayna out in the park, chatted with her about things no one asked Nayna about, things that were pipe dreams in her head, the arguments her parents had, telling her to be kinder to her mother, asking her about the books she read, the pictures she painted. At times, Nayna did wonder how Ana knew about all these things, and was flattered that Ana found her interesting to chat with. Adults mostly treated kids as irritants and pests, to be either spoken down to or just about tolerated. It was lovely to find an adult who actually wanted to talk to her, a child. Their conversations were interesting. And she was pretty, Ana who came and went, with her liquid gold skin, shiny black hair that ran down in waves, and a laugh that bounced off the sky and earth, her voice husky with too many cigarettes.

The window had now gone dark, swallowing Ana up. Nayna turned to go back into the house. An owl flew past, hooting a casual greeting at her. She waved back.

It was a different world she lived in from the world of her mother. She saw people with shifting colours around them, animals and birds spoke to her, as did some trees; she could sometimes hear what people were thinking. Her mother thought she was making up things, but it was a real world to her, just not what it was to her mother. Or her father, or her grandmother, or her Pinky Bua, or her Lovely maasi, or Nandi maasi, or to Rajeev, Saachi, Bubli and Chamki, her cousins. She had learnt to keep her strange world to herself because it made her mother cry and her father would furrow his brow in worry and take her to Dr Shanbag, who would ask her many, many questions and then tell her father he should not worry, it was just the result of an overactive imagination, and that she would grow out of it. And her mother would berate her father for encouraging her strangeness by buying her all the children's books he could lay his hands on: fairy tales, exquisitely illustrated books with witches called Baba Yaga who lived in a house standing on chicken legs in a dense forest in the USSR, trolls and gnomes and cupboards that led to strange lands with white witches who created perpetual winter, yakshis who enchanted gullible men and led them to their doom, Joan of Arc who heard the voice of God and led her people into battle, women who didn't fit in and refused to do so, Nayna read them all and knew that no matter how strange and unbelievable their world was, she lived in a world that was even stranger. But she tried to fit in. A world she couldn't speak about to anyone, or they called her mad. Half crack. Children were cruel, they were quick to shame what they couldn't understand. She was old enough to know that survival meant camouflage and fitting into the other's understanding of what one should be. And she needed to be an ordinary girl, not one who saw sparkling lights around people, dead people asking her to convey messages to the ones they had left behind, and trees and animals that chatted with her.

Ana was the only one she could speak with about these things because, strangely enough, she knew. Nayna didn't know how she knew, but she knew and she was completely okay with it, because she saw them too she said.

The housing society, built decades ago, housing middle class respectable government officials, some living in the flats they had been allotted here, some having sublet them from those officially allocated to them, was to put it politely, decrepit. An incestuous cauldron of crumbling four-storey buildings hiding crumbling lives, fading hope and diminishing dreams. Everyone knew everyone, or knew someone who worked or had worked with the other, or had worked together at various points in their transferable careers. Transfers and promotions were the pins on which the charts of the lives were plotted. They came from all over India, from the small towns of Bihar, from the paras of Kolkata, the mofussil towns of the Gangetic plains, the earnest academic homes of South India, from wherever in India parents aspired to safe public sector jobs for their children, with assured promotions at regular intervals and the guaranteed pension and provident fund. Middle class lives with middle class ambitions that dared not aspire for more than what they assumed was within their grasp. Middle class homes where life became faded nightgowns, starched cotton sarees, shirt collars frayed with scrubbing, with an accepted open-door policy that allowed the children to rampage through each home in turn, like pack hounds from a boisterous hell, that respected no nap times or maternal headaches. Within these quarters, with the walls that needed a slick coat of paint and the windows rusting from the proximity to the sea, lives lived out for the few years they were posted there, or until a promotion elevated them to the next level of accommodation, one more bedroom with servant's quarters, or until death or retirement took them away to private residences built brick by brick back in ancestral towns.

Was Ana an airhostess, Nayna wondered. That would explain why she was so glamorous and smoked cigarettes, cigarettes she asked Nayna to get for her from the shop round the corner and laughed when she saw the pack. 'No gruesome tumours!' she had exclaimed. Nayna didn't have a clue what she meant and Ana didn't choose to elaborate. And then Ana had been gone the next day, only to return now, in the night, at a time when the country was dealing with the loss of a prime minister, and rivers of blood flowing in retribution. Not that Nayna worried about that, concerned only with whether they could go to the movies next Friday as they always did or if cinema halls too would be closed for a week to mourn the departed politician.

Nayna helped her mother set the table for dinner. It was frugal everyday fare. Boiled rice, not the basmati of the festive days, rotis, a pale yellow dal tempered by jeera, just about redeemed from being turmeric water, okra, potatoes and onions, all made palatable with liberal helpings of the mango pickle that her mother made in early mango season, when raw mangoes flooded the market, after days of chopping, drying in the sun, adding oil and spices, and bottling in the white and brown ceramic pickle jars every household possessed. Pickle-making was a chest-thumping exercise of sorts among the women of the colony, both the ones who were working and the homemakers. Each set to outdo the other in the number of kilos of raw mangoes they had pickled. Jars of camaraderie had gone out to the homes of those who hadn't been able to make their own pickles, a favour that would eventually be repaid with a bowl of kheer or payasam making its way back in gratitude. This is how communities knit themselves together, through food, through taste, through giving. Nayna loved pickle, she could scoop it out with her finger from the jar much to her mother's annoyance and eat it without the need for rice or dal to soften the sour. They waited for a bit for her father, and when it was 9.45 p.m., her mother stated they would eat without him; perhaps he'd got stuck with something urgent in office. He was a manager, he had important responsibilities. And even if he hadn't, her mother had learnt that waiting for her father was a game of unpredictability and that it made sense to eat when one was hungry.

They ate their dinner staring unblinkingly at the television, through the English news, no word voiced between them. When they were done, Nayna helped clear up and packed her school bag and put out her uniform for the next morning. She looked outside the window; a fruit bat flew past making those strange clicking sounds.

'Ana is waiting for you.'

Nayna's eyes widened, but before she could ask why, the bat had flown off with languid smooth flaps of its wings. The next morning, she would be packed off to school by her father, and her mother would be busy in the kitchen.

Perhaps Ana was really her new best friend. She always smiled at her, and asked her about herself. Not any of the other kids, mind you. Not even Kamakshi, tall and strong and the alpha female of the pack, who had divided them all into teams and decided who was a kachcha limbo and had unhesitatingly put Nayna into the kachcha limbo squad with kids years younger than she was. Ana didn't speak with any of the other children or the adults. As her mother cleared the table and changed into her cotton nightgown, creaming her face with Afghan Snow and the feeble hope of a complexion unwrinkled by life's insidiousness, Nayna settled into her bed in the living room, divan by day, child's bed by night, thinking about Ana. Ana was different. She was ethereal, beautiful, unhardened by the causticity of the daily grind. When she grew up, Nayna decided, she would be like Ana, she of the pensive expression, who came and went as she pleased, her hair a black ocean flowing down her back. Ana of the smile so very familiar and yet so distant. She would go to her house tomorrow, she decided, and she would ask Ana what made her so sad.

2

On the Other Side

'Nothing is ever really lost to us as long as we remember it.'

—Lucy Maud Montgomery, *The Story Girl*

'I AM ANA. I AM THIRTY-TWO YEARS OLD. I LIVE IN MUMBAI. The year is 2008.'

'I am Ana. I am forty years old. I live in Mumbai. The year is 2016.'

'I am Ana. I am twenty-eight years old. I live in Mumbai. The year in 2020.'

'I am Ana. I don't know how old I am. I don't know what year this is.'

I stopped. I was spat out. The mirror paused. I turned around, looked at myself now reflected within, the surface calm, none of the churning that had reached out and sucked me in. I was deposited in front of the basin, exactly where I had been when I had been sucked in. Was it a moment ago, a day ago, a week ago, a month ago? I did not know yet. I would figure out lost time or time gained soon enough.

When was I? Where was I? Who was I?

These were questions I was never quite sure of the answers to, they changed each time I crossed. The surface would ripple again, soon enough, I knew not when. The reflection looking back at me was the same as it was in the then, in the now, in the there; my hair a tangled mess, my face much the same from when I'd last seen myself in the here, the only addition on my person a dupatta I had pinched from an unguarded clothesline. I had been flung across the multiverses wearing just the thin black vest and faded old pyjamas I had on. If I could predict when it would happen, I would ensure my feet were shod and my clothes were unremarkable enough to allow me to step out in times that were not now, not then. All of me, tissue, sinew, organ, neuron, cell, atoms compressed to a pinpoint and flung across the chasm of space time. Deposited somewhere, elsewhere, I knew not where, I did not know how. I travelled to meet us. All of us. I didn't understand it yet. Not me, not us. We were still trying to wrap our heads around what this was, what this meant, how it began and how it would end, if at all it would ever end. I didn't know. We didn't know. All I knew was this was my penance. This was my reparation.

So here are the facts as I understand them. I am Ana. I am Nayna. We are all Ana. We are all Nayna. It took some getting used to thinking of oneself in the plural. But for now, I still thought of myselves, think of myself, in the singular. It was easier. I was me. I am me. We are us. We are ghosts and memories, hopes and dreams, walking parallel interloped paths, we converge, we diverge, we intersect, we collide, sometimes we fuse.

'Here you are again,' she had said, the furthest ahead of the us I had visited, the first time I had been caught and thrown across what I knew now to be the abyss of space time. Loaves of space time, sliced by travellers like me, flinging ourselves across infinity in the span of a thought, unable to control where we went or why we went where we did. We were energy and matter, frequency and vibration. I didn't understand how I did it, but I knew how to in the way I knew how to breathe, how to walk, that my heart beat within my chest, and my body functioned every single moment. I knew that I could move beyond this time, this space, this moment. I also knew I couldn't choose how or when it would happen.

She was older than I was now. Much older than I was then. Younger than I could have been.

'You are chosen.'

'Who chose me?' I remember asking her.

She laughed. 'You chose yourself. You've come here before. And after.'

I didn't understand it then, I didn't understand it now. The first time I had been a child, five perhaps. I had been sticking my tongue out at my reflection in the tiny face mirror above the wash basin that had then frowned back at me and burst into tears. The mirror began swirling and sucked me into its vortex – the next moment I was in a strange room with no ceiling, no wall, no floor, much like the inside of an egg. The woman within saw me, gasped and reached her hand out to me and then in the blink of an eye I was back, throwing up everything in my stomach incessantly in the same small basin, running a high fever for the next couple of days. Dr Shanbag gave me a shot and a prescription, warning me sternly against eating ice golas from the street. I protested my innocence; I hadn't eaten anything from the street after school. I'd been washing my face when I fell into a room like an egg, with a lady sitting within, wearing flowing silver water. Maa said it was a dream. It was a dream, I told myself. I forgot all about it in the way one forgets things no one else pays attention to.

It was one of the many things that made me what I was, an abomination. These crossings, the animals I spoke with, or the dead but not gone, hungry for someone to notice them. When they learnt a young girl could see and hear them, they flocked to me from around the neighbourhood. The dead never scared me, the living did. As the years passed, I forgot it all, the conversations with animals, birds and the undead, falling into the mirror, and then Maa passed away. I was alone, I was twenty-eight. Then I was thirty-two. I had no life here and now. Nothing that would keep me here, tied to this place, to this time. Nothing, except Aman. And now I had started falling into mirrors all over again.

Four years had slipped through my fingers, my brain, my body. All I had to show for them was Aman. He was all I needed, my magnetic north, my polar south. The man I went away from and came back to, whom I waited for and didn't, in the here and now and the everywhere else. I was here for him. I was there for him. I had him here. I lost him there. Aman Bajwa, of the hawk eyes and the sharp nose, the one who gave me the silences I deserved, asked no questions and expected no answers. He gave me the buffer of sanity and drove me insane.

Aman. I breathed him, the feel of him, the smell of him. My beautiful man. His long pianist's fingers that worked on business plans but made music whenever they touched my body. His eyes molten copper, his voice with its smoker's rasp and languid ennui, concealing a mind sharper than a blade after the whetstone. Aman was the only person who deserved the truth about me. He was the one person I couldn't dare tell.

If there was love, it was him. If there was fear, it was the fear of losing him. Myself, I had already lost, scattered across the vacuum. I longed to go back to what I had been; it was simpler, so much simpler to live life out in a straight line, to be born, to grow up, to age, to die. That, we thought, was the natural progression of things. Little did we know what would happen after the singularity, or what we, in all our innocence then, called the singularity. I'd seen them, seen me, there where we couldn't imagine humans go. I had what they hadn't been able to figure out even though they had managed to extend human life indefinitely and transfer consciousness to an everlasting life, lived out in genetically extended lifespans, bodies that were synthetic models, carapaces one pulled on over one's consciousness, which could remain sentient through aeons when uploaded to the grid. The aeolian interstellar winds had buffeted us far and wide across spaces we could have never comprehended being able to build the capacity to travel to. Wormholes, warp speed, the stuff of the science fiction books and movies of my time, had become reality. We had terraformed outposts in our galaxy. Humankind had found immortality, and now they did not want it anymore. They longed for death. What was life anymore in these times, I wondered, but they were not my times to contemplate. I would return to my own time in a flash. Who was to tell, perhaps somewhere in some unknown corner, one of us, one of me, was doing the same, shuttling herself across galaxies and telling herself this was déjà vu.

There was no advance warning when it happened; all it needed was a reflective surface, any reflective surface, a sudden buzzing in my cranium, sparks and lights exploding in my eyeballs, a falling into, then a falling through, and a falling out, with the breath crushed out of me and then whooshed back into me as I unfolded every corner of me, finding myself disoriented in a dusty room. For the first five minutes, I threw up all that was in my stomach until I was throwing up pure bile because there was nothing left to disgorge. This was ten hangovers in one go and not even a single drink the previous night. I stood up, feeling like I had just been assembled by an apprentice carpenter. The air in the closed room was fetid, cobwebs tumbled down in veiled shanks from the ceiling, damp mouldy Rorschach patterns spread from door to ceiling, claiming what those who might have resided within may have fought. Faint breeze from a gap in the shutters, feeble light pushing through the glass, a heaviness I could not define. I staggered with great difficulty to the window, unbolted the rusty latch with a fair amount of difficulty and pushed it open, ignoring the protests of its disused hinges. I stuck my head outside and breathed in deeply the clear air. It smelt different. It smelt of yesterdays I had left behind.

The sky outside was the crispness of an early winter morning from memory, a pale pink creeping up from what I surmised would be the East. Or was it the West? In the worlds I went to, I could never be sure if things were what I was accustomed to. Pastel streaks from a distance would soon spread to the rest of the black purple vault and light it up into the familiarity of day. Where was I this time? And then it hit me. This is where I had been. I was where I had been all those years ago. I looked across to the building opposite, surrounded by many others the same size and shape, with the same box balconies and indifferent windows, painted the same stolid regulation cream and brown, faded in patches, ruined by damp and fungus at others. Clothes hung from lines in the box balconies to dry, some wire, some plastic cords, some at waist level on the outside, some on lines high up within the balconies, sheltered from the elements. Feeble attempts at amateur horticulture flourished in used Dalda tins and weathered pots. The familiar stench of the marshes hit my nose, invisible but predatory, the threat of drowned children's corpses within. I had been there, a run to the back of the compound, a broken gate, a dirt track down an overgrown, disused, no man's land, and beyond it, the nallah running out to the marshes. An unpaved lane from the main road also reached here, a dead end with a huge boulder as indicator and warning. This far and no further. Few paid heed. Some didn't and flung themselves in, only to have their bodies dragged out days later, when they floated up to the edge, bloated, green and decomposing, bursting with putrescent gases and grief.

The rundown gate nearby, the narrow lane out, a short walk to the main road and the bustling city in its everyday hurly-burly. This was familiar. This was home. Bombay of the mid 1980s, back when it was still Bombay. And there, standing in the balcony of the building right opposite, feeding a crow a biscuit was a young girl. Was me. Was Crow. Was us.

She was familiar, yet unfamiliar, a ghost from my memories. Would she recognise me, would she look at me and know who I was? Did I know who I was? Perhaps I was locked in one of those lucid dreams, unable to move, to escape the weight of the dream pinning me down, breathing into me, dragging me kicking and screaming into a world from which the only escape was waking back to life or drowning in one's subconscious, into an eternal greyness, from which the only awakening was death. But this was real, this was me and there, across the quadrangle, was I. Breath a lump in my throat, vomit on the floor, pain shooting through every limb, and the curious fatigue of many lifetimes lived and loves lost.

I blinked into the sunlight. This was a different sun from where I came, the light gentler, softer, further. My eyes were adjusting to the invasion of light after the infinite unending tunnel I had just fallen through when my reflection sucked me in. I waved unthinkingly. She waved back, a child's unwavering trust in the world. She ran back into the house, a call perhaps, from her mother, my mother, to get ready for school. I stepped back into the shadows: I could see no one, no one could see me. An hour later she clambered on to the back of her father's Bajaj scooter, my father's scooter, cream and with its chrome polished diligently every Sunday, wearing her starched and ironed blue pinafore, a too-white shirt, socks modestly rolled right up to her knees, hair in two tight plaits, a tan canvas school bag on her back.

The day passed, it was evening. Time moved as one wanted it to in the other side, there was no waiting. I went down the stairs, pulling a dupatta off a clothesline as I passed, wrapping myself in it. I needn't have. No one saw me, no one would see me, sitting on a bench in the corner of the garden. She was swinging listlessly, lost in her own thoughts, studying the sky, the stars; did she know yet that she could fall through to the others? All the other children had returned home when darkness fell. She was awaiting her Maa. My Maa. Our Maa. Maa had gone to the market and instructed her to wait until she returned, and so she waited. She was an obedient child. I had been an obedient child. I had waved to her, she walked across. We chatted, strangers to each other, strangers to oneselves.

That was the first time. Years ago, for me in my time. A few months in her time. It had been January in her time when I had first come through. It was almost winter again, winter meant nothing in this part of the country. Four years, five years, ten years, twelve years in my times. Years moved differently under different suns. This one was older than the one I knew. Time looped strangely, stretching and narrowing, as it hurled itself across expanses of infinity. What I knew now is that time wasn't linear, what we experienced of time in our regular life was just one strand of a complex tapestry. Perhaps just the diameter of the circle. Time, the entire circle, with solid, pulsing, multidimensional bubbles one within another, intersecting with the other, an ant on a line, walking all around it, the top, the bottom, front, back. Time, elastic and inelastic, snaking around itself, galloping ahead in a straight line. A cotton candy mesh of stickiness impossible to extricate oneself from. When one fell into it, one sank straight in, helpless, until time itself decided to spit you out again. It was unpredictable, uncontrollable, ductile, malleable and immutable. Time was an arrangement of moments boxed into each other, like those exquisite Russian dolls my father had once bought me from a handicraft exhibition in the grounds next to his office. I had thrown them away in anger because I had wanted a doll that would open and shut its long-lashed blue eyes, with long blonde hair, a doll that came with a battery-operated voice box that said 'Mama' when you pressed a button. Time was unfulfilled desires for dolls with blonde hair. Time was languid summer afternoons filled with mindless sucking on white and black striped boiled sweets that left the tongue a gruesome black, stealing pieces of raw mango from the sheets spread out on the terrace to dry out for pickling. Time was the summer breeze that blew in from the sea bearing microscopic motes from lives unknown across the ocean, loves and longings unknown to those who would breathe them in on this side of the water. Time was this moment and the moment running alongside it, and yet the other running towards both from the opposite side, all destined to collide with each other. Time was a mercury pool closing over a hand put into it and withdrawn, leaving no trace of ever having parted. Time was now. Time was forever. Time was never ever.

I could hear the thunderclouds smash against each other outside. Jagged bursts of lightning sparked up the world outside the slatted glass panes. I flickered in the reflection. I was this instant here. That instant there. This instant back here. A mere flickering to anyone looking on, static, a buffering of an image, a hologram that was still finding acuity. Days, weeks, months passed in that flickering instant. The flickering paused. I was here. I splashed water on my face, once, twice, thrice, then in an uncontrollable flurry that left me breathless and the bathroom floor slick with water and dissolved despair. It made my bare feet wet and muddy. I should remember to always have my feet shod when I looked into a mirror, I told myself. Travelling between universes barefoot was rather undignified.

Switching off the lone CFL bulb that had probably stayed on for the days and weeks I had been there, I opened the door and stepped into the bedroom. The room was as I had left it, undisturbed, tidy. No dust on any surface. Gauri-tai had been coming in diligently, little knowing I had not exited via the door but the mirror. I went into the living room to find the newspapers kept in a neat little pile on the side table after being picked up from the doormat. A small pile this time, the news they bore of no relevance now that the days had marched on. It had been a couple of weeks here, the newspapers told me, when I scanned the front pages. A morning to evening there passed in the blink of an eye. Gauri-tai knew that Baby, as she called me, having seen me grow from a terrified, gawky child into a terrified, gawky adult, came and went as she pleased. It was part of my job, she knew, to go away and to come back. The world continued outside my walls. A door shut with a bang somewhere, a child wailed, whether in pain or hunger I could not tell, a woman's voice was raised perhaps shushing the wailing child, a man grumbled, a pressure cooker whistled, cutting insistently through the sound of the pouring rain, somewhere else a television set was blaring a cricket match in progress. The sounds of everyday were the same in the here or the there. A car honked impatiently for the gate to be opened to let it in, the wind wailed as it made its way through the narrow slats that kept the outside from invading the stairway. I opened the window and looked outside at the here and now, this world, this city, this universe, this time that was mine. A solitary pigeon cooed from its perch on top of a window ledge, looking askance at me for intruding. Then it fluttered away after giving me a reproachful look. There were no sounds in the house, only the thudding of my heart and my blood whooshing through my veins. I lived alone, with only the ghosts whispering in my head. Those gone before me, the father, the mother, the dead sibling, the unborn children from my womb, the husband I had left, the lover I shared with his wife and other lovers.

My phone lay face down on the bedside table, probably from where I had been checking it before I drifted off to sleep that night. The last I remembered, I had woken up to visit the bathroom. Then I had been flung across, a blinking, a moment, a crossing.

I called him the moment my phone chimed back to life as the electricity poured into it. I was breaking a rule, calling him on the weekend. I had been gone weeks with no contact. The call went straight to his voice mail. 'Leave a message and I will call you back soon.' His voice was velvet and honey, smoke and kiss. It wrapped me up, strong and protective, keeping the world at bay. Every world at bay.

'I'm back,' I said to the emptiness of the voice mail box.

Monsoon had hit the city between my going and coming; the earth was still warily soaking in the rain after the scorcher of a summer, the air washed clear of all suspended particulate matter, wet, clean, green. It still smelt anticipatory, fed as we were on the romance of the season, lovemaking under the canopy of clouds, seduction under umbrellas, wetness around us, in us. The heaviness of damp earth, petrichor redolent with the infusion of childhood, hitting the limbic system like a sledgehammer, churning memory and emotion. The heaviness inducing an indefinable yearning in all those who lived under its canopy until a couple of days morphed the yearning into a fecund eternal dampness, the sickeningly sweet smell of rotting, uncleared garbage mingled with stagnant water, clotheslines strung across living rooms with ceiling fans on full speed, slush to be waded through in order to get anywhere. The walls would get damp patches, spheres of alien landscapes, ridged, serrated, flaking to the touch, microcosms within. Grey-green moss and fungus would bloom on the balcony walls, arranging themselves into ghostly faces screaming in silent agony at all those who gazed upon them, the unspoken terror they heralded still to come. Walls would bubble up and plaster would crack and sprinkle down from the ceilings, dropping on heads, into plates of food, into precious water hoarded in pans and vessels. On a Sunday morning, the committee members of the society would go officiously from home to home checking the damage caused by the leakage, planning for the waterproofing to be done post the monsoon. Then would come the men, tied by ropes to a flimsy bamboo scaffolding, crawling across the surface of the buildings, keeping out the damp for those who lived within, a respite that would last for barely a year or two, before nature seeped in, staking her dominion.

I could sense the grey day outside making an inglorious descent into dusk, the muted night noises slowly intertwining themselves with the intermittent rhythm of the occasional raindrops. The white noise it created was strangely comforting to my frayed nerves. Beyond, in the marshes beyond the lane, unseen, frogs sang their mating songs.

The silence in the house was gnawing. There were so many of me, I knew, out there, sprinkled across existence. Were any of them so utterly alone as I was at this moment?

I was an orphan, I had no siblings, no husband, no child. There was Lovely maasi, my fierce dragon of a maternal aunt, her wings soft mul dupattas, her fire breath fortified with her nightly peg of Scotch neat. She had graduated over the years from Old Monk to her own rather prestigious collection of single malts that no one else was allowed to touch, leave alone imbibe, not even her son Rajeev when he visited every few years from Canada, or us nieces, or Saachi, Lovely maasi's daughter, my little or not so little cousin who had made her way to Mumbai a few years ago, met and married the love of her life, and expanded in girth and generous giving love exactly like her mother had. She was all the blood and shared DNA I had in the city, the only one who checked on me and worried if I didn't reply. Friends WhatsApped and left it at that if I did not reply; I had pushed away all those who had tried to stay in touch, and now no one did. What was family but people connected to each other through tenuous bonds of double helix amino acids and love or hate, spliced over and over again to make humans a species. Saachi was my only connect to Maa here – bits of me connected to bits of her etherically.

I called her. The phone rang interminably before she answered, the laughter from a conversation put on hold echoing in the lilt of her voice.

'Ana?'

'Hey, Saachi.'

'Where the fuck have you been, bitch? Maa has been guilt-tripping me every night for not watching over you. That too after two Patiala pegs. I have holes in my eardrums from her yelling at me. I want to kill you.'

'I love you too.'

'I've been calling you for days. At first your phone rang and then it was unreachable. No replies to messages. What's with this disappearing act?' The reproach in her voice was love, concern and disappointment. I had always been a disappointment to my family, I didn't apologise for it. They had reacted by holding on to me tighter, afraid I would skitter away and never return.

'Had to go away.'

'At least reply to messages and emails. I finally called Aman. He told me you had gone for some Vipassana retreat. You didn't even mention it... I even came and sniffed outside your flat in case... you had...' The words hung unspoken in the air. In case I'd decided to do what first my father and then my mother had done before me, ending it all.

'I'd forgotten to carry my phone.'

'Seriously? What if there had been something urgent? What if Maa had fallen ill? What if I had fallen ill? What if there was an earthquake? What if there was a terror attack? What is the point of having a phone if you won't carry it along? They don't let you keep your phone with you, I hear.... so how do you actually survive without social media? Oh, I forgot, you don't do social media, you're one of those weird ones. It makes it even more difficult to keep track of you, do you realise? If you're posting a couple of times a day, I know you're fine. I'm going to open an Insta account for you.'

I cut her short. Saachi could talk in full pages and not pause to breathe if one allowed her.

'They don't allow you to keep a phone and, no, you're not going to open an Insta account for me.'

'Why do you do this Vipassana thing, constantly going away?'

'It calms me down. Keeps me sane.'

'Did you go alone for this Vipassana thing?'

'Yup... just needed some time to myself.'

'Aman called yesterday, you know. To check if I had heard from you. If you were back. I found that strange, given he'd told me that you were at Vipassana. When did you get back? Come home now, there's biryani on the stove, wine, vodka and rum, nothing fancy just Army canteen stuff. If you want something else, bring it along. If you want to eat something else, I'll order.'

'I just got back barely an hour ago....'

She would not take any excuses, I knew that from past experience. I also knew that I didn't want her to take my excuses. Her mom was like that, she would impose herself on you and insist you needed her around and then when she was around you realised that you did need her. And she would feed you until you burst. After all, what was feeding another person but a form of love? 'Just call an Uber and get yourself here. We'll drop you back home if it gets too late. Promise. Or just stay the night.'

Loneliness skittered menacingly through the house I sat in, icicles exploring niches and crevices with skeletal fingers, slithering through gaps between the window and the pane, prodding impudently, asking annoying questions like, was one really alone in multiverses containing an infinity of alternate selves. The wind had let up outside and the rain was an indifferent drizzle. Streetlamps shimmered, refracting through the rain and the frosted window panes. Owl was sitting on a branch of the mango tree touching the ledge of the window. It had been decades since he had visited. Crow hadn't come for decades too. I had almost forgotten all about them. Now I remembered. Seeing Nayna chatting with Crow when I'd first crossed, I remembered it all. And they had returned. I went to the window, part of me feeling a tad silly. Perhaps they had been all figments of my imagination, my childhood conversations with owls, bats, crows and dogs. Perhaps this was just an ordinary owl who had landed outside my window, and had nothing particular to say to me. But this was Owl, and he seemed to have something to say, I could tell by the way he cocked his head at an angle and was looking into the tiny room as I made my way to the window, twenty steps across. I had a long stride. It bobbed its head as I approached, the mock-spectacled markings on its face making it look as wise as they assumed the species was. Athena held an owl – she distributed wisdom, her owl was associated with wisdom. In India, the goddess of wealth, Lakshmi, was accompanied by an owl – she was Alakshmi, the older sister of Lakshmi, because wealth was always accompanied by strife and disharmony. In the city, they were rare. 'Ana,' Owl said, his voice gravelly with the weight of the aeons. 'Why are you going back?'

'I need to change what happened. Make amends for what I did. I need to find the one. The right one.'

'The choices are not yours to make now. You could create something else which could be even worse than what you're trying to make amends for.'

'What could be worse? And where have you been all these years?' I asked.

'In another time. You have grown up since I've been away.'

'I would, wouldn't I?'

He nodded.

His voice was deep and soothing, like Dadaji's voice, a distant memory from my childhood, before I had words to define it. It had a smooth, measured timbre to it, one that came from judicious thought before speech, as well as a daily intake of the finest Scotch on the rocks. One large peg before dinner without fail, at 8.45 sharp followed by dinner at nine. It was the Armed Forces background. How disappointed he had been that his son hadn't followed him into the military. Bad eyesight, spectacles, flat feet. He never mentioned it, but Pappa had always carried failing his father with him like an invisible lead jacket, the weight of which curved his shoulders and hunched his spine, made him mean-spirited and callow.

'I'd forgotten about you. And Crow. How did you find me? I moved houses since. I moved suburbs.'

'Your time is shorter and memory even shorter. I find you not by geography but by what animates you, all of you. By anima and animus.'

'What is anima? And why does it feel like we've had this conversation before?'

He chuckled. 'I've just come back from chatting with you in another time. And we've discussed anima and animus. Think hard and you'll remember, you've studied it in another time, later....'

'I was eight years old.'

'You are eight years old. We just chatted. Before I came here.'

'The soul. You find me through the soul.'

'The splintered soul. Jung, of course, had a variant on the theory. He gave it a masculine and a feminine. He left out those who don't choose to conform to the binary but that was purely him being a product of his times. But there was a kernel of truth in what he said. You know Jung, don't you? Never met him, I know, he was a little before your time. Just a couple of hundreds of years, I think, it's tough to keep track of your time. Clever chap, rather morose most times, always fainting and trying to get away from school when he was a kid, you would have got along well. You do know you are not a she everywhere you are. In some places you are a he. I wonder if you've met any of the male variants of you. A he.'

'How could I be a he?'

If an owl could smile, this one did. One couldn't actually see his beak curving upwards at the side, but there was a smile, a hint of one, a gentle smile, one that was not derisive or condescending.

'You don't need to understand it. You just need to accept

it and that you might come across yourself in a body you don't recognise. Male. Female. Both. Neither. Not necessarily flesh and blood, sometimes metal and synthetic skin.'

'I will figure that out when I come across it. How did you know about me going back?'

'I know everything you do. It is my job to watch over you and guide you. Me, and the one you call Crow. We are your tutelaries. Guardian spirits. Guardian angels, as some religions like to label us. I'm here to tell you to stop this back and forth. It will take its toll and you won't achieve what you set out to achieve.'

'It just happens.'

'That's where you are wrong. Every single thing that happens in your life is under your control. You are the programmer of what you do, to use a term you are familiar with. You give up responsibility over your actions by assuming you don't have any control.' He paused. 'It will kill you, this back and forth. The human body is not made for this. Pay heed. What is done is done. You cannot make amends.'

I sighed. The moon moved swiftly behind a passing cloud and Owl looked up at the sky as it did. Its light shone out from the ragged borders of the cloud, enveloping it in an unearthly nimbus. Owl turned its head back towards me, bobbed its head up and down as though trying to assess me, and then with a huge swoop of its wings, hurled itself off the branch and flew away into the darkness, flying higher than I had ever known an owl to fly, high into where clouds made love to the night, and further up where the air thinned out into vacuum and chaos scattered the light of dead stars millions of years before it hit our eyes.

'It will kill you, this back and forth.' His words reverberated in my ears. I knew what he was talking about, or at least I thought I knew what he was talking about. I could see it around my midsection, pinpricks of absence where matter had once been, molecules of me now missing. No one else could spot it, but I knew. I could feel the winds of the universe corral through the missing spaces, whistling eerie tunes of nothingness. I could feel the dance of the universe through the newly formed channels passing through me, connecting all I'd been to, past and future, with skeins of light and thought.

I switched the laptop off, charged my phone, showered and changed into a pair of trousers and a faded t-shirt. I was careful to not look at myself in the mirror. My wardrobe was pitiful, but I didn't have the luxury of indulging myself and I wouldn't accept anything from Aman. Maa's treatment had eaten into my little savings like termites boring through a sheet of ply, rendering it hollow, knocking it down, crumbling into dust once what had been solid wall, medical insurance exhausted, company policy limited, and then I had quit in order to care for her. I had nothing now. No savings. No stable income. Whatever came in from the occasional project was barely enough to keep body and soul together. And I couldn't even take up a proper job now; I was unpredictable. I had no idea how long this would continue – it had been two years that I had been living like a resident in a motel in my part of the universe. I needed permanence somewhere. Here, where I belonged. Or there, where I visited. Perhaps Owl was right, this back and forth would kill me. Perhaps I wanted to die.

I hailed a desultory auto rickshaw that had wandered down my lane. We took off through streets below skies so black that they felt like a velvet black curtain stretched across a dome. Rain sneaked in through the fluttering plastic sheets that hung ineffectually down the sides and flared out into batwings as the vehicle picked up speed, drenching me. We turned through lanes and by-lanes. The road glistened wet, a magical upside-down city in an alternate world just beneath the surface. What if I looked into it, where would I end up? Did I dare?

We turned into the lane leading to Saachi's home. Auto rides gave me gooseflesh, a crawling finger of ice up my spine, a panic grabbing my throat and making me want to jump off while it was still running, the breath knocked out of me, leaving me with no voice and coherence. I shivered as the wind hit skin. It was uncharacteristically cold, a cold unfamiliar to this city, a sludge of humidity most months, spare a week of mock winter. Saachi and Prashant lived on the first floor. It was a rented one-bedroom apartment. Few made the transition from living on rent to owning their home in Mumbai. That was true upward mobility in this city, being able to afford a home of one's own here, this city where land crept inch by inch into the sea and the sea bided its time, waiting to take back what it had lost to human greed, warning us by flinging our garbage back at us during high tide and the monsoon, and sending in the occasional cyclones, a warning of how it could bring us to our knees.

The building was a government-subsidised construction allocated through a lottery draw. They were small, these houses. Just enough to have the cement concrete walls wrap around one's body, something to keep the elements out. Perhaps that was all one really needed, enough space to wrap oneself into, to stay warm, dry and loved.

'Saachi & Prashant' the nameplate outside the door said. It was a simple one, tiles with letters that spelt out their names and a flower on the last tile, bought from a store at the mall. Emblematic perhaps of how they were: simple, glazed to shiny, happy and boxed in. They were happy to be boxed in, I wasn't. I was a coward. I disliked certainty. Or perhaps, I liked certainty too much to see it collapse around me. I had lived it, middle class respectability smashed to smithereens in a matter of seconds. Sweaty hands all over my body, the pain spreading from the most private of me to all of me, the tearing of skin and tissue, the violation, the blood, the pain.

'Jump, Ana, jump.'

When I closed my eyes, I could still see the spreading stain of red on the paving of the path below, the gentle drizzle washing it out into streaks that blended into the mud, the earth soaking it in, life leaching out from the broken body that lay askew on the concrete. I had landed on the mud patch next to the concrete. It was soft. I'd survived, the damp mud saved my life. The me in this time had survived without a scratch. A minor concussion. The others of me had not escaped so easily. Some had not survived. Some had it worse. For them it would have been better to have died. There were horrors the past held that I had been peeling back, scabs I had not allowed to heal, picking on them incessantly, seeing infant skin, puckered, pink, shiny and thin enough to burst again and bleed.

'My name is Ana, I'm twenty-eight years old, the year is 2002, this is Mumbai.'

'I am Ana, I'm thirty-two years old, the year is 2018, this is Mumbai.'

'I am Nayna, I am eight years old, the year is 1984, this is Bombay.'

I was here. Now. Standing in front of Saachi's door. I had been here before. In another place, another time. I took a deep breath, steadied myself, and looked back at myself from the glass fronting the square of the door camera. I shimmered in the reflection. My reflection spoke to me.

'My name is Ana. I'm thirty years old. The year is 2008, this is nowhere and everywhere.'

I closed my eyes and rang the doorbell. When I opened them, my reflection had turned around and was walking away. I stared down at the floor until the door swung open and light from within the room spilled into the landing, warm and welcoming.

'That was quick, was there no traffic? It's Sunday evening, there wouldn't have been any traffic.' Saachi beaming from end to end, asking and answering her own questions as she always did, encased in a voluminous kaftan that had seen better days, wiping her hands on a grubby apron that needed a deep soak in detergent and then a determined scrubbing. Saachi was a million wonderful things but a stickler for cleanliness she was not. Her home was always a dishevelled space where you threw bundles of clothes off the sofas in order to find space to sit, and smells of cooking wafted out of the kitchen no matter what time one visited.

She walked the fine line between voluptuous and matronly already. Curvy and comfortable in her skin; not all edges, angles and prickly like I was. Her face was rounded, eyes calm. It suited her, this expansion; she was an expansive person who took you into her fold unquestioningly, engulfed you, made you hers, brooking no resistance. It didn't even occur to you to resist her. 'You're a mess. No umbrella?' she commented, registering the drenched clothes.

'Nope.'

'You will die without buying an umbrella ever in your life. I'll cremate you with an umbrella and a raincoat.'

'I won't need one then.'

'That's true too. Come in and change quickly.' I did, pulling on a wine-coloured satin kaftan she threw at me, drowning in its folds, checking the phone for a message twice over even as I changed. Saachi noticed it and shook her head disapprovingly. She poured some Shiraz into two glasses created for Burgundy, and handed one to me, uncaring of the fact that the wine and her glasses did not match and she wouldn't care if she had to serve it in a paper cup or a beer mug.

'Drink up, it will make you feel better. You want a white? I have a Sauvignon Blanc if you do. Or do you want something stronger? I have some Old Monk too. It will warm you up quick if you need it. Shall I get that? Okay, drink this first since I've poured it out and then tell me if you want the rum. There's some single malt too but Prashant is terribly fussy about that.'

She moved seamlessly to her next topic. Me. 'You are half your size since I last saw you. Intermittent fasting or Keto? You are too skinny! Do you plan on becoming a ghost? You will become invisible if you become any thinner. You'll disappear...'

The doorbell rang and she went to answer it. I was left with my thoughts for a moment. Saachi did that, she filled up the void where thoughts swirled. Perhaps I was a ghost, a creature that didn't live in the here and now but kept flitting around, hankering for release. And I couldn't explain to Saachi why I had shrunk, not yet at least. She came back with a food delivery bag that she opened directly on the small coffee table, without bothering about cutlery and serving plates. Kebabs from the local takeaway, tangy mint chutney in a small plastic container.

'Eat,' she commanded. 'Now tell me why are you a skeleton.'

'I'm fine,' I replied. 'Is your biryani cooked yet?'

'Ten minutes more and then we are good to eat. But let's have some more wine first... Prashaaaant... We have company, Prashant,' she called in a tone that brooked no argument or negotiation. 'Come, say hello.'

Prashant emerged from the dim room like a deer caught in the headlights. He was a huge man, shaggy and dishevelled as a norm. He gave me a bearlike hug.

'Where do you keep going off to? You had Saachi all worried. Then that chap told her not to worry because you were off on some monastery type thing.'

That chap. Prashant didn't like Aman much and never failed to make his displeasure open and vocal, he was rather old-fashioned like that. When had hormones ever agreed with societal approval? Maa had not known Aman to offer her approval or disapproval. Neither had my father. He became a part of my life after they had left it – chosen to leave it – and he would never know those I came from. He knew nothing of me except the edited story of me I had told him. Weren't we all guilty of editing our stories to suit the moment, the person we were telling it to, adding tucks and seams, fringes and lace, to hem in the ugly?

Aman was the antithesis of everything Prashant and Saachi were. To be honest, Aman was the antithesis of everything I was, with his posh boarding school, B-school old boys' network, tropical wool and linen suits rotated by the season, silk ties, handcrafted leather briefcases, monogrammed travel luggage, corporate club membership, business class travel, a planner that was always full, time stapled and glued into place by Google Calendar and an executive assistant to make sure the days were scheduled up to utmost efficiency of time. I was the gap in his packed schedule.

'What is going on, Ana? Why can't you tell me what the truth is? I am family. The only family you have here, and the clan back home has entrusted me to keep a watch on you. Something is wrong, isn't it, tell me, tell me the worst, I can take it, what's wrong, why are you wasting away? Is it what Mandira maasi had?' The dreaded word would not be mentioned, naming things aloud gave them power and contagion.

'The only thing wrong is that I am really hungry right now and will die if I don't get food.'

'That's what is wrong. You are never hungry. You never eat. You were always lean but look at you now, all skin and bones. Naanu would have given you two tight slaps and made you eat properly, ghee, butter, everything, none of this cut the fat nonsense.' She stopped. We both missed our maternal grandmother, she of the soft, crumpled, parchment skin speckled with liver spots and freckles, smelling of love and a peculiar rose ittar she used all her life and had insisted should be sprinkled on her shroud when she went, taking with her that special magic in her fingers that made even the most ordinary, everyday dishes heavenly.

'Come, help me set the table.'

The table was an inadequate rectangle for two wedged against the wall with a couple of bucket chairs on either side. Saachi hastily dragged up a stool to the unoccupied side. The table cloth was covered with a diligent householder's precaution of a plastic sheet to prevent inadvertent spills from ruining it. We set out three places and Saachi hauled in the degchi with the biryani in it, the dough sealing yet to be broken. Prashant followed her with the raita bowl.

Saachi had been my saviour after Maa died; she kept me fed and functional for the weeks I could barely drag myself into the bathroom or even splash water on my face. She nursed me through the greyness of grief for months. Her mother, my Lovely maasi, had come down for some time. Frail herself, she could provide me with only the emotional support of her presence, so wrapped up was she in her own grieving. Saachi sent her back home after a couple of weeks when it became apparent that neither of us were competent enough to take care of each other. How was it that two sisters had ended up having such different lives, I wondered. Lovely maasi, so generous with her love, had gone on to live a life that expanded and brought more people to love within its fold. And Maa, with her constant resentment about having been wronged, first by her father, then by my father, and then life, had closed in until her circle, and by extension mine, shrank until it was only us, the two of us, and now it was just me, alone in the house, with only Saachi coming and going with food, love and caring, keeping me from putting knife to wrist in the intervals between her going and coming, and Maa's coming and going, and Pappa's coming and going. And then, a couple of years later I began coming and going myself too, back and forth, into times and spaces I could have never imagined.

'Settle down,' she said. 'You need to be with people. You can't live completely alone. Find a job. Get out of the house more often. Get married. If he is not willing to divorce his wife, leave him. We will find someone for you, someone kind and loving and settled.'

'Settled' had become Saachi's favourite word. Tea leaves settled. Mountains remained unsettled, rising a centimetre or two every year. Evil earth remained unsettled: shifting, spewing up magma from its depths, remodelling its contours, alive, angry, in constant ferment. I remained unsettled. To settle was to die.

'I will think about it,' I replied, more to get Saachi to drop the topic. 'And, anyway, I have you. There's Lovely maasi, Raja bhaiya, Punam bhabhi, the kids. I'm not alone. And you will have a baby soon and I will be a maasi, so there's always going to be more people to love.'

She smiled, her eyes going soft for a moment, and I was instantly envious of the child who would be the recipient of all the love she contained within herself, running like a vein beneath her skin, just waiting to burst at the cry of her child. She was meant to be a mother, I was not. I had never known what mothering meant, raised by a mother who had always treated me like an inconvenience. Lovely maasi had always hinted at it, but never quite said it outright, that I was the reason Maa's plans for her own life had gone awry, I wasn't quite the preterm baby she had told the world I was. Pappa knew it. Lovely maasi knew it. And I knew it, when I grew old enough to know a baby was carried for nine months in the womb, and that I had been born six months after my parents' wedding. I had counted the months off on my fingers, all of twelve years, after the bodily function lecture from a gynaecologist the nuns had organised for all the girls. I had been born early into the marriage but I was not a preterm baby. What had helped was that my mother shifted to another city with her new husband, a city no one knew either of them or the wedding date to count the months on their fingers and look askance at me.

'Anyway, come to the point. Why are you so thin? Are you keeping well? I worry, you know, after what happened with maasi.' She meant Maa. Maa had gone from diagnosis to the pyre in four months. There had been no autopsy done, it hadn't been deemed necessary, after all she had been terminally ill. It was release. Perhaps I had released her by placing those painkillers within easy reach, with the bottle of water at her bedside.

'There is this,' I had told her that night. 'You have a choice.' It had been cruel but necessary. The suffering was too much, death was better. It had made her decision easier. I hadn't mentioned that the bottle of painkillers was full when I'd last seen it, empty when I'd found her the next morning. I had just cleaned up the vomit and called Dr Shanbag for the death certificate. If he noticed anything amiss, he didn't mention it either. It had been a release for me, too, a release I sought. He knew it too. It hadn't been easy growing up with Maa as a mother. It had become more difficult with her illness. Sometimes she told me I was an evil child for wishing her dead. Some nights, when she tossed and turned in the bed next to me, screaming in pain, I replied she had been an evil mother who deserved it. Then I woke up to an empty bed.

My head was now heavy with wine, food and the exhaustion of crossing universes.

'I'm fine, Saachi, don't worry about me.'

'How can I not worry about you? That's my job definition, has been since we were kids.'

She was the younger one. She was the mature one, the one more likely to think things through. She would have never gone through a deserted alley in the hope of a short cut, unheeding of Crow telling me to take the longer walk through the main road. She would have never jumped into an auto rickshaw after running through tangled lanes in a slum, chased by a gang of men intent on preying upon her. She would never have let Pappa jump. She would never have told Maa to kill herself.

The comfort of the old and the familiar lay between us, curled and purring, like a content kitten, bringing warmth and joy to a drab day, the presence and solidity of the other's affection and concern. Some people were like that. They were home. Saachi was home to me in a way no one was, not even Aman. Aman was a storm I was struggling against, a force of nature I hadn't even tried to resist. There was nothing comforting about him, there was only chaos, and it was chaos I had wittingly stepped into, from the moment I got into his car, accepted a ride from him, a stranger, invited him home and unthinkingly put my lips to his when he stepped into my house.

'Get a job,' she repeated, her voice was now languid with the wine and the biryani.

'I will,' I replied, wondering if I could ever get back to a regular life, a job, a husband, children. It all seemed so alien to what I was going through right now, and completely unthinkable. I snuggled against her, my rock, my little sister who was my big sister.

Outside, the rain had just about begun beating impotently down the little awnings that covered the window, some droplets finding their way in, settling into a fine mist over the divan, the coffee table, the house plants.

'Get married,' she said, sounding much like the stuck record she was on the topic.

'I like this impermanence, I don't want to be tied to him.' I didn't mention the other women in his life, those who came and went. A fuck. A forgetting. Use protection, I had told him. Don't bring anything back to me. He had raised his eyebrow, I had sighed. Had his wife used the same words about me?

'How long has it been now? Three years?'

It had been four years, actually, but I was not going to correct Saachi. Four years since I had shared an elevator with him, riding up to his office trembling with the proximity and six hours later become his lover, a fucking that I knew was inevitable when we first laid eyes on each other. We were strangers. I was there to conduct a research orientation workshop for the new interns. He walked in and had sat through it, right at the back of the room, with an unreadable expression, never taking his eyes off me, except to look at his watch and step out midway. When I had exited the premises at the end of the workshop, the rain had begun pelting down in buckets. I was waiting desperately at the gate of the business park in the pouring rain, trying to hail an auto rickshaw, drenched to the bone, feeling the embarrassment of the cold day and the thin kurti sticking to my body, my nipples visible to all those who chose to look at me, their eyes lingering, stripping me, doing unspeakable things to my body. A car drew up next to me, a window rolled down, he looked at me. Meeting his eyes was like being hit by lightning.

'Get in.'

There had been no refusing. His voice brooked no argument. I knew that I would get into the car, go anywhere he would take me. Introductions seemed unnecessary. He didn't ask me my name, I didn't ask him his. I set the directions on his phone. He stopped at my gate; I asked him to come up. He would like some coffee, he said, when I asked him if he preferred tea or coffee. Black, strong, without sugar. He didn't leave after coffee, I didn't expect him to, and when he sat at my feet and kissed my foot, I knew this was what it was. I drew him to me, kissed him hard, slapped him harder, felt him grow hard against my body. He obeyed me. I commanded him, his every movement. It was what we had recognised in each other from the very first moment, a dance that only we knew the rhythm to, never spoken, never mentioned, a knowing of the needs of the other that came naturally. I gave him all the pain he yearned for, he gave me the power that life had taken away from me. He stayed back for dinner, I ordered in.

It was inexplicable how our bodies drew together even as my mind kept telling me I was being ridiculous. Rules had been thrown out of the window. It was a yearning beyond lust. I could feel him in my heartbeat, in my breath, and I didn't even know him. He left when morning was about to break. It was then that I asked him his name, and he told me he already knew mine. It was honest, this relationship, we based it on lust, on an equation few understood and fewer accepted. Lust soon became comfort and routine. He would land up home after work, stay for dinner, leave past midnight or early in the morning before the sun rose. He left stealthily, without putting the lights on, without making a sound, vanishing like a demon lover, leaving behind no evidence of his presence except the stickiness between my thighs and the smell of him in every crevice of my body, the acridity of the cigarette smoke that wreathed him in my hair, in my pores, his skin under my nails.

I slid easily into the other woman's role. It didn't matter to me that he was married; if it mattered to him I didn't know or ask. What I gave him no one did, not his wife, not the others. It was not sex he needed, it was pain and release. I couldn't tell Saachi this.

The bottle of wine was empty, the edges of my awareness were blurred. Saachi rose to her feet.

'Shall we open another one?'

I nodded. She padded away to the bar cabinet on soft feet and returned with another, a strong red. I sipped, feeling the warmth flooding me.

'Stay the night. You can go home tomorrow morning.'

'You sure I won't be a hindrance? I'll just call a cab.'

'Don't be silly. Just stay. It's too late to go home, and it is pouring again.'

It was nice to feel wanted. The mellowness was beginning to take over my head. Was there a word for the comfort one felt when one was fed and sated and with people one loved?

'What are we going to do about you, Ana?'

'Nothing. You're going to feed me and ply me with wine once a week and stop worrying about me. I am a big girl now. I can take care of myself.'

'Anyway, good night, I'm off to sleep. I can barely keep my eyes open,' Saachi said, rising heavily to her feet. 'Sleep tight, Naynu.'

I had dropped Nayna for Ana. But Nayna would never leave me.

And so I slept while the light drizzle morphed into pelting rain. Thunder crashed and lightning crackled, the clouds hung low and menacing, black ominous puffs of vapour and wrath. When I wake up the clouds would have moved on, I told myself, before allowing myself to drift off into sleep. The distant east, where the low hills framed the horizon, would be glowing faintly beneath an uncertain pale sun. I would wake up, change into my clothes and go home, back to an empty house.

I knew it would be another day, in this year, this time, and I would be here, in this city, in this home, and all that I saw around me would be real and present and not whispers of memory making themselves real in my head. Sleep overtook me, hushing my fears. I woke up with a start when the night still lingered. The steady patter of the rain outside had ceased. I got up, dressed and went home. I lay on my bed and then sat up again to look at the mirror opposite the bed. I wasn't there. If there was someone in the room I had just left, at that moment, looking into the mirror, they would see me lying sprawled in a greyness that had no beginning and no end and began closing in on me, tighter and tighter until it enclosed me like a shell would enclose a yolk, and me reaching out my hand to touch hands yet to be formed. And there were the other hands, the hands of the one I had pushed there into the Greyness, the one who should have been me in the here and now. The image would dim and pop and fizzle and disappear from the reflection and all it would reflect would be the room it was in, the curtains opposite it, the half open window, the pre-dawn slowly staining the sky a tremulous pink. The bed I was on was empty, and then the mirror smashed outwards with the ferocity of a thousand thunderbolts, a blast no one would hear in this time and space. I returned, slammed back into my time. I never seemed to have slippers on my feet when I went – I now stood on shards of glass, the blood from my cuts flowing to the floor, mingling with the rainwater coming in from the broken window, before I fell right back on the bed into blackness.

3

Good Morning. Or Good Night.

'Everybody needs his memories.
They keep the wolf of insignificance from the door.'

—Saul Bellow

WEDNESDAY MORNING. LIBRARY DAY. ON THAT DAY, FOR A long delicious hour, they were allowed go into the high-ceilinged, musty library presided over by an equally musty and wraith-like Miss D'Silva who wandered about the room redolently perfumed by the smell of old books and dust. The library was to Nayna what heaven would be to a pious soul; she could spend all day in a library and not tire. Today, she would give back *Great Expectations* to Miss D'Silva and ask her for HG Wells's *The War of the Worlds*.

Her parents did not understand her love for books, though they indulged her. Her father was never happier than when given a pile of numbers to tally or an odd job to repair a gadget around the house, and her mother found her small joys in songs, the little portable transistor radio going with her from room to room as she did her chores for the day. She would hum along when a favourite song came on, at times bursting into full-throated song, in moments so rare that when they did come, they startled Nayna. The voices of Lata Mangeshkar, Asha Bhosle, Geeta Dutt, and her mother provided the background score of her childhood. Singing and dancing were not skills for girls from a respectable family to cultivate. Lovely maasi told her of how her mother had once participated in a talent contest in college and their father had stormed on to the stage, dragging her off in a rage. Her mother had never sung outside the walls of their home after that. Girls from respectable families didn't make a display of themselves for people to gawk over. They erased themselves, bit by bit, slowly and steadily over the years, until they acquired a matronly respectability. It kept them safe.

Maa had not learnt to stay safe. 'She was too beautiful,' Lovely maasi had sighed. 'Boys would peek over the boundary wall of our compound just to catch a glimpse of her. Even if we stepped out to the market, he insisted we put our chunni around our heads. That was only for married women, you understand, but Babuji didn't want us to be seen. Mandira more than me. She was the lovely one, I don't know how I got the nickname.'

Years later when she thought back, she would only remember the discontent that had permanently crumpled her mother's exquisite features, discontent that if erased would have made her mother beautiful again. She was yet to know of the accumulation of little betrayals and disappointments that ended up creasing up one's face and soul, of how beauty was a curse and desirability was a double-edged sword that society insisted on smashing into two before a young girl could realise how it could be wielded to gain power and currency in a world of men.

Nayna was still to be disillusioned. Happiness to her was a new Archie Comics book, tutti frutti ice cream in a cone, Coca Cola in a bottle with a straw, Phantom candy cigarettes, gold coin chocolates, a much-coveted Walkman, a double-recording cassette player.

This morning, her father dropped her off to the bus stop on his scooter and waited until she was safely ensconced in the red BEST bus that would take her across two suburbs to school. One fine day her parents had decided Nayna was now big enough to travel on her own. They taught her how to navigate the bus route and the roads by herself, all of eight. The key to the main door sewn on to a long cord attached to the inner lining of her school bag, the courage to travel alone sewn into the inner lining of her little-girl soul. After all, it was just a couple of bus stops, a short walk from the bus stop to school, no roads to cross. What could go wrong, they thought. They didn't factor in men.

She learnt early on that a young girl travelling alone was easy prey. The first time a man sitting next to her flashed his penis at her, stroking it gently as she stared, she was curious and repulsed. It was on her way back from school and the bus wasn't empty. The others around looked away embarrassed, no one interfered or stopped the man or lambasted him for his indecency.

'It looks like a sea slug I read about in *National Geographic*,' she had told him earnestly before bursting into laughter, totally flummoxing him, shrivelling him up instantly. He quickly zipped up and scampered to the door, hopping off as the bus slowed down. Her father would have one like that too, she realised. Black and hairy. Did her father show it to young girls sitting in buses, she wondered. Did all men do that? She felt a swift flash of sympathy for men. To go around with a flaccid and purposeless thing hanging between their legs, interfering with their walking, running. She had seen little boys' penises, tiny little stubs, before but what she saw on the bus was a different species.

Why, even the banyan tree behind her house was safer than the bus. The one rumoured to house ghosts. She could see it from her balcony, spread across the rear of the complex, foreboding and imposing. Across the worn-out patch of cemented courtyard was a water tank in the centre, serving as a makeshift stage for impromptu musical performances. And behind it the banyan tree, spreading, spreading, spreading, grabbing air with its branches, its aerial roots hanging down to the ground, the dishevelled locks of a witch, for children to swing with, for another to hang herself from one of those branches, back when the land was bare and unoccupied. The children didn't know about the one who sat there, watching them as they played. Sometimes she tried to join in their play, but they couldn't see her, feeling her as a cool breeze against their skin, following them as they ran.

Nayna the only one who could see her, she of the grey eyes and black wavy hair. She terrified Nayna at first when she called out to her, but Nayna bravely stayed and chatted with her, in a language that she had never learnt to speak but somehow understood. She introduced Nayna to the others. They told her about the times they had lived and died in, much before the city was ruled by the white-skinned, when kings came in from the north and the south, conquered, set up their ports and dominion, only to be defeated by others. Her mother warned her against going there time and time again, and it wasn't just the otherworldly creatures haunting the periphery around the tree that worried her mother. There was a gap in the compound wall leading to a wasteland occupied occasionally by vagrants who lit fires and set up their makeshift tenements there until the police and the residents shooed them away. And beyond the scrubland, the creek and the marshes that filled in when the tide came in.

It was cold under the banyan trees, both the one in the building compound and the one in school. Nayna shivered under them. Sometimes she sat under the banyan tree and chatted with the faces above until her mother called her home because night had fallen and it was dangerous for a little girl to be out unsupervised. She needn't have worried, Nayna was safe. She was watched over. The faces above watched over her and scared away those who climbed in through the gap in the wall and reached for her, wanting to assuage a momentary lust. When two vagrants were found inexplicably dead below the banyan tree, the society had the wall rebuilt and barbed wire put above a layer of glass shards set into the cement.

Nayna took the bus every day. And in the bus she knew she was dreaming that day because it was daylight in her dream and she was standing at the window looking across the courtyard at the building across hers.

Ana was standing at her window, the one with the broken slats and the darkness within, her expression inscrutable. A wind from nowhere began blowing wildly, whipping up leaves and dust and whirling them around. Both buildings began moving towards each other until the windows were barely a hand's grab away. Ana put her hand out, taking Nayna's hand.

'You have to come with me,' she said. 'Get up, Nayna, we have to go.' And then she burst into an explosion of blue sparkles that seared Nayna's eyes.

Nayna woke up with a start. The bus conductor was shaking her shoulder.

'We are almost at your stop.'

When she dismounted at the bus stop, the clouds were hanging ominously low and dark. It was monsoon, it could rain anytime. The books in her bag were wrapped in plastic to keep them dry. With pink flowers on a white transparent background, her new raincoat was her pride and joy. This year she had outgrown both her raincoat and school uniform, much to the dismay of her mother. It entailed extra expenditure of two new sets of uniforms, a new raincoat, new school shoes, new rain shoes. If she was without socks in school, she would get a caning. Five sharp ones on the calves with a thin bamboo cane by Sister Theresa. The dog was waiting. It got up from the bus stop as she began walking down the road, and trotted next to her. It had done so every single day, ever since she had begun travelling to school alone. The first day the dog accompanied her, she kept up a steady recitation of the

Hanuman Chalisa. She reached the school gates and the dog waited until she was safely in, before turning off and trotting away to take care of other important dog things. She didn't know yet whether it was a boy dog or a girl dog. Both were equally dangerous, that she knew. 'Maa, a dog follows me to school,' she had told her mother the first day it happened.

'Does it scare you, does it attack you?'

'It just walks with me to school every morning.'

'That's a good thing then, just think of it as your bodyguard.'

'Or my guardian angel.'

She discovered after gathering her courage and going down on her haunches to pet the dog, that it was a girl dog, and named her Angel. She had Owl and Crow. Now she had dog. But she called the dog Angel, not Dog. This morning, Angel fell into step beside her as she walked the short distance to school from the bus stop. Perhaps the dog would talk to her too, like Crow and Owl did. She decided to try.

'Angel, why do you walk with me every morning to school?'

Angel replied, like dogs and humans had always been conversing, in short barks that Nayna understood.

'Just for something to do. To watch out for you. Don't you want my company on the walk, Bitto?'

Only her grandma had ever called her Bitto. Was Angel Daadi?

'Are you my Daadi?'

'No, I'm not, I'm just a dog.'

'How do you know my nickname is Bitto?'

'I just know, I don't know how. It is like you knew my name is Angel.'

'Is it really Angel?'

'Now it is.'

'Angel, can you talk with other people?'

The dog barked a short rough laugh. 'I can talk to everyone, but not everyone listens.'

'Why can I understand what you're saying?'

'Because you are paying attention. If we all paid attention, we would all understand what the other was saying. There was a tower built, you know, in ancient times, before which we could all understand each other. But we built that tower to reach the heavens and we lost the ability to understand each other. Humans went a step further and created many languages to complicate things even more. We animals stayed true to our original languages at least. You humans like to feel special and different. Break yourselves down into barriers of language, religion and more until finally you have small little cocoons where you isolate yourselves. Perhaps we need Babel fishes in our ears, all of us, to rid ourselves of what the Babel tower wrought.'

Nayna's mind had drifted off; for a dog Angel had really long, ponderous opinions. Long opinions were wearying. A dog would have no opinion on movie stars or comic books or music or studies.

'So, what do you do all day, as a dog? I mean, I have to come to school, then go home, finish my homework, help Maa with the chores, then I go down to play. On Saturday evenings we go for a movie, on Sunday mornings we go to the beach or the museum or a park and to the bookstore. What about you?'

'Oh, I ramble around all day. Sometimes I get into fights, but now the other dogs around know I'm quite a bitch so they leave me alone.'

'Here's school. Bye, Angel!'

Angel raised a paw in acknowledgement and trotted off towards the market where the generosity of strangers awaited her. Nayna was early as she always was. The first bell would ring at 7 a.m. and it was just about 6.50 a.m. on her shiny new HMT stainless steel wristwatch that Pappa had bought for her on her birthday. She was the only girl in her class who had a wristwatch. It was a status symbol she flaunted incessantly, annoying her classmates who called her a show-off behind her back because she was constantly telling them the time despite the big clock right in the front of the class. The cleaners were still swabbing the stone floors, going around from class to class, putting the benches back in place. Sounds echoed, bouncing off the stone walls, stone floors, reverberating through the still premises, throwing themselves at each other, playing catch. The windows were thrown open class by class as they finished cleaning each, letting the dampness of the monsoon outside drift in and settle unasked in the rooms, intensifying smells, glistening mist on the surfaces of the wooden desks, carved with initials of students past, dotted with ink blots from careless spills in the present. Nayna walked up the three flights of the sweeping stone stairway with its imposing wooden balustrade to her classroom on the third floor, settled her bag on the bench she had been assigned, went to the bathroom, and came back to the classroom. It wasn't empty anymore.

A girl stood by the window, looking out. She was in a regular frock, not the mandatory school uniform.

'Hello, are you a new admission?' Nayna asked.

The girl nodded without turning around.

'You can't just sit anywhere, you know. You have to wait for Miss Shirley to come and assign you a seat. You are lucky you can wear a dress until your school uniform gets ready. You can wear a dress for a week at least, unless you have a super-efficient tailor who will get it done immediately. We are allowed to wear a dress only on our birthday. Last year I wore a pink lace dress with ribbons to tie at the waist. Is it your birthday?'

The girl shook her head to indicate a no, and began turning around ever so slowly. Nayna couldn't see a school bag anywhere.

'Don't you have a bag?' she asked. 'Don't you have any books? You have to go to Janta Book Depot and give your name and class and division and buy your set of books. Don't forget to buy brown paper and red border labels. Plain ones. If you buy fancy ones, they will make you cover them again.'

Voices floated down the corridor, early arrivals, chattering happily about things young girls chatter about. Sangeeta and Anita, twins who lived down the road, entered the class chattering at the top of their voices.

'Do you know we have a new girl in class?' Nayna said to them as they entered, turning around, pointing towards the window. There was no one there. She looked around puzzled. There was no way the girl at the window could have exited the classroom without them noticing.

'Did she go out, the girl in the white dress who was standing at the window?'

The twins shook their heads. 'There was no one in the class when we came in except you,' Anita replied. Nayna dashed to the door and looked down the long corridor; the first stragglers were coming in, but there was no sight of the girl. Above the city, the clouds cleared lazily, spotlighting the swamps and marshlands that separated the island city from the mainland, over the throb of the buildings piled untidily against each other, washing over the muddy ground and the small squat stone and cement building that made the school.

How strange, she thought, but the first bell rang then and the class became a den of chattering magpies in pinafores and braided hair in ribbons, socks up to their knees and polished shoes, with books and other missiles hurled across the classroom until the second bell and the arrival of Miss Shirley whose single sweeping gaze promised the application of the wooden ruler to the knuckles.

'Good morningggggg, teacher,' the class sang in unison as she walked in. The public address system in each class blared into life with the hymns and the national anthem along with the thought for the day that constituted the morning assembly.

Miss Shirley took the attendance mechanically and moved on smoothly to the French Revolution, adding juicy titbits of how the peasants sat knitting in front of the guillotine as the heads of the aristocrats were severed from their bodies. 'Knit. Pearl. Knit. Pearl. With each stitch one head lopped off,' she said, much to the delight of the bloodthirsty class of prepubescent girls who had never been in more physical danger than being chased by a stray dog.

She went on, 'Let them eat cake, Marie Antoinette said when the peasants cried they didn't have bread. This upset the peasants and they called for her to be guillotined.'

Nayna thought this a very impractical solution. How could you eat cake with gravy? The guillotine, though, she thought, was a very practical invention to end someone's life.

Marie Antoinette's hair went grey overnight when she had to be brought out to the guillotine, Miss Shirley told them. What she didn't mention, and what Nayna would read later, much later, when she grew up and read more than what the textbooks told her, was the speculation on how the original champagne glass or coupe was modelled after Marie Antoinette's left breast. Of course, the champagne coupe had since fallen out of favour, but the girls didn't know this, or that a glassmaker somewhere cast a mould over a woman's left breast, according to myth and legend, immortalising the teenage queen's breast for generations to come. Right now, all they knew of history was what was filtered through the prurient prism of the textbook and Miss Shirley's retelling of it.

After the class ended, and Miss Shirley had gathered her bag and books to go to her next class, Nayna followed her out.

'Miss Shirley, was a new girl to join our class today?'

'No, child, not that I was informed. Why do you ask?'

'There was a new girl in the class when I reached, and then she went away I don't know where.'

'She must have come to the wrong class then. New admissions are still coming in and some transfers are due too.'

Nayna nodded, secretly deciding to be friends with the new girl. She now had to find out which class she was in. During recess, she went into all the other divisions of her grade to look for the new girl, but she was nowhere to be seen. Perhaps she was on another floor, in another grade. She would see her at dispersal time, and would ask her which grade she was in, on which floor. It was a small school, three floors, but bordering over eight acres of sprawling grounds. It would be easy to spot a girl in a white dress among a throng of girls in school uniform. But the girl was nowhere to be seen. Not in the milling crowds as the girls tumbled down the stairs and spilled out onto the quadrangle before straggling out onto the street. Not at the gate where Sister Theresa monitored declining morals by rising skirt lengths, administering justice with a smack from a cane and detention. Not outside the gate where the gola wallah, the ber wallah, and the stickjaw sweet vendor did brisk business, earning the undying gratitude of the local dentist. Nayna looked down the road, at the school gate. The new girl was nowhere to be seen. Nayna then looked up at the window of her classroom, and there she was, her eyes boring into Nayna's, her expression the saddest Nayna had ever seen all her life.

4

The Heavens Tipped Over

'The past is a foreign country; they do things differently there.'

—L.P. Hartley, *The Go-Between*

'ANA,' THE MAN SAID, THE MAN IN MY DREAMS OR WAS IT THE MAN IN my reality, I never knew what was what anymore. 'Sit up straight and eat with your mouth closed.'

'Yes, Pappa.'

'Ana, finish all your vegetables.'

'Yes, Pappa.'

'Ana, I'm going to jump.'

'Yes, Pappa.'

'Watch me jump. Jump after me.'

'Yes, Pappa.'

I stood at the door to the balcony, watching him climb on to the ledge, stand there for one undecided moment and then fling himself off in one sure, smooth jump. His reflexes, trained from college football days, a little dulled with age, nonetheless still miles ahead of regular folk who had never trained. Landing on the concrete where kids played every evening, the quadrangle between the buildings, where grass grew unkempt. I went into the balcony and looked down. The screams began as in a chorus from a Greek drama, muted and distant at first, ominous and terrifying as they increased in a crescendo. From the balcony, I saw the blood fan under his head and run off with the water pelting down from the skies, the earth soaking it in where concrete ended and mud began. People begin to mill around him, whistles from the security guard, children breaking into loud wails of distress. Faces looked up, at me standing in the balcony looking down, confused.

The ground rose and with it my father's broken body, askew, straightened itself and stood up as I watched in terror. I ran to the main door of the house and opened it, terrified. Manjari aunty from next door swooped in and hugged me. 'Were you here when he jumped? You poor child. Where's your mother?' She was suddenly huge, layers and layers of fat that spread and rippled, smothering me, closing around me, making me gasp for breath in her embrace.

'She's gone to the market,' I panted. 'To buy me Poppins.'

Manjari aunty's mouth formed a small O in shock. 'That's all you can think about, you wicked girl, Poppins? Your father is dead. Think of your mother.' I thought of my mother and how happy she would be that my father was dead, and how she would exult that she was no longer tied to him. I laughed. Manjari aunty gasped. Her eyes were huge saucers that stared into mine, and then she looked over my shoulder. The ground was now level with the balcony and my father was stepping over into the balcony, holding his cracked skull in place with his hand. Brain tissue and blood dripped to the floor out of his nose.

'Ana, why didn't you jump?' he asked.

I shrank further into Manjari aunty's voluminous embrace.

'Come, Ana,' he said, one hand reaching out for me, the other still holding his skull, oozing blood and brain across the floor as he advanced towards me.

Manjari aunty turned me towards him.

'No,' I pleaded. 'Don't let him take me, help me.'

She laughed, her eyes black saucers in her puffed face as she pushed me hard towards him.

'You have to keep your promise, Ana, you promised to jump.'

He grabbed me and jumped again. The ground rushed at me and I woke up with a start just before it slammed into me. I was dead. I was alive.

It was morning. Pale light came in from the window and fell gently on my face. The pouring rain of the night had dissipated, the sky outside was clear. I sat up and looked around for a moment in a fair bit of confusion before it all came back to me. I had been to Saachi's house and had decided to come back home late last night while she was asleep. I vaguely remembered changing into my own clothes and leaving Saachi's home before dawn broke, climbing up the stairs to my home. The last I remembered was lying down in my bed, too exhausted to change out of my clothes into my sleepwear, kicking my shoes off. And then catching a glimpse of myself in the mirror opposite the bed. I should have known by now that to look at myself in a mirror, in any reflective surface, was stupidity.

A discombobulating of self, sifting through solid and vacuum and liquid, a wetness strangely familiar, and then I was slammed into the greyness, and hurled back into my time, my space. I had been there, in that place, for barely a flash, in the centre of a pulsating palm before I was thrown back, and here I was lying in my own bed. I had been there before. I had escaped, put another me in my place. It was a guilt I lived with every day.

Morning sounds were already percolating through the drip of the receding drizzle. A pressure cooker whistled somewhere, a conch shell blown in worship, the bells of the Hanuman mandir just across the gate clanging with grim determination and hope, a distant muezzin calling the faithful to prayer. The syncretism of the city I lived in, the routine of the everyday, the sounds of normalcy, were reassuring. The world as I knew it went on. And somewhere, elsewhere, worlds as I was yet to know them went on too.

I sat up in the bed and looked around me; something was off, but I couldn't quite put my finger on it. I was dripping wet, like I'd waded into a lake or gotten out of a bathtub. Not cold, but warm and salty. Amniotic fluid. Sea water. Cocooning, comforting. The room I lay in was destroyed like a cyclone had passed through it, wrecking every single thing in it. The window panes were shattered, there was glass all around, the cupboards were open, doors off their hinges… The water on the floor, could it be from the rain that had been lashing the city through the night or was it the same liquid that had drenched me and carried me here, the mirror above the dressing table smashed, like something or someone had been hurled into it? I had been hurled into it, I realised. My body hurt, every bone hurt, I was weighed down by a pain I had never experienced before, a crushing pain that made it impossible for me to move.

The Greyness, the wetness, had followed me back here. Somehow. My intestines bunched up and my body went cold and clammy. It sang in my ears, my brain.

'I'm Ana, the year is 2000. I live in Bombay, no, it is Mumbai now.'

'I'm Ana, the year is 2020. I live in Mumbai. I am thirty-two years old.'

'I'm Nayna, the year is 1986. I live in Bombay with Maa and Pappa. I am eight years old.'

'I am Sue. The year is 1995. I live in Bombay with my Maa. I am sixteen years old.'

'I am Anantya. I live beyond the Mother Planet now. I have stopped counting my years because I no longer have the Sun of our elders.'

The doorbell rang, but the weight of a thousand gravities held me down, the dampness of the Greyness slick on my skin.

It was Gauri-tai, on the dot. She always arrived at eight in the morning, hair in an oiled bun at the back of her head, a neat centre parting that revealed no grey, and a mouthful of brown teeth brought on by chewing more gutka than her body deserved if it was to live without succumbing to an oncologist's ministrations, and skin that was leathered by the sun. She had once told me she was seventy years old, and at another claimed to be merely forty. I'd given up trying to guess how old she was as long as she kept my home clean and functional, and cooked food for me to live on. I heard her let herself in with the key I had given her and sauntering into the kitchen, with the assurance that the house would be the same as she had left it the previous day.

I called out to her, my voice weighed down by the same heaviness that held me down on the bed, crushing my bones. She rushed into the bedroom.

'*Aaaiii ga*,' she squealed as she surveyed the destruction. '*Ithey kay zhala?*'

'I don't know,' I replied. That was as honest as I could get.

'Are you okay?' she asked me. 'Did they take anything, did you see them, did they do anything to you?'

Them. The scale of destruction was such she was convinced it was a break-in by more than one person from the magnitude of it. I put a hand gingerly to the back of my head; it was bleeding, perhaps from the impact with which I'd rebounded back into my space, my time. She saw it, and rushed into the kitchen, muttering to herself. She came back with the ice tray, hastily dislodging a couple of ice cubes, wrapping them in a handkerchief and pressing them against the bleed.

'We need to call the doctor and the police.'

Before I could argue or protest, she had pulled out her tiny phone with a long-suffering sigh and jabbed at the buttons. '*Haan, mere ko* late *hoga*,' she informed the owner of the next house she was due at on her daily rounds of cleaning. '*Idhar pura sab chori ho gaya.*'

She then turned to me, suddenly realising that we hadn't actually taken stock of what precisely had been robbed. '*Kya chori hua*?'

Who could have entered the house, she wondered, the windows had grills and the door was closed, there was no sign of a forced entry. She wore the key to my home on a long chain around her neck, tucked tidily into her blouse so she didn't misplace it and no one could rob it or make a duplicate. She was fiercely loyal to me, she wouldn't have let the key out of her sight. Surely, I didn't believe she would have let someone else have the key?

I knew I could trust her with my life. She had been with us ever since we moved to this home after it happened, seen me grow from child to woman. She'd seen Maa go from a beautiful woman in her prime to a withered, shrunken corpse. She helped me up and I moved from the wrecked bedroom to the living room, the blood from the cuts on my feet leaving trails on the wet floor.

The weight of the unseen gradually came off my bones; I had gone without conscious knowledge of how I went where I was not supposed to go, the land of the grey, the realm between creation and destruction.

Gauri-tai marched out and returned with the society chairman, a retired government official in shorts, collared t-shirt tucked in neatly, and running shoes with socks pulled up to his knees. The very grumpy night watchman followed them, vociferously protesting that no one who wasn't a resident had entered the premises on his watch. Sister Theresa would have been pleased with the society chairman's socks, I thought. No cane to his calves.

'We will have to inform the police,' Purandhare kaka said, his rheumy eyes taking in the destruction with disbelief.

'They hit her on her head,' Gauri-tai explained, turning my head and showing him the wound. 'She was unconscious, poor thing, when I came into the house. She has just came back to consciousness. She is lucky they didn't do any *galat kaam* with her.'

There was a momentary change in Purandhare kaka's expression from disbelief to worried, but it returned to the prosaic and practical.

'Do you remember their faces? Were they delivery boys?'

'The rain came in through the open windows,' I said, neither agreeing nor disagreeing with his story.

'Do you want to call the police? And you do need to see a doctor about that blow to your head. You passed out?'

I nodded. 'I think so.'

'Have you checked for anything missing?'

I hadn't had time to check, but there were no valuables in the house. I shook my head. 'I think not. Nothing is missing. Everything is in place, the laptop, the television. Just the bedroom seems to have been ransacked. And I have no jewellery for it to be stolen.'

'You live alone, *beta*,' Purandhare kaka said, his eyes concerned, 'ever since your mother died. It isn't safe. We all worry. I've seen you since the time you were a young girl and moved in here with your mother. Such a tiny thing you were. Fifteen years ago, was it?'

I nodded again. It had been twenty years, give or take a couple of months. I had moved into this flat with my mother on a rainy morning, much like the one on which my father had jumped. It had been less than a year since he'd passed away; it had taken Maa time to find a new place to move into. Maa's gold and Pappa's funds that had come in post his death had funded the new flat, along with some generous loans from Lovely maasi, repaid in due course of time, with gratitude and no interest. We had bundled all our belongings into a small tempo van and shifted bag and baggage into this tiny apartment on the outer fringes of a distant suburb in Mumbai. From our fourth-floor window we could see the stretch of the mangroves right up to the silver of the sea. During the monsoon, the stench of the creek beyond made us close all the windows the first year; by the second year we had grown accustomed to the waft of dankness that swept in and infiltrated the rooms, filling every nook and cranny with a staleness that only fresh sea breeze could evaporate once the sun was out.

There was nothing here that would remind us of him. This building had an elevator, something that would be easier on Maa's knees as she grew older. This flat had no balcony. All the windows were grilled, there was no getting out if you were in except through the door. Maa had made sure of that. But there was the terrace above us, and Maa hadn't factored that in. I had, but had never found the courage to go up to it, to stand against the narrow wall and look down at the ground, wait that long moment before one flung oneself, when everything compressed and elongated into white noise, and the only thing audible was the incessant thudding of one's heart in one's ears.

The new home we moved into was located to the far north of the growing city, a city that lengthened itself having no space to spread horizontally, the main business district connected to the rest of the newly developed suburbs by the train lines that stretched down the Western Line, the Central Line, and the newly developing Harbour Line, which went off on a tangent to the mainland, calling itself New Bombay where the sprawl was ambitiously trying to develop an alternative to the crowded island city. We now lived in a suburb on the Western Line – swathes of fields in parts could be seen from one room, and swamps and marshes from the other side of the house. The railway station was a bus ride away, the Link Road meant to connect the suburbs parallel to the arterial SV Road was still coming up in broken patches. The new and affordable building complexes in these outskirts sprouted like so many mushrooms, feeding on the decay of lives and souls that the city thrived on. We had lived in this complex, staid, middle class and cocooned in its insularity for almost two decades now, Maa for five years less than I had.

Purandhare kaka was still talking. My mind had wandered off.

'Perhaps we should call the police in, though I don't really have much faith in their abilities.'

'No, it's really okay.'

'I am going to fend off all those coming up the stairs. Just lie down, I'll tell them there was no robbery and you fell and hurt yourself. It wouldn't do for word to get around that there were intruders in the house. These people can be nasty gossips and do a one two *ka* four when not required.'

He stepped out. I could hear his booming voice instructing everyone to go home, that there was nothing to see here, I had just fallen down and hurt myself.

My head ached. I could feel the buzzing within begin. It could happen again and again and again, it did not bear thinking of, me bringing the Greyness into this, the world of the living, the here and now. If I had gone there once, I would go there again. And there was only one possible reason why I had gone there: in that time in that Greyness was a part of me, a part of me I hadn't been able to salvage. I needed to get her out from there, I knew, but I didn't know where would I put her once I plucked her out of the Greyness, how would I take her where she needed to be. I didn't know where I was supposed to put her, what time, what universe. And when I put her back where she belonged, I would have to stay where I'd plucked her out from, I would have to return to the Greyness. That was my punishment. Perhaps I needed to do it now. It would never stop until it took me.

I stood up shakily, feeling my head throb. In the bedroom I took a sedative from the bottle in my drawer and gulped it down without water. And then another, and another. Maa handed them to me as I swallowed them down. I stopped counting. I then lay down on the sofa and waited to be found. Waited to find myself in the Greyness.

Gauri-tai, uncaring of what I was swallowing down, was on her haunches, sweeping the broken glass into black garbage bags, tut-tutting at the wanton destruction of a perfectly good full-length mirror.

I could hear the shards of glass tinkling as she poured them into the bag from the dustpan, a tinkling that took me back years and decades, to the tinkling of ice as it hit glass and then the slosh of the golden liquid poured over it. And his voice, gentle, mellow yet threatening, velvet and thorn, scratching on my memories. I sank into bed, melting into it as the waves of darkness came.

'Ana, be a good girl, won't you?'

'Ana, jump after me, won't you?'

'Ana, come with me.'

The sound of his body hitting ground, flesh and bone slamming into concrete. And the dull thud of the next body, barely a couple of seconds later. Mine. As the blood flowed out of me, I looked up at a dull sky, the rain falling into my open eyes that could not shed tears anymore and that could not close on their own now. The Greyness closed over me, wet and warm, salty. The brine we all came from. The ocean. The amniotic sac. Washing over us, erasing all our memories, bringing us back, over and over again, to live, to die.

When Aman came, called by Gauri-tai when she realised I had passed out, I saw him pick me up and carry me down to the car, traces of vomit still at the sides of my mouth, my skin pale and blue. He drove me to the hospital with a speed that made me dizzy watching him. You can see it all, hear it all from within the Greyness. But no one can see you within, no one can hear you scream.

5

The New Girl

'When the remembering was done,
the forgetting could begin.'

—Sara Zarr

WHEN NAYNA CLAMBERED ON TO THE BUS EARLY THE NEXT morning, there was only one other passenger right up front in the single seat next to the driver. The indeterminate blue rexine seats were clean, freshly wiped for the start of a new day. She settled into the window seat in the last row, the one she preferred. The conductor smiled at her genially, displaying a mouthful of paan-stained teeth as he gave her a ticket.

He sat on the seat across the aisle and turned to her.

'And what have you got in your tiffin box today?'

She dug into her bag, pulled out her tiffin box to check.

'Jam sandwich.' It was the standard she was used to. Jam sandwich or chutney sandwich. Her mother's repertoire in the early hours of the morning extended to just this. Nothing more. She subsidised her hunger with visits to the school canteen from money she palmed off her father on Sundays, when he felt indulgent. There was exciting fare in the school canteen, like medu vada sambar, idli sambar, masala dosa, sabzi, puri bhaji, samosa, batata vada; the menu changed regularly. For a five-rupee coupon it offered her what she craved for, enough calories to keep her going till she reached home again.

She would not tell her mother that the tiffin box was inadequate. Her mother might just decide to not send any tiffin box, she was unpredictable like that. She was terrified of her mother but she loved her too. Sometimes. She loved her father and was not afraid of him. She knew he loved her unreservedly. Her mother could be cruel with a word, a glance. And then a sudden outpouring of guilty love that completely threw her off-kilter. She never knew what to expect from her mother, and she had learnt to keep herself distant. She spoke when spoken to and replied as was essential. It protected her. She needed to keep herself safe from her mother who hated her for what she reminded her of. For whom she reminded her of. She would never tell Nayna who that was. Sometimes her mother would look at her, examining her features with her eyes, touch her nose, her chin, her lips and cry softly, whimpers of pain. 'You poor child,' she would say, over and over again, and never tell Nayna why she was a poor child.

At others she would be curt, dismissive, scathing. 'I didn't want you, you know,' her mother had told her once. 'I could have been a heroine in the movies, you know, or a model, I was so pretty. Or a Miss India. Everyone called me Miss India in our town. But everything changed...'

Her voice had trailed off wistfully, and the story would never get completed. What it was, Nayna would never know. But it was so horrific that it had warped her mother completely. Nayna had asked her aunts about the story her mother would never tell her. And her grandmother. They would all pat her head and tell her to not bother herself with stories of what had happened before she was born. Her grandmother would say in a disapproving tone to the others, 'Mandira should love this child. It is not the child's fault.'

Nayna had grown up with the guilt of having been the reason her mother had to give up her dreams. When she grew up, old enough to have dreams of her own, the weight of her mother's shattered dreams would sit on the chest of her own fledgling dreams and choke them until they gasped for breath and died.

Angel was waiting for her when she alighted from the bus stop, ran up, sniffed her crotch in friendly camaraderie and then walked with her down the early morning road to school. The road glistened with the dew of the morning, or perhaps a late-night drizzle. The streetlights, still to be switched off, made the road gleam. An inverted world. Nayna looked down at herself, inverted, looking back with a frown. She smiled at herself. The girl in the reflection didn't smile back but stuck her tongue out.

'You know,' she told Angel. 'There was a new girl in my school yesterday. She was there in the morning in my class and then suddenly she wasn't and I saw her after I left the building, standing in the window of my classroom, looking down at me but I don't know where she went off to when class was on, I couldn't find her all day in the short break or the long, or even between classes. No one believed me when I told them about her. They thought I was making her up. Do you think she's shy?'

'Possibly,' Angel replied. 'Ask her if she is shy when you see her today, and tell her to sit next to you. Be her friend so she doesn't have to be shy.'

'Yes,' Nayna replied. 'I will do that today. Do you have any friends, Angel?'

'We don't really have friends as dogs, Nayna. We just roam around in packs but we forage for food on our own. And when I have kids, they grow up and go off on their own, not like humans who stay put with their parents for years and years.'

She entered school early as always, bounded up the stairs to her classroom where the lights were yet to be switched on. The new girl was there again, standing by the window, looking out. From that vantage point she would be able to see the main gate and the entrance to the school. Today she was dressed in a dress similar to yesterday's; not white though, but, an indeterminate colour between beige and biscuit. Nayna reached out and switched the lights on. The lights did not come on.

'The electricity has gone off again,' she said to herself and then turned to the girl. 'Hello there, where did you disappear to yesterday? I was looking all over for you.'

The girl turned around. Her face was sallow and pinched, her expression indecipherable.

'Come here, sit next to me on the first bench. Are you in Six C or in some other division?'

The girl nodded.

'Where is your school bag? Are you sure you're in this class? You seem like an eighth grader or a tenth grader.'

The girl stood motionless, not replying, not reacting.

'What's your name? I'm Nayna. My mom is from Meerut, my dad is from Jalandar, but now all the families are everywhere. My mom doesn't speak to her family because she didn't want to get married to my dad. She only speaks to one sister, Lovely maasi, and my father's father is dead anyway. My grandmother and his only sister live in Delhi, so I don't really have any cousins or anyone from my family here in Bombay to be with. I'm all alone. Do you have sisters and brothers?'

The girl shook her head.

'Oh, that's sad then, you must feel bored like I do. I wish I lived near school, I could come to your house and you could come to mine. And we could play together. But what's your name?'

The girl came round to the desk and sat next to Nayna, her face sad in a way that could not be defined, a sadness that wafted off her and entered Nayna, making her suddenly and inexplicably morose.

'I'm Sue.'

'You are the first Sue I know. Where did you come from, Sue, and why did you need to join school midterm?'

'My father died and we had to move homes.' Sue fell silent. Nayna was stymied into silence too. What did one say when someone just told you their father died? The silence though lasted only a few seconds, before her natural curiosity took over and refused to be restrained by the niceties of what construed polite conversation.

'How did he die?'

Sue looked at her, weighing carefully what she could share with this girl, ebullient with the joy of not having faced any grief in her years as yet.

'He jumped from our balcony on the fourth floor. His head cracked open on the cement of our building compound.'

Nayna shuddered involuntarily. A goose walked over your grave, as Sister Lucy would say, only Nayna had never seen geese anywhere, least of all in graveyards. All she had seen in the graveyard attached to the church down the road were stray dogs and an occasional cow who had created a good amount of hullabaloo when it refused to be shooed out by the gardener.

'Why did he jump?' It was the lot of young children to ask the questions that adults would hesitate to. It was also the lot of young children to answer these with all they knew and nothing more, no analysis, no opinion, no inference.

'I think he was very sad.'

'About what?'

'I don't know. He was always sad. He's passed his sadness to me now. Now I'm always sad, I don't know why.'

Nayna put her arm around her in an uncharacteristic gesture.

'Don't be sad, I'll make you happy. I will be your friend.'

Sue hugged her back and got up.

'I'll be back.' She walked out of the classroom towards the end of the corridor where the bathrooms were.

The lights flickered on a second after she stepped out of the classroom. It was a dark rainy morning. The clouds would not let the sunlight pass through. The other side of the corridor echoed with the sounds of squelchy footsteps and voices of young girls chirping in conversation with each other as they came tumbling up the stairs and through the warren of corridors to their classrooms. Nayna began setting out her books for the first period of the day and quickly finished some geography homework she had forgotten all about. Map work, she enjoyed it, marking out the mountain ranges of the world. The Himalayas, the Alps, the Atlas Mountains, the Rockies, the Appalachians, the Western Ghats, the Eastern Ghats, the Aravallis, the Caucasus, the Karakoram Range, the Pamir, the Hindu Khush… she crosschecked them with the textbook and carefully made the requisite sharp zigzag lines to indicate the ranges. Then she marked out the important peaks each had, writing their names and height in neat capital letters with a dark pencil. The pictures in the textbook intrigued her; some day she would go see these peaks, climb them, she told herself, like Edmund Hillary and Tenzing Norgay, like Bachendri Pal. She would stand on the summit of the Chomolungma, the Sagarmatha, one day and look down on the spread of the earth from that vantage point. Her father had indulged her this dream, her mother had scoffed at her. You can't sit through a road trip without vomiting, how will you ever climb the Everest? That was Maa, intent on crushing every dream she had because she was the reason Maa had crushed her own dreams.

The class had filled up, the bell rang, Sue didn't return. Nayna kept looking towards the door of the classroom, expecting her to come in at some point, but the entire period passed and she didn't. At the end of the class, Nayna excused herself and went to the toilets to check if Sue was hiding there, perhaps nervous about facing a classroom full of new faces and curious questions but there was no one. Confused, she went back into class. Miss

Shirley was now walking towards the staffroom. They had art now, and it was a class she happily bunked by flitting around aimlessly between the library and the laboratory and happily indulged in by custodians of both places, much to the dismay of the wren-like art teacher, Miss Koyal, who earnestly tried to teach a bunch of giddy pre-teens still life, composition in monotone, and nature studies, all of which they were thoroughly disinterested in.

'Miss Shirley!' she called, scampering behind her class teacher who walked on, her back ramrod straight, her legs two straight lines, accentuated by the high stilettos she always wore, no matter that all day she needed to climb up and down three floors relentlessly.

'Yes, my child, what is it?'

'The new girl, she was there again this morning, and then she disappeared again. She goes away when the other girls come in and then I don't see her anywhere for the entire day. She only comes when there is no one else in class.'

'This is the second time you've been talking about this new girl, Nayna. I asked at the office if there had been any new admissions. There is no new girl joining our class.'

The corridor began spinning around Nayna. Served her right for not having those Parle-G biscuits with her milk in the morning as Maa insisted, and only gulping her milk down. Perhaps she would faint right there in the corridor and have to be sent back home early.

'I spoke with her, Miss Shirley. She said they had to move homes after her father died and that's why she had to change schools. She was very sad. I hugged her. But she looked like she was an eighth grader. She's tall.'

'So, she probably is an eighth grader and had come to your class by mistake and went back to the eighth section.'

Nayna nodded. The corridor was still shaky around her. She put a hand on the banister of the stairs to steady herself.

'But, Miss Shirley, this is the second day she's come to our class. Perhaps she wants to be in the sixth grade.'

Miss Shirley laughed, her laugh was rare and precious and Nayna was pleased with herself for having evoked it. She patted Nayna on the head, thinking to herself the child had managed to develop such a vivid imagination.

'The next time you see her, you must ask her name and why she comes to the sixth grade.'

'She told me her name. She said her name was Sue.'

Miss Shirley's face went ashen for a moment, and her hands began trembling. 'What did you say her name was again?'

'Sue. That's what she told me. And she was very sad.'

'What does she look like?'

'She's very fair and tall, she has long hair, and she has light eyes like mine but green, not grey. She wears a dress, not a school uniform.'

Nayna looked up at her class teacher's face, now taut with an anxiety that had arrived from nowhere and settled all across her pinched features.

'What happened, Miss Shirley? Do you know her?'

Miss Shirley took a deep breath before putting out a hand that shook just a little bit to hold the banister. 'I don't. And the next time Sue comes to our class, please bring her to the staffroom. I'd like to meet her. I will come in early from tomorrow, and wait in the staffroom. Or you could come to the staffroom if you're early and the lights are still not on in the classrooms. It would be safer.'

'Why safer, Miss Shirley?'

'I don't want you to be alone in the classroom if no one is in yet when you arrive.'

'Why, Miss Shirley?'

'Tomorrow when you reach school, come straight to the staffroom and call me, and I will call Sister Theresa and we will all go together to speak with Sue. She shouldn't be going to the wrong classroom every morning.'

Nayna nodded. 'Okay, Miss Shirley.'

Miss Shirley patted her on the head and sent her back to class. She then went into the staffroom and had a quick glass of water before mopping the cold sweat off her brow. She went across to the wash basin in the corner of the room. The mirror over the cracked and weathered basin in the staffroom was blackening around the edges, the face that looked back at her was her own, perhaps from some twenty years ago. And behind her, blurring into the darkness at the fringes of the staffroom, now deserted, was a thin, pinched, sorrowful face. Miss Shirley turned around, her heart in her mouth.

'Sue,' she said, her voice shaking.

'What happened, Miss Shirley?' asked Mrs Rastogi, the Hindi teacher for the senior classes, who happened to be sitting at the other end of the long staffroom, having her morning tea and biscuits. 'Did you say something?'

There was no one there. It was all her imagination, of course, what else could it be?

'No, Mrs Rastogi, I just thought I saw someone I needed to speak with.'

Mrs Rastogi returned to her biscuits and her back copy of *Woman's Era*. Miss Shirley was a little off, the rumours went in the staffroom. An excellent teacher, no doubt, but a little off. Everyone kept a distance from her, there was no telling what would set her off. But no matter how unhinged she seemed to the rest of the staff, she was immensely gentle and patient with all her students. They loved her and she loved them like she would have loved all the unfertilised babies that tumbled out of her womb each month when she bled.

Miss Shirley walked over to the bench by the window and sat there, looking out, trying to collect her thoughts.

There had been a Sue who had joined midterm when her father had suddenly died by suicide and they had shifted homes. She'd been an eighth grader. This was before the school had expanded and reorganised its classrooms; what was the grade six section now was then grade eight. Miss Shirley had not taught Sue. In fact, she had been her classmate, she had sat next to Sue and shared tiffin boxes. They had been best friends, cross my heart and swear to die kind of best friends for that entire year. Sue had left school suddenly at the end of term, and never returned. Miss Shirley had never thought to find out what had happened, she hadn't even known where Sue lived to go ask about her. No one spoke about her after that year, it had been like she'd never existed in anyone's memories except Miss Shirley's. Sue, the girl with the two plaits to her waist, the green eyes and skin like milk with a thin film of cream on it. Nayna, all these years later, looked exactly like Sue, but was smaller, younger, not the same grade. Nayna was Sue a couple of years before she would be Sue. Miss Shirley realised why she had been so inexplicably fond of Nayna. Nayna, the girl who somehow subconsciously had reminded her of Sue, the girl who had been too pretty to be real, that's what one of their classmates had said about her. Perhaps she had never been real. Perhaps that's why no one had known her or missed her. Perhaps that was why she had slipped in and out of Miss Shirley's life without a ripple, disappearing into the nowhere she had come from.

6

The Clouds Fell Down

'Memory is the diary we all carry about with us.'

—Oscar Wilde

'ANA, EAT YOUR BREAKFAST.'

'Ana, close your mouth while chewing.'

The door to the bathroom opened and my father came out, dripping blood and brain, his limbs as twisted as they had been when he collided with the asphalt.

'Ana, aren't you going to jump too? I'm waiting for you. You promised me. Come on.' He stretched out his hand, the flesh rotting off the bone.

I woke up. All I had needed to do was to convince him not to jump. Instead, I had promised that I would jump after him and chickened out. It was a huge promise to expect an eight-year-old to stick to. It was my haunting, one I deserved. A day had passed since my return to my time; I had gone to a self that hadn't yet been formed, contained in the Greyness, waiting to be born. I had rebounded with double force back into my space, my time. I was glad of the mirror though; I had wanted to replace it for a long while. I saw Maa's face when I looked into it. I realised that my face was now Maa's. She was me. I was her.

At the clinic they pumped my stomach out. The Greyness spat me back when they brought me back to consciousness, I had failed yet again in doing what I'd set out to do. I was being kept there, saline drip in my vein, to recuperate and for what the doctors called observation. When I opened my eyes, I saw Aman, white and drained, by my bedside. I was here and now.

Aman, my lover, my keeper, my caretaker, my protector, my heart, my soul. He was everything and nothing, my words and my silences and also the space between the silences. He was the container of all I was. He was all that I had wanted from my life but had come into it too late to be all I needed. He stayed till he was sure I was out of danger, then he left and didn't come back for the next three days. When I called to tell him I was being discharged the next morning he arrived within twenty minutes. He must have driven like a maniac, I thought. Luckily it was against the morning rush hour.

'Don't do that, you could get hurt,' I said, as always selfish, worried about him not being there for me to turn to when I needed him.

'I'll be fine. Nothing will happen to me. Are you okay?'

He grabbed me and held me tight. I drowned in him, pulling him into my lungs, breathing him deep, choking on him.

'Shall we go?' He held my face between my hands and looked deep into my eyes. I nodded. His eyes were molten caramel, fire and warmth to mine, mine with the charcoal and copper flecks in indeterminate faded grey. I had Maa's eyes. Maa's face. Maa's skin. Maa's hair. Nothing of my father. I didn't know what my father looked like. Perhaps that was for the best, Maa always said it was. But sometimes Pappa had looked into my face, long, searching looks, trying to find glimpses of him in me and failed. It was a hope that was stillborn. I had nothing of him in me, except the love he had given me.

Aman drove me home. I shivered all the way back, the cold was within me, was me. Crow sat on the windowsill and looked at me with a beady, disapproving eye as we entered. I stuck to my story. Attempted robbery, I told him, the same story I'd given Purandhare kaka. I opened the door to what I thought was a courier delivery, turned around to find a pen to sign. And the chaps had pushed me and stormed into the home and then destroyed the bedroom when they couldn't find anything. I fell on the edge of the dining table and blacked out. The truth would have been unbelievable. The pills? I didn't realise I was taking too many, my head was aching, I wanted to sleep. He didn't buy it, I knew, but he wasn't going to argue with me right now over it.

'I've been telling you to move out of this old place! The ceiling is leaking, the building is falling to pieces and it is completely out of the way in the back of beyond. I'd feel better if you were in a complex with proper security systems in place instead of this old geezer who couldn't scare a stray dog away, and spends all his time scratching his balls and picking his nose.'

'You know I can't afford that.'

'Let this place be, lock it up, give it out on rent if you want, sell it off. I'll find you a place that's more...' he hunted for the word for a long moment, '...convenient.'

'Convenient for whom, Aman? Me or you?'

Impermanence was convenient. I was convenient. My location was inconvenient, out of his way; he would have preferred it closer at hand, possible for him to nip out when he could and drop in. And of course, I would have to be waiting, that was what my primary job was now – as mistress, a keep, relinquishing all claim to myself. Existing purely as a convenience. How had I let myself fall into this? Because it was convenient. I had slipped into being a convenience, without giving it a second thought. It was convenient to be a convenience.

'Let's not get into that discussion again. I would just feel safer about you if you were in an apartment complex that had better security. Just don't you dare keep disappearing on me, okay? I can't deal with it.'

I kept silent.

'Sleep it off. Bye,' he said, kissing me on the forehead. 'I'll drop by after work. We'll order in or I'll bring something, don't bother cooking. And think about what I said, about shifting to somewhere better. Safer.'

I wouldn't think about shifting. I couldn't afford it. But I would wait for him as always, feeling my heart sink every moment he didn't arrive. And then he would. Ring the doorbell, take up all the space of the narrow door, fill the room, fill the house, fill my heart, fill my cunt, until there were no empty spaces left inside me anymore. Until I couldn't feel eternity whistling through the gaps in my body.

'Okay, then find me a place and pay for it. I'm not selling this place. This is my home. And I am free to leave that one and come back here whenever I feel like.'

'Done! I'll find you a place by the end of the week. Keep your bags packed and ready.'

'So, I'm officially your keep now, is it?' I laughed. I didn't mind.

'You could be better things. You could be worse things. This is completely your call, of course. Perhaps it is time now to move on. You don't have to live your life hanging on to what your childhood handed you. Pack all that trauma away and move on.'

I couldn't. And I couldn't tell him that rather than moving on as he wanted me to, I was moving back, revisiting that trauma, exulting in the pain going back brought me, the physical and the emotional.

Maa had pushed me to get married when I was barely twenty-one. Only fair, she thought, that I get married and be off her hands. She accepted for me the first halfway decent proposal that came along. We were divorced soon. That was the end of that escapade. Marriage was not for me, I told Maa. She had narrowed her eyes, her beautiful almond eyes flashing fire.

'What will you do when I die?' she moaned. 'The world is not kind to women who live alone. You need a man to keep you safe, Ana, you need a man, a child, a family. They are the suraksha kavach that keeps the demons at bay. Without these, the world will eat you up and spit you out.'

'Don't worry about me,' I'd told her. 'I'll keep myself safe. I'll be my own suraksha kavach.'

She was kinder after my divorce. I wouldn't say she loved me more, but she didn't hate me as much. I'd had grief too, and she had been the cause of it. It was the closest I would get an apology from her. That she stayed detached from how I led my life henceforth was freedom enough. She continued teaching in the convent school she'd begun teaching in when I was a child, where she'd moved to teaching the secondary section now. Mandira Ma'am. Hindi teacher, class seventh to tenth, and Class Teacher 8A. The year she retired they gave her a huge framed tapestry of Radha and Krishna, ironic considering how devoid of romantic love her life had been. She'd hung it proudly above the divan in the living room. 'All the kids contributed to it. Imagine.'

She hadn't given any opinion about the men who came and went in my life. Her detachment helped, she cared and she didn't care and made no attempts to hide her indifference. Where libido stepped out, love stepped in. And then came the early menopause. It would have been easier, I told myself, to have been in this only for the sex and the money. Love messed up things. When had lust morphed into love I didn't know. Perhaps I was just too alone to know better. Aman was everything I shouldn't have had in my life and more, churned my stomach, made me weaker and stronger, sadder and happier, and all the things I didn't know I could be altogether, all at once. He was mine and only mine and he wasn't.

I had never known ownership of a person all my life, but now I knew the release of allowing myself to belong to another. We fitted together, two broken souls, to run our fingers over where we had been broken and glued ourselves back together so that we could get on with the business of living in a world where broken bodies were healed and broken souls were left unrepaired.

It was a Wednesday morning. Wednesdays are indeterminate, unlike Thursdays or Fridays that were only a hindrance to the arrival of the weekend. The morning was spent sorting out and replying to unanswered emails, lying neglected in my inbox for the past so many days. I had meetings to deal with, projects to be closed, commissioned projects to be delivered and discussed, payments to be chased with invoices and reminders that would progress from the gentle to the belligerent. I had been away, unscheduled. It suited me, being a consultant on long-term research projects. I worked at my own pace, and deadlines were always long and generous for the kind of work I took on. I was good with it, it was impossible to schedule anything now, there was no telling when I would cross. Crossings happened. I was slowly learning to recognise the symptoms of when one would happen. A buzzing in my ears, a sudden glimpse of myself in a reflection and then falling through and emerging where there were the others of me. A fraction of a second was all it took in my time, I had no idea what it took in other times. I'd crossed over and over again. It was against the order of nature, I'd thought, but now I knew that nature had no order, that we existed in multiple times and multiple universes, much like a slab of bread loaves, ladi pav we called them, the breakfast of my childhood, butter on bread freshly delivered from the bakery, still warm in the bread bag hung on our door knob, dunked in a steaming hot cup of sugary tea. We lived out in parallel universes, in our individual loaves of space time, all multiple selves of ourselves, each living out a version of our reality, shifted, altered, perceptibly, imperceptibly, and each unaware of the existence of the other. As it should be. Me, I was the traveller, I was an aberration.

At first, I thought I was losing my mind. I began taking pills to knock me out, to put me into sleep so dead that only the alarm would wake me. There was no point in reliving the pain, in scratching scar tissue already healed. It was strange, recognising myself and then not, seeing the girl I was, seeing the woman I would become. A few minutes at first, here. Hours there, and then days here, across the darkness that wrapped itself around me like a coil and shot me through it.

There was no one I could talk to about it. Aman wouldn't understand. And I couldn't tell him. To him I was the strange one who came and went without explanation. He had learnt to live with this, my idiosyncrasies as he thought. To him, I was this strange creature, completely different from the very regimented childhood he'd had. Civil service parents, a childhood scattered across the country, playing tag to the parents at their more convenient postings, and then boarding school when he was old enough to manage on his own. Economics honours, then an MBA from an Ivy League university, and straight into one of the most prestigious multinationals in the country. Married at the right age, produced the mandatory two kids, his wife morphed into a trophy wife groomed to within an inch of her life, content to dabble in art and social service as they shuffled around various positions within India and abroad. This was when our paths crossed. Or collided. And we found in each other what we needed. Pain, solace, release, love. Depending on which world you looked at us in. The marriage was dead, that's what he told me and I chose to believe without questioning. Questions were inconvenient.

It had been four years now, here. We were just starting off elsewhere, in others, in some we had ended it. In yet others, we were together, after he'd left his wife, we had kids, we were married. In others we were yet to meet. In some, he would die. In others, I would. Every stage of this I knew existed somewhere, in some time. In every life, he was with me, and I with him. Infinite versions of ourselves looped into infinite versions of our story together.

The water was cold as it hit my body as I showered. The bathroom fittings were still the original ones, put in when the building was built, and like the rest of the building were old and spasmodic. The water sputtered indecisively, and the lone CFL bulb flickered in a strange synchronicity to the water pressure. I towelled myself off with the roughness of one for whom the body is no source of pleasure, but rather a bulk to be tolerated and which demanded to be bathed, fed, clothed. Dragging my bathrobe off the peg, I put it on, the little bathroom eerie with the flickering bulb. My reflection in the mirror above the little basin quivered with it. It hit me then, I would cross now. It was a new mirror, one I had picked up from the hardware store down the lane. I could feel my head still heavy from the last crossing that landed me where I was not supposed to go. I couldn't understand why I had been sent there. But then there was nothing I could explain about all this. I didn't have the vocabulary for it. I just got carried along whenever it opened and took me, and sometimes it took me where a version of me wasn't and sent me back. And then it opened again, a yawning craw that devoured me whole, spat me out again, covered with the slime of the spaces I had visited.

I drew the robe closer to myself, wishing I had time to pull on more appropriate clothing for travelling across time space. Of course, such travel did not demand vanity but comfort. But before I could react or respond, I saw myself dissolve in the reflection right in front of me, into a flash of bright blue sparks and then fell through that vortex of undecipherable dimness, with the sparks flashing past me, popping circles and streaks of light on my retina until the tunnel curved suddenly and dropped me soft as a feather into the other room I had seen in the mirror before I saw my reflection dissolve. The afterglow of the brightness still was a circle on my retina when I saw her standing there, at the end of the darkness, as she looked all around her trying to make sense of her surroundings. Such a curious little thing she was, so different from the other girls who were only keen on playing and discussing the latest Hindi movies in the park. And she was beautiful, hauntingly so. A beauty that came from hope and innocence and trust. She was me. She was not me. She was us.

She was never quite all there, her nose in books she borrowed from the school library and the library down the lane, lost in the adventures of white-skinned children called George and Anne in the England of yore, imagining what scones would taste like and what would it be like to live in homes with a garden and a fireplace, and where everyone dressed for dinner and supper was had in the evening.

The house had allowed Nayna in. It would, wouldn't it? Had I expected otherwise?

'Here you are. I was searching for you, I wanted to give you this.' She held out a book, cloth-bound in dull green with golden lettering on it. *Grimm's Fairy Tales*. An illustrated copy, so exquisitely illustrated that it brought to life the unicorns, the cannibalistic witches in candy houses, the thumb-sized little girl, the beanstalk and the giant, the Pied Piper and all the magical people who lived within. It had been my most precious possession when I was her. I had forgotten these stories as I had grown up. We were doomed to forget magic and lose our belief in it as we became adults. It was the price one paid for growing up.

I knelt down beside her, holding my bathrobe together, marvelling that it hadn't disintegrated on the journey here, that I hadn't disintegrated between the there and the here.

'Thank you, I will read this.' She was holding some flowers in her other hand, picked from the shrubbery at the back of the housing complex. Where the elderly women of the building picked fresh blooms for their puja. I had loved them as a child, these flowers, and I had forgotten them too. Five petals, white with a yellow centre, a strong fragrance that was childhood, play and nostalgia and all I had left behind rolled into one. Champa. The name hit me out of the blue, the limbic system kicked into action. Frangipani, as I had learnt they were called much later.

'These are my favourite flowers,' I said, not untruthfully.

'Really?' Nayna's eyes sparkled in response.

'Yes, I love these and I love lavender, but you don't get lavender stalks here. Someday when you are older, you'll fly to another country in a plane, and you'll stay a while in a country called France where they grow lavender, you'll see the fields of lavender and never want to come back home.'

'Will you take me there?' Nayna put her small palm in my hand, all admonishments from her mother to steer clear of strangers who sought to take you away clean forgotten.

'I will,' I promised. I didn't know how I could make that happen.

We were, I knew, a day away from the before and the after of her life. I now had a chance to change it. What would anyone do when given a chance to play God but to grab the opportunity, uncaring of the potential chaos it would unleash in the universe. I knew then just what I had to do. I did it. The second time I chose to play God. It was barely a moment, a second to decide, a nanosecond to cross. It was time, it was space, it was crossed. Barely a step across the darkness into another room, another time, another place. In her eyes danced starlight that was aeons in the making, from another part of the universe, from the beginning of time and space and existence. There was no sound, except a whine that went on interminably, then a hushed silence that drilled at the tympanic membranes. A tunnelling darkness. A falling through. She was silent, unafraid as I held her hand. I had always been brave, braver than I thought myself to be. Had she been through this before, I wondered, was this familiar to her? We now stood opposite the mirror I had been facing a few minutes ago. The drop that had been suspended at the tip of the mouth of the tap when I crossed now fell and was swallowed by the drain. It was loud, the sound of it hitting the basin. There was no longer any silence. Time had unpaused itself.

I looked down at her confused tiny face, the eyes too long-lashed, the nose too tiny and the lips too finely shaped. She was exquisite. Had I been this exquisite and not realised it?

'Where are we?' she asked, her voice quiet with fear, strong with courage.

'The right question is perhaps when are we. But don't you worry, you are safe here with me.'

'Is this your house?'

'Yes, this is my house.'

'This is not your that house.'

'No,' I replied, as honestly as I could, 'This is not my that house.'

'Which house is this?'

I had no reply to that so I smiled. She frowned back. In her face was puzzlement. She walked out of the bathroom and into the house, examining every room, her steps careful and measured with the unfamiliarity of the situation she found herself in. She was still holding the champa flowers in her hand, and I had my old book of *Grimm's Fairy Tales* in mine, the copy she had brought across to lend me. This was still brand new, the gilt letters embossed on its cover still bright and shiny, the pages yet unyellowed by the patina of time.

'I've come here before,' she said with a definiteness I could not refute. 'You were sleeping in your bed. Then I went back home.'

She walked to the window that looked out into the marshlands in the distance. The marsh birds flew in and out, diving into the waters, roosting on the stumpy marshland shrubs, sentinels guarding a liquid world. On the other side of the island city, to the east, a sea of pink covered the mudflats every yearend. Flamingos arrived from the cold of Siberia every November, with the unerring navigational compass that genetic instinct and migratory routes conferred upon them. With their pink bodies and long legs, they flew in to escape the Arctic winters and stayed a while until it was summer again. Parents flocked to show them to their children, the flamingos of Sewree. There were other birds too, that were denizens of these wetlands. The Curlew Sandpiper, Eurasian Oystercatcher and Bar-tailed Godwit. My father used to take me to see the birds, with his binoculars around his neck and his cap perched jauntily on his head. I remembered his joy at spotting a rare bird, and how the joy quickly transferred itself to me when I realised that birds were the only creatures on earth who were not constrained by gravity. When would man be able to fly independently, I had wondered. Why had mankind stopped after Icarus, why had we not pursued devices that would let us fly independently, apart from the single-seater airplanes that were cumbersome and needed hangar space and money, or paragliding which was more an adventure sport rather than being refined into a legitimate mode to travel around the city? Why had we not gone on from the genius of Leonardo da Vinci and his magnificent sketch prototype of the personal flying machine he envisaged, the human ornithopter, with its bat inspired wings of the immense wingspan? Why had we not moved into the future with the personal jetpacks like The Jetsons, allowing us to defy gravity and fly off wherever we chose to? Why were we all not Superman, traversing interstellar space, escaping gravity and human limitations? I missed my father and the glimpses he gave me of not needing to be bound by gravity and the earth. Perhaps he had wanted to fly when he jumped. Perhaps he hadn't realised that he would crash.

'I like your this house. That house was very dark and old and dirty.'

'Thank you.'

'How did we come to this house without coming out of the building?'

'Let's just say we took a short cut,' I replied. 'I can't quite understand it myself to explain it to you.'

It involved time warping, parallel universes, the chequered fabric of time space, thought travel and multiple existences. I didn't know how it happened. All I knew was that she was here. And she was there. And I was wherever we went—back or ahead. And she could move through like I could. Perhaps we all could.

I saw my home as Nayna would, a confused mix of the old and the new, threadbare and the shiny fresh from the store. The new windows just put in, the old furniture, the Godrej almirah, the teak sofas with the tapestry covers, the new bookshelf with the clean lines, the television on the wall, sleek like a painting, reflective like the time tunnel it was.

'Why do you have two houses? Are you very rich?'

I laughed. 'I don't have two houses, I'm not rich at all.'

'Don't show your teeth when you laugh, only wicked women laugh out loud and show their teeth. Like Shoorpanakha. It brings ruin to the family,' Nandi maasi's voice rang in my head. I wondered which dark recess of time she was now haunting. I never wanted to run into her ever again, she with her penchant for picking out the worst in a person and forever focusing on it in her interactions with them. She died a miserable death, her innards rotted beyond removal, her body shrunken to bone and skin topped with a hank of hair. All her misery turned on her, settling itself deep into her cells, making them putrid, turning her organs against her, until she imploded, a putrescence of negativity.

There had been a simmering resentment between these two sisters that I had never understood nor attempted to understand. Could it have been the imbalance of appearances? My mother so delicately beautiful, a beauty that her grandmother had often called the cause of her ruin. And Nandi maasi, bovine as her name would indicate, stoic in the placidness she had inherited feature by feature unmercifully from her father. The complexion that no amount of gram flour and milk cream paste application would subdue into the realm of the wheatish, the nose too broad and flat, the eyes too tiny, the face that was too square, and beneath it all, a young girl who had grown up ugly in the shadow of a beauteous sister who could wake up in the morning, splash water on her face and have the morning star smile down at her, the fading moon rays linger a bit to caress her. Lovely maasi stayed out of the quarrels of her two siblings.

Nayna had inherited her mother's beauty, the nose that was fine and straight and the small nostrils that flared impatiently when she was angry, the eyes that were wide and full-lashed, moving from grey to green depending on the light and her mood, the hair that was a tumble of waves, skin that was blessed with a smoothness no amount of store-bought jars could ever promise to replicate. In ancient Greek mythology, beauty was a curse from the Gods. It only brought unhappiness in its wake. Nayna would learn that soon enough, as I had.

'Where's your office? My mom goes to teach at a school near my house and my father goes to Nariman Point. It takes him over an hour to get to office from our house in the morning by train. He takes his scooter to the railway station and parks it and then takes the train to Churchgate. He drops me to the bus stop in the morning. I go to school by bus. It takes me half an hour to reach school. I stay the furthest from school and yet I reach first every day. Our principal mentioned me in the assembly last week as an example of a determined student who travels from very far but doesn't miss a single day of school or reach late. I even got a certificate of appreciation. Even my best friend, Sangita, was jealous. She lives in the next lane. But she's always late to school, every morning.' Nayna lowered her voice to a whisper. 'She even cut her hair into a fringe. A Sadhana cut. Sister Theresa made her pin it back with bob pins. You know we have the same colour eyes. Why aren't you married, Ana?'

Nayna's thoughts scattered themselves around the room and she plucked them as she chose to voice them. There was no filter, no coherent flow; she spoke as her thoughts tumbled. Unfettered, unthinking. The world would soon teach her how to put her thoughts into ordered streams, and dam them up, to be released bit by bit to those who chose to listen to her, to those she chose to share them with.

'Because I didn't like anyone enough to want to live my life with.'

Nayna took in this answer, her eyes widening and unquestioning. She had come across few women of my age in her eight years who were unmarried, and seemed content to be so.

'Crow told me to go with you when you came. And so I came.'

'Crow?'

'Yes, Crow. He told me I had to listen to what you would tell me and that you would take me away and I should go. What are you going to tell me?'

I sighed. What was I to tell her, this child who was me and not me? I hugged her, feeling the bones beneath her thin frame, their fragility a reminder of just how delicate she was, and just how easily she could be snapped into two. The mirror in the room in which we stood reflected the two of us, a grown woman hugging a young girl, who stood confused, looking all around her, trying to make sense of her surroundings, and the sudden shift from where she had been to where she was. And beyond us, a reflection of an older woman, her silver curls tied carelessly at the nape of her neck, her unwrinkled face golden and glowing in a pale light, her robe flowing like water around her, a tear trickling down the side of one eye, fading imperceptibly around the edges and then disappearing from view.

Outside, the clouds had darkened and the rain began pelting

down with a force that smacked against the walls of the building. Soon the compound would get flooded if it continued raining this way. The world outside would be a watery morass, inaccessible, and we were stuck here, she in my time and I in my own, with no idea what I was supposed to do with her in this time, in my time. How long did I need to keep her with me? Would I ever be able to take her back, and if I did, how would she live out the rest of her days, how would life change for her if the incident had bypassed her, if she had been away? All I could do now was to wait until the doors opened again and we were thrown back across the vortex of time and space and the universe, so we emerged together at a tick-tock one of us had already lived and one would hopefully never live.

7

Drowned In

'Memories are killing. So you must not think of certain things, of those that are dear to you, or rather you must think of them, for if you don't there is the danger of finding them, in your mind, little by little.'

—Samuel Beckett

POST-LUNCH AN APOCALYPTIC CLOUD SWAM OVER THE CITY, A black lid of doom, impenetrable, unmoving. The rain began coming down heavy, then heavier, until the sky upturned itself in a deluge with no beginning, no end, only water flowing and blurring everything.

An occasional flash of lightning split the horizon at a distance and thunder grumbled angrily a few seconds later. A waiting held its breath in anticipation of what might come. There was a sense of the sky falling, filling gutters already overflowing, filling up every crevice, every hollow, every gap, until the damp seeped through skin. Rain that threatened to swallow the city whole. A sense of sinking, of the self, of the city. The city a watery grave. A day when the earth and purgatory merged into each other, and souls crawled out of the netherworld, trying to find their bearings in this one.

'You better go find her and bring her home,' the father said, pulling off his sodden shoes, which had left mucky stains on the grey speckled terrazzo tiles. He had come home early as offices had shut in the middle of the day after reports that the railway tracks had flooded. 'Did you see the children anywhere when you came home? I can't see her from here,' the mother said, her tone not quite worried, because she knew Nayna would be around as she always was, somewhere, playing hopscotch with her friends in the covered spaces where the rain couldn't get them, or singing Hindi film songs. A quiet finger of disquiet tap-danced up her spine, reaching the nape of her neck and turning into an icy grip around her throat, squeezing it, releasing it, making her gasp for air.

Her husband didn't notice her expression slide from the mildly worried into the panicked. But then her husband didn't notice her expressions at all these days; he rarely looked at her face, into her eyes. When she served him tea he was looking at the newspaper, when she served him food he was looking at the television, when he entered her body her eyes were shut to shut him out. They looked at anything but each other. It made for peace.

'They are probably in the stairwells or in the garages or behind D wing,' the father said, the disdain he felt for his wife falling off his words like the fat raindrops he had shaken off his umbrella just outside the door.

The mother wiped her hands on the little rag that hung from the handle of the noisy second-hand refrigerator they had purchased a couple of months ago, and unconsciously smoothed down her hair, straightened her faded cotton home saree, the pallu of which she had tucked into the waistband of her petticoat to keep it out of the way when she was trying to chop and cook. Her face, reflected in the screen of the television not yet switched on, was puckered with stress. The compound had begun to flood up.

She was probably in a friend's home. There was always a simple explanation for most things, a simple explanation that was almost always overlooked in the quest for the complex.

'Let me go down and find her,' she muttered, not expecting a response from her husband, and not getting one. He was like that, responded to her only when it suited him. She was used to this. She didn't expect better. He changed into his home kurta and pyjamas, the drawstring hanging out inelegantly, and was now sitting on the divan watching a newscaster drone on about the derailment of a train up north that had taken many lives and was already cluck-clucking in indignation over the laxity of operations in this country and why India and Indians needed a dictatorship to get things running like clockwork. Perhaps, in some corner of his brain, he saw himself as the ideal person to run the country, never mind that he was hard-pressed to efficiently run the five-member minor department he was in charge of at the office.

The light was dim on the landing and a bulb flickered half-heartedly in the stairway as she made her way down. Climbing down the four floors and climbing up again multiple times was something she was used to on a daily basis, but this time her stomach caught itself in a panicked twist as she went down. Her mind did a rough calculation, and icy water pooled in her limbs.

No, she didn't want another child, though her husband did; he wanted a son, to carry on his name, he said. Fat lot of good his name had done in the world while he had borne it aloft all his forty years. What did he care, he didn't have to deal with the feeding, cleaning, the sick days and nights, the body thrown out of whack for over a year, the sleep deprivation, the darkness of motherhood no one spoke about when they exhorted you to have a child.

She would buy raw papaya, she told herself, eat it so it cramped her up and pushed the blastocyst out of her uterus. And that black tablet, the one with the ingredients guaranteed to make the womb inhospitable to any implantation. Her husband would never know. He had never known of the ones earlier, expelled out of the womb by a steady consumption of heaty foods and herbal concoctions she had gleaned from a friend who was not in a profession her husband would approve of. She didn't want to bear this man a child, he didn't deserve to have his genetic material propagated in this universe. All she worried about was how to keep her daughter unaffected by his sly vitriol; her daughter was all that mattered to her. Her daughter was all she had, a memory of a love that was once within her grasp, and then ruthlessly snuffed out. The family never spoke of it. But her cousins and her father coming home, the blood still fresh on their clothes, their voices hushed and her being married off within the week was her truth and her reckoning. And the child burgeoning in her belly, making her presence felt a few months later, born too early into the marriage, born healthy and full term.

'Naynaaaaa....' she called, knowing that the rain was drowning out her voice.

'Nayn......' She looked around. None of the kids her daughter played with were to be seen anywhere. There was no chattering of little voices riding above the sound of the rain falling. She opened the umbrella she'd carried with her and held her saree up higher so it wouldn't get soaked. She went up to the watchman who was seated in the little cabin by the gate.

'Jaywant kaka, have you seen Nayna around?'

He said, 'She went into A Wing.'

She took a step back, a sudden fear gripping her stomach and twisting it.

'Who are her friends who live in A Wing?'

'No one from A Wing she plays with,' he replied.

She narrowed her eyes and two lines appeared vertically between her eyebrows; her lips compressed into silent rage. She turned round, swiftly marching up to the A Wing, climbing up the floors to the third floor as swiftly as she could. This was the first time she had come here. The door to A-302 was shut. She rang the doorbell of the flat opposite. Mrs Pathankar lived there, she knew. She lived alone after her husband had passed away a couple of years ago and her children had all moved to different cities in pursuit of academia and employment. There was a faint stirring within and then the sound of heavy feet shuffling towards the door.

'Who is it?' Mrs Pathankar called from within, before opening the door with the safety chain on, her expression wary and just that bit annoyed.

'Arrey, it is you, Mandira. Sorry, these children keep ringing the bell and running away, so annoying.'

'Sorry, but have you seen Nayna? Jaywant kaka told me she came into this wing, and she has no friends here, except for your neighbour whom she waves out to and chats sometimes in the park she tells me. But the house is locked and I can't find her anywhere.'

Mrs Pathankar looked over her shoulder at the door opposite, her expression inscrutable. 'There is no one in that house, Mandira, not for a long while. I haven't seen Nayna either… So pretty she is growing up to be, just like you, Mandira. Thank God she didn't get her father's looks. I am sure she is around somewhere. Always wandering around, that child, lost in her own world.'

Mandira shrugged, faintly embarrassed at how she was always put down for being better looking than her husband, almost as if it was her fault. Where could Nayna be? On a parallel track her mind, this strange thing that could hold simultaneous thoughts and worry about both equally, wondered whose child was in her stomach, was it her husband's sperm that had reached her eggs, or was it the other's, the one who came to her when the child was at school and the husband at work, the gloriously beautiful one she had taught touch by touch, move by move, thrust by thrust, how to please her until her body spasmed into ecstasy. She put a hand to her head and clutched the banister with another, breaking into a cold, clammy sweat.

'Come inside, Mandira, have a glass of water. I am sure Nayna will be around somewhere, playing. Or in someone's home watching TV. Don't worry.'

Mandira shook her head, face pinched with worry.

'I can't find her anywhere. I thought she would be here.' She looked at the door opposite again, where the cobwebs hanging down it were long undisturbed.

Perspiring madly, she turned towards the steps. She was faded now, but she must have been pretty once, Mrs Pathankar thought, looking at the other's pale skin, the thick plait hanging down her back like a snake, her frame tall and lithe, her eyes red-rimmed with unshed tears of fright. She must have been lovely before marriage and childbearing had wrung her hollow. What ogres of parents had married her to the man who was her husband, Mrs Pathankar wondered; such an ill-matched couple! She so exquisitely beautiful, despite the crumpled saree and the lack of any adornment. He like a toad birthed him; beady, suspicious eyes, balding, bespectacled, shorter than her, puffed up with misplaced self-importance and a potbelly that entered the room before he did. Mandira couldn't have been more than thirty and already fine lines had carved themselves into her skin: two lines from her nostrils to the edge of her lips, a furrow between her eyebrows and crinkles around her eyes that came not from laughter but from a constant squinting against the sun, and a deep vertical one between her brows from frowning. She had bestowed her beauty upon her daughter, Nayna, a gift made generous by her complete renunciation of all efforts to beautify herself. If she as much as applied kohl in her eyes, her husband would have something to say. 'Have you asked her friends where they last saw her?'

Mandira nodded. 'They told me they had all gone home, but Nayna said she had something to tell Ana, and came up here. And the door is closed... But Nayna sees her standing in the window and waves to her. And talks to her in the compound some evenings.'

'Don't be silly, I'm sure she was imagining someone. This flat has been empty for years. A girl supposedly committed suicide here, but that was much before I came here.'

'But where is my daughter then if she's not here?'

'I'm sure she is in someone's house.' Mrs Pathankar patted her hair down purposefully, picked up a key from the hook right next to the door and came out of the house, closing the door firmly behind her. 'Come, let's find her.'

They went down the stairs, Màndira on swift feet that found new wings and Mrs Pathankar with steps that echoed down to the ground floor with the effort of hauling her weight around. Within a few minutes, most of the residents of the colony were down in the quadrangle underneath open umbrellas, in deep conference about where Nayna could have disappeared to; all those Nayna played with had been summoned for their inputs. The verdict was clear – she had told them she would be going to meet Ana in A-302. But there was no Ana in A-302. A-302 had been closed for years and years, there were cobwebs across the door. No one had been in, no one had come out.

Her husband came down, noticing the racket from the balcony, having hastily pulled on his office shirt and trousers. His spectacles had droplets of rain and his sparse hair was plastered across his scalp wetly, the ridiculous comb-over he adopted giving him neither camouflage nor dignity in the pouring rain. Yet, in his diminished soaked avatar he still commanded respect; he was, after all, a senior manager and these things mattered to the men who were the breadwinners. When all other things were equal, rank and file were the only thing they had to distinguish one mediocre man from the other.

'Khosla saab, don't worry,' said Mr Khare. 'She will be here or there somewhere, we will all look for her.' And so they did, going off in different directions, calling out Nayna's name.

After a couple of hours, the residents gathered again at the quadrangle, defeated in their search. The ones who went to the wall behind, where the banyan tree stood and watched over the children, scampered back because there were voices and shadows that moved but no Nayna to be found in the torchlight. No one clambered over the wall and looked across the marshes in the distance. They knew the child would not go there voluntarily and if the child had indeed gone there, they didn't want to be the ones who found her. Voices had dropped to a hush, children were yelled at to stay within their homes and not to step out. Mr Khare and Mr Inamdar, the two stalwarts of the retired gentlemen's club that generally occupied the bench next to the main gate to scrutinise the comings and goings of all that mattered in the colony, stepped up and pulled the father aside, murmuring to him in concerned undertones that now all that was left was to file a missing person's complaint. He nodded and went off with a couple of more men from the colony to the police station.

The women helped Mandira to her feet, walking her up the four flights to her home, murmuring words of hollow reassurance. Her husband had left the main door open, she noted, in her worry. Not out of any consideration for her, she knew, but because he didn't know where the house keys were. It was *her* job to keep the door closed. He came and went with the privilege of knowing someone would always open it for him.

The rain, unknowing of the devastation it was wreaking in the heart of a mother, continued to pour down here, in this city, in this suburb, in this year and in this city, in this suburb, in that year, where Nayna stood at the window and looked out at a view she had never seen, wondering where she was, not realising that what she really had to worry about was when she was, and that the when she was in was far, far removed from the when she came from.

And Ana had no idea how to get her back. Or where.

8

Swimming in the Tears of a Cloud

'And the moral of the story is that you don't remember what happened. What you remember becomes what happened.'

—John Green

AMAN CALLED UP AT AROUND EIGHT IN THE EVENING. NAYNA WAS by the window, looking out at the impenetrable darkness. 'Are you okay?' he asked.

I was okay, I assured him. I was home, I told him, I was safe.

'Sukanya and the kids are home too, so they're safe. I'm going to stay in the office tonight. The roads are flooded, the Western Railway and the Central Railway tracks, both lines, are down, so most of the staff is staying back in the office. I could try driving back home, but it just seems more sensible to stay back. I might just book myself into a hotel down the road if I need some proper sleep and a bath. Or sleep on the sofa in my office.' He paused. 'You just make sure you stay put at home. No need to step out of the house.'

I had stepped out of the house and come back without getting caught in the floods. This was not something he would understand

and not something I could tell him. Not yet, not right now.

'I'm at home,' I replied. I didn't add that I now had with me a young girl who was me. A me from another time and place, a younger me who had the potential to become so much more than what I had become, who still had to pull together the floating, silvery strands of fate and destiny and free choice to weave the tapestry of what would eventually become her life.

'The city is drowning.'

I knew. I'd seen it in the microscopic fragment of a second as I re-entered my world, my time. A broiling wall of water encircled the city, alive and seething, engulfing everything within.

'Love,' he said, his words truncated, the 'I' and the 'you' missing. All we needed was the assurance of love and the boundaries between us dissolved. Strange how a relationship that began on the premise of pure lust had now curiously morphed into something beyond me, beyond him, something the world called love, a word completely inadequate to express how we felt.

'Love,' I replied. A word hopelessly inadequate for the burden of belonging and implicit surrender that it bore.

Nayna was eating a quickly rustled together meal of dal and rice with pickle and curd by the light of a candle. This was the zenith of my culinary abilities and she was hungry, the child. All food is delicious when tempered with hunger, I realised that now. She served herself some more and ate it quickly, her hand moulding the rice, dal and curd into a convenient morsel that she ferried to her mouth with ease. I watched her indulgently.

Outside the window the marshlands were submerged, tips of the stunted trees now barely visible. The tide had come in, barrelling back rainwater that should have flowed out into the sea. The rainwater waited politely on the roads, the streets, the bylanes, waiting for the tide to go out so it could follow it out into the sea. In the building compounds, in the back alleys, the swelling wall of water climbed higher, held back by a recalcitrant sea that would not ease, would not give, would not cede space in its welcoming bosom. The sea would not be denied, it would claim back what man had taken from it.

At around six in the evening the electricity went. We were plunged into a darkness unrelieved by distant stars or a pale, undecided gibbous moon. A dark now settling over the city like a benediction and curse.

The whispery light of candles could be seen in homes all around. It was a routine they were familiar with every monsoon, the residents of this area. Torches, matchboxes and candles were standard household essentials during the monsoon. Every home had enough stocked to see them through nights of no electricity. Homes filled up buckets of water when the downpours showed no sign of abating, awaiting the electricity to be switched off and the water pumps not being able to carry water up to the rooftop tanks. Water in every bottle, steel utensils on kitchen platforms filled with water, enough to keep them hydrated for a couple of days until the electricity was switched back on and the water pumps became functional again. And the contingency plan for those dependent on gas cylinders to cook their food was a kerosene stove with bottles filled with kerosene stored safely for days just like these when the city would be flooded out and gas cylinder deliveries would go on hold. The drainage system for the city had been built by the British over a century ago and hadn't grown to keep pace with the growing city. There was no telling when life would return to normal this side of time and the multiverse.

'Do you want any more?'

'No,' Nayna shook her head from side to side, and patted her belly to emphasise her satiety. 'I'm not hungry anymore. Maa must be worried. How can I tell her I'm okay?'

'We can't, unfortunately, until the rain lessens.' There was nothing more I could explain to Nayna. All we could do was wait until the mirrors decided it was time to send us back to where we had come from.

Nayna nodded, she was an understanding child, one who didn't throw tantrums, an obedient child. Maa had told her that often enough, that she was a good girl, she behaved herself. Maa could trust her with her secrets, to not tell Pappa. She hadn't. Maa's secrets were all safe with her because she was a good girl. She didn't tell Pappa about the one who visited Maa when he was not at home. It was their secret now. Maa's and hers. She would never tell Pappa. She had learnt early on to keep out of the fights between her parents; the rancour was so deep and acidic, an accidental splash from the bickering would scald. Even Crow had told her she was a good girl. She looked at the television on the wall.

'What's this?'

'The TV.'

'It looks like a painting. Where is the knob to turn it on?'

'We can't right now, alas, there is no electricity. But I can put my laptop on for you if you want.'

'Laptop?'

I went to the bedroom and fetched it, my old HP laptop, clunky and outdated, large as a briefcase, setting it on the dining table. The screen blazed into light and her eyes lit up.

'Wow!'

I realised I had bypassed the desktop altogether in introducing her to the laptop, a technology completely alien to her. She touched it gingerly, afraid it would disintegrate if she did something wrong.

'What do you use it for?'

'My work,' I replied. 'I write my reports on this, reply to my emails, and things like that… Emails are like messages or letters, but they go from computer to computer.'

'So, there's no postman?'

'There is a postman, but there is also something called the internet, which connects all the computers in the world.'

Nayna nodded. The mobile on the table caught her eye next. She picked it up, curious.

'It's a phone.'

Nayna laughed. 'No, this is not a phone. If this is a phone where are the buttons with the numbers? And the wire?'

She had no phone at home. She was used to the push button phone at the milk booth down the road where Maa went to call Lovely maasi. With an uncertain hand she jabbed at it, and then leaped back as the numbers popped up on the screen. She then grabbed it with both hands.

'I know Gadgil uncle's phone number. Can I call my mother and ask her to come and get me?'

I shook my head slowly, looking at Nayna with eyes that were the same shade, only with the hope dimmed out of them.

'I don't think you will be able to call your mother with this phone.'

'But I know the number, see...' Nayna recited it back to me and it came flooding back, the telephone number of a forgotten childhood.

'Can you dial it for me?'

'Sure,' Ana replied, punching the digits in, putting the phone on speaker.

'The number you have dialled does not exist,' came the automated voice. 'Please check the number you have dialled.'

Nayna's face fell.

'How can that be possible? Perhaps their phone is dead with all the rains.'

'Yes, that could be it.' I grabbed at the only possible explanation Nayna would swallow and appropriated it. 'Phone lines go dead all the time when it rains.'

'How can I tell Maa that I'm okay? When I get back home, she will call me a monster put on earth to shorten her life.'

I laughed. 'My mother told me I was a monster often enough.'

'All mothers think their daughters are monsters,' Nayna said with a wisdom beyond her years, her eyes twinkling with the sudden camaraderie that this revelation brought about. 'They love them even though they are monsters. Fathers think their daughters are angels, but hate them.'

It blindsided me, a sudden pang of longing for Maa and her sharp rebukes flooding my insides.

'I will take you back as soon as I can. The way we came here, I can't control it. It decides when we come here and when we leave.'

'Okay. What's it?'

'It is travel through time and space.'

She nodded sombrely almost like she understood all that I was telling her.

'Why did you bring me here?'

'I don't know, I didn't plan to, I just wanted to keep you safe. You see some days from now something terrible would have happened…'

She frowned and nodded as if she already knew what I was going to tell her. 'Pappa will not jump and he won't make me jump. He will make Maa jump. He will make Maa cry so much that she will jump. With the baby in her stomach.'

'How do you know that?'

'That is what will happen. Maa will jump. And I will watch her.'

'How can you be so sure?'

'That's what you told me would happen the last time you came. You told me I was not to jump.'

'Me? I didn't tell you that.'

It didn't make sense. What was Nayna talking about. But she had said what she had to, and would say no more. She was now distracted by my easel, examining the painting on the frame with a great deal of attention. She would lose Maa. I had lost my father, but my father had loved me. Hers didn't.

'I got an A in art last year in the elementary art exam, and I won the Camlin district competition and a certificate of distinction at the Shankar's art competition and the Rotary Club drawing competition,' she informed me with no small measure of pride. 'I drew a rainy-day scene, children with raincoats and school bags, puddles on the road, people walking with umbrellas and the rain falling down. I'm good at art. They always call me to decorate the blackboards whenever there is a celebration or a special day. Or to make the charts. I can draw flowers very well. All kinds of flowers. My art teacher says I am a natural. I asked her who is an artificial.'

I laughed too. The art teacher was right, Nayna was a natural but it was a talent she had abandoned, I had abandoned, on the path to a secure career, a management diploma, internships, moving from organisation to organisation quicker than was seemly. Art did not pay. I had been a woman in a hurry, until everything had come to a complete stop. Now I painted again, but for myself. 'What do you like to paint, Nayna?'

'Flowers. And candles. And faces.' Her list was precise and finite. I wished I could be as specific as that when it came to what I painted. My works were a chaos of all the infinite things I wished to include and which resulted in nothing being quite what it was.

From the window I could see the tops of the cars that were by now almost submerged with the water level up to the compound wall, the gates themselves were ajar and held open by the force of the flowing water which sought the swiftest route out to the marshlands and the sea beyond, which was right through their little scrappy compound. There was nothing humans could blame this on, except the fury of nature and their own idiocy that had clogged up all the outlets for the rain to flow out, making the entire city a sink bowl of horror. Humankind had been kneaded and re-kneaded into existence by mythical floods, from the Pralaya of Matsya, the fish that guided the sage Manu and all the creatures on his boat to dry land, to the forty days and forty nights of rain that had Noah build his ark, the universal myth of the great flood across civilisations, across geographies, across aeons, a collective consciousness of an event so great, so overwhelming that all branches of mankind remembered the prehistoric destruction they had survived. The floods of the last glacial era, a mere blip in the memory of a planet. This was our version of the primordial flood, not devastating enough to annihilate us. This little flood here in the western corner of a country on the edge of the Asian landmass, a bit of land that had floated up through the Tethys millions of years ago, this was an inconsequential minor little flood in the list of the floods through the epochs.

'Can't I just go home down the stairs and across the compound? I know how to swim. Pappa teaches me to swim in the sea every Sunday, he says it will make me strong.'

'I know you can, but this is a different place from where you entered, you cannot swim across.' I paused. 'A different world. A different time. This is not where or when your home is.'

Her face crumpled a little and she went to the window, watching the rain lashing down on a world far removed from the one I had snatched her from.

'I'm hungry again,' she said eventually, having possibly considered all that she could say to assimilate the situation. Hunger was, after all, the only bodily truth that kept us human. Hunger and sex.

'Would you like some Maggi?'

She nodded her head in glee, her eyes lighting up.

'You have Maggi? Maa doesn't buy Maggi.'

I pulled out a packet from the kitchen pantry shelf, boiled the contents in the mandated two cups of water and set it down on a plate before her on the table. Had I really been such a perennially hungry child? I couldn't remember. Maa would have gone nuts trying to feed me, given how she hated getting into the kitchen and cooking.

I looked at the child's face indulgently as she slurped down the noodles. This had to be figured out. I had been impulsive, I had shifted things against the order of time. But then, as anyone who had passed through and passed back knew, time had no order except what we decided to impose upon it, time was everywhere and nowhere, here and now and then and there, and thereafter. Time was the Alpha, the Omega, the beginning, the end, and we all lived out our spiralling existences unknowing and uncaring of what lay across the curtain, just a step away, just a glance away. Déjà vu. That's what most people called it. But I knew better now. It was the living out of the experiences, over and over again, experiences the soul remembered but the mind forgot. And the ghosts we told ourselves we had seen were nothing but the people in our lives coming back or coming forward through time and again, trying to warn us, to tell us to stay on the path, to make the right decisions, gently deflecting us from peril.

I couldn't keep her with me, it was against the rules and, anyway, how would she last? She would fade gently, blur along the edges at first and then there would be the gradual erosion of layers of her until there was nothing left of her here. I had to take her back, as quick as I could. I had no power to take anyone back or forth across times and worlds unless they had the ability to cross themselves. Nayna could cross on her own, she had crossed before she had told me. I was not the only one of me who could cross.

'Crow,' Nayna said all of a sudden, moving to the window from the dining table. Sitting on the ledge outside, bedraggled and as dark as the night it came from was Crow, my old friend. And hers too.

He spoke – a voice that was a caw to the world, but words to us – to Nayna and me. 'What do you want to do, Nayna? Do you want to stay here or do you want to go back?'

'I want to go back home to Maa,' she replied without hesitation.

Owl hooted softly in the distance and then flew down to sit on the ledge of the balcony, a little distance away from Crow.

'What are we to do with these girls now? They have broken the rules.'

Owl sighed, a long drawn-out sigh, the mock-spectacled markings around his eyes imparting the illusion of wisdom that he would now display. He fluffed himself out and shook himself down with the aggrieved air of someone much pu*t upon.

'Don't worry,' Crow said. 'Her spirit knows where she has to go, just go with her, just make sure it happens soon, before she discorporates completely.'

And with that they both flew off noiselessly into the still pouring rain, above the clouds, into the universe beyond the sky and the stars, in the gaps between time and space where they resided.

9

When It All Drained Away

'I stir in bed and the memories rise out of me like a buzz of flies from a carcass. I crave to be rid of them...'

—Barbara Kingsolver, *The Poisonwood Bible*

IT WAS A FRAUGHT TWENTY-FOUR HOURS. MANDIRA AND Pawan Khosla waited, for a call, a knock on the door, some news, any news. There was no sign of Nayna anywhere. The entire neighbourhood had been combed, all the buildings in the lane, right down to the stalls and shops on the main road. The suspicious vagrants who loitered around the tea stall at the junction of the lane had been picked up and taken in for questioning. The rain continued to pour down, inverting the sky, leavening the mud, percolating through cracks in the concrete of the city.

Sometime between the night ending and the morning beginning, the rain halted, and the accumulated water in the compound drained out, gently at first and then all at once as the tide went out. The ground was soggy and bedraggled, overwhelming the shrubs and the straggly trees that made up the piteous patch of greenery the residents called the garden.

The door to A-302 remained resolutely locked. No one was sure who had the key: the society office or the resident real estate broker, Sunil Deshmukh, called Barkya for his skinny frame. Mandira insisted Nayna would be inside the locked flat; she was probably being held captive, rendered unconscious, or worse. It didn't bear thinking about. Nayna did not return when morning came and Mandira insisted the closed door, with its flaking paint and rusted hinges, be broken open.

A pestle was procured to break the lock. A silvered mirror hung by a nail at the back of the door fell as they pushed the door open. It didn't break, there was no bad luck to be dealt with. All the members of the society stood by as Mandira stepped in first, their faces arranged in careful worry. The smell of dust and disuse hit them. The air within the rooms had not stirred for years. One naked bulb, which did not respond to the flick of the switch. Cobwebs hung like valances from the corners of the ceilings, draping themselves elaborately on the abandoned furniture left behind by a tenant. Windows jammed shut, no footprints on the dust on the floor. But Ana lived here, Nayna had insisted she did. Ana whom no one had seen or spoken to or noticed Nayna have long conversations with in the park. Mandira herself had never seen her.

'No one has been inside this house for a long, long while,' said Mrs Pathankar, swearing on her kuldeva and all the devas in her ancestral temple that no one had lived in that house ever since the suicide of that young girl who slit her wrists and held them out of the window, letting the blood drip while she stood there looking for the local layabout who had broken her heart and possibly impregnated her.

No one from within the colony had seen anyone fitting the description of the woman Nayna called Ana, ever. Mandira went cold and faint at the thought that her daughter would never be found, there was no evidence that the one who had supposedly abducted her ever existed. Nayna had vanished into thin air. Girls who vanished into thin air stayed vanished, they were never found, and if they were, you wished they had stayed unfound.

But there, just behind the door to the inside room, was a faint light, perhaps from an open window, a muffled groan and Mandira pushed through the men blocking her path. The laws of motherhood are fiercer than all natural laws. Nayna was lying on the floor, in what seemed to be deep sleep. Her eyes fluttered beneath closed eyelids, the way they did when she was deep in the throes of a dream. Her clothes were dusty, her hair was still tied back neatly in the thick plait Mandira had tied for her before she'd stepped out of the house.

Mandira grabbed her. 'Naynu....Naynu...' she cried, trying to shake her awake, and then looked piteously at her husband standing at the door of the room, trying to comprehend what was happening.

'What's happened to her, why isn't she responding?' Her voice was shrill with panic.

Dr Shanbag, still in his vest and shorts, having been dragged from his home on the ground floor by a panicked Mrs Pathankar, bent down and checked her pulse, checked her eyes. 'Just seems to be in a deep sleep. Probably sedated.'

He added, as an afterthought, 'She'll be fine.'

Mandira repeated those words over and over to herself, repeating them in her mind like beads on a prayer chain. The train of unwelcome thoughts that had inevitably followed her every waking moment for the past twenty-four hours had stopped, the what-could-have-beens had been erased—a kidnapping, a rape, a killing, a body not found, a body sunk into the marshlands extending far beyond the periphery of their compound walls, or a curiosity about the marshy waters causing a fall. All worries were now at rest. Her daughter was here, she was fine.

'I'll carry her,' Pawan told his wife in a soft but firm voice, squeezing her hand tenderly, all the emotion he felt appropriate to display in public narrowing to this. His delicate, beautiful wife, more precious to him than anything else in the world. He was lucky to have married her, an off chance with a distant relative of his figuring out that the Chaturvedi girl needed to be married off immediately and calling him to Meerut instantly. It was tough to find a family willing to give their daughter to a man who seemed jinxed when it came to wives. He had lost his first wife in a difficult childbirth and second wife to malaria. His third wife had been a blessing beyond his belief. He had worshipped her all his life and she had made his life comfortable, and his home a happy one. Thankfully, she had not passed away young, breaking the jinx, had given him a lovely daughter and was now bearing his child again. A boy this time, he was sure, he could feel it in his veins. She was carrying low, the older women in the society had noticed and remarked. His mother was due to arrive soon, just in time for the birth; she would be overjoyed with a grandson.

'You have not rested since yesterday, and it is not good in your condition. She is fine, don't worry.'

'Maa...'

Mandira thought she heard a voice, soft, hesitant, confused.

'Naynuuuu...'

She was coming around, Nayna. Her eyes fluttered, then they opened slowly and for a minute they had the wonder of the universe shining through them, lighting up the dim passageway, before it faded.

'Okay, I'm back home, bye,' she said to no one in particular.

'She's okay, she's okay,' the doctor said. 'Take her home and let her rest. And go to the police station to close the case as soon as you can.'

Pawan nodded, and set Nayna down gently on a step. 'Are you alright, *beta*?' his voice was the gentlest Mandira had ever heard him speak. 'Can you walk?'

'Yes,' she replied. 'I can walk. Why do you all look so worried?'

Mandira grabbed Nayna in a hug that encompassed the earth, the sky and the oceans, and crumpled her into her as if she could fuse with her child. Every mother was once a daughter, a daughter would perhaps be a mother. Smashed between mother and daughter was the yet to be born son, feeling the relief flood through his mother's body. Nayna felt a feeble embrace reaching out to her from the womb.

'Maa, I'm sorry, I should have told you I was going up to Ana's house, and then I went so far away, I don't know how, and I couldn't come back and you must have been so worried.' She flinched from the slap she expected coming, but she was gathered swiftly into an unexpected embrace.

'It's okay, *beta*... Where *were* you?'

Nayna looked at Mandira, perplexed. It felt uncomfortable. Perhaps, she thought, Maa was pretending to be loving because they had an audience. She would beat her when they reached home and no one was around to hear her scream. 'I knocked at the door and then fell into the mirror and inside, then with Ana, and then she couldn't get me back but now she could get me back so she got me back. Have I missed school? Miss Shirley will be angry with me. I went with her and then I got stuck in her house and it was raining so much, but she got me back. She said something about it being safe now for me, that the time had passed, and she would put me in a different universe. I couldn't understand what she was saying. Is dinner ready? I'm hungry.'

Mandira's ears were listening to the words coming from Nayna's mouth, and they passed straight through the eardrum, through the inner ear, through the auditory nerve to the brain but didn't get processed. Her eyes were still taking in her daughter, living, in front of her, looking, if anything, rested and well fed, far from the horrors she had imagined being unleashed on her. Her hands were touching her daughter's face, her hair, hugging her to her body, feeling her slightness, her warmth, inhaling her, devouring her with every sense she had.

'You must be starving, my darling child,' she said; food was always love in physical form. You mixed love into every morsel. Have you eaten, eat your food, come to have your lunch – what are these except declarations of love? The word spread amongst the residents that the Khoslas had gone into the disused flat in A wing and found their lost daughter inside. With the door still locked from the outside. The residents of the colony emerged like ants to a cube of sugar, collecting on the stairs to see the girl who had disappeared into nowhere at dusk and had returned from that same nowhere the next day, seeming none the worse for her disappearance. Nayna continued to describe her adventure, unaware of the eyes on her, listening in to what she had to say.

'It's all different there where she is, she has hand phones with no wires like compass boxes, you can hold them in your hand and walk anywhere and call but I couldn't call here, maybe the phone lines were down, and there they have computers you can open like a book, the size of my drawing book, Maa, with no wires. You can watch movies and the TVs are on the wall, flat like a painting....'

Pawan Khosla looked at his wife, and she looked back at him in consternation. He went down on his haunches to be at eye level with Nayna.

'Where did Ana take you, Nayna?' There was the briefest of silences as Nayna looked at the faces of both her parents.

'I don't know, Pappa. She took me to her house which was here, but not here. It was different. This is not her house, Pappa. Her house is across a mirror and fog and lights.'

'Okay, let's get her home and rested,' he told the assembled crowd of curious onlookers that kept swelling as the word spread. They walked down the steps and across the landing and the quadrangle to their building, where they went up home with definite steps. The people from the building who had gathered around to watch slowly parted to let them through; concerned matrons touched Nayna, patting her shoulder, grabbing her face and kissing it. Someone brought some chillies and insisted that the evil eye be removed instantly. The girl had been found safe and sound and asleep behind a locked door in a house no one had entered for years. This had to be a miracle. The crowd dispersed to their homes and the Khosla family went into theirs. Nayna looked around with consternation at the reversed arrangement of the rooms, the living room led to the kitchen and there were two bedrooms branching off from the passage.

Nayna trundled into the living room and flopped on the divan.

'I'm feeling very sleepy, Maa, I want to sleep. I'm so very tired.'

'Eat something first,' Mandira urged. 'Then go sleep in your room.'

Nayna widened her eyes in surprise. 'My room? But I sleep here on the divan in the hall.'

Mandira laughed. 'You're tired, sleepy and confused. Go to your room and sleep.'

Nayna had already begun closing her eyes, heavy with the tiredness from distances unfathomable to her parents. 'Maa, I'm tired, very tired, so tired, and all those lights I fell through, they were so beautiful... they were...' Her words trailed off as she fell asleep in a second, almost like a button had been pressed. Her breathing deepened, and her head turned to the side, her chest rose and fell gently with each breath. Her parents stood over her, looking on with a strange mixture of relief and puzzlement. Mandira felt it more keenly, the subtle shift, perhaps it was the symbiotic connection of the now severed umbilical cord that made it so. This was Nayna, but it was not. She was changed. There was something that had changed in Nayna that Mandira couldn't quite put her finger on, something so insidious that it hovered carefully in the air around them, feverish, trying to conceal itself in the realms of what would seem normal and yet, trying to make its presence felt.

How had Nayna gone into that deserted home in the first place? And, most importantly, who was this Ana from A-302 that she had always been talking about, and how had Nayna seen her standing at the window of that house in separate incidents over months when it had so clearly not been lived in for many, many years?

These were questions Mandira would ponder over later, right now she expelled all the sighs she had collected within. They rushed out with a whoosh, a mass of cold icy air that contained the deepest, darkest despair of a mother's heart, now racing on the wind, off to find other mothers who would inhale them and keep them safe and warm for a while, while they worried about their offspring. She looked at her husband. He was sitting on a chair in the living room, looking at his sleeping daughter, his hands cupping his chin, his forehead in a frown.

He had too many questions himself and not enough answers. But for now this would have to do. Right now, there was the relief that their daughter had been returned unharmed. Mandira stroked Nayna's hair as the child slept, breathing deeply. Her other hand rested on her belly, enlarged and almost ready to give birth to new life.

Unseen by all of them, I emerged out on the other side of time, a time I had yet to enter in this body, a time I would perhaps not live to see while I was in this body. A time that had no measure for me to comprehend right now in my time.

10

Because Tomorrow is Here and Yesterday Too

'You forget what you want to remember and you remember what you want to forget.'

—Cormac McCarthy, *The Road*

WHEN I ENTERED THE ROOM, SHE WAS SITTING BY THE window. Her face, as I came into her line of sight, was ageless and calm, a pond which had no wind of emotion ruffling its surface. Nothing surprised her anymore; perhaps when you lived that long, nothing could, not even a version of yourself from another time and universe. From within this egg-shaped room with no ceiling and no floor, just a transparency and opacity where walls should be, where everything stayed in its place held by some strange magnetism that allowed me to walk all around, I could see the angry purple sky outside, dust clouds swirling and subsiding within seconds, dancing their dance of destruction and resurrection over and over again. This, I knew, was not a home of these times, this was a holding room for those who had outlived their utility to the community, for those who would be ended.

This is where we all would end up eventually, in a room meant for people with no one to care for them. Her face, that strangely ageless eternal face, lit up as she saw me. I went to her and hugged her, ignoring the strange feeling that I was hugging Maa, because she looked so much like Maa before the illness crept over her body, drowning her in rivers of pain, turning her cells against her, taking away her hair, her smile, her control over her bodily functions. She looked like Maa because I looked like Maa, and I would look like her, too, if I lived that long. How long had she lived, I did not know. She was me, only older. Much, much older. Or much younger, depending on which side of the time divide you came from.

'So many years since you last visited. How have you been?' she said, her arms reaching out for me, a hug that spanned space time and multiverses.

It had been decades in her time since I had visited this place. Less than a year in my time, my universe. It stretched and contracted, it did, time. It was unpredictable, recalcitrant, it ebbed and eddied and bloated and shrank as it pleased. Time had its own rhythm, it filled up space, or it withdrew from it, and no one could quite predict what it would do. No one could hold it, shape it, manipulate it. Perhaps in some future they already knew how to, and had moved on to manipulating other things that were more worthy.

They had written about this, centuries ago, in all we called our holy scriptures, before my time, much before my time. We hadn't paid heed. The cyclical concept of time and space, the yugas that we must go through where all that has happened will happen again, there will be beginnings and there will be ends, and beginnings again. That the day of the creator was as long as one could imagine infinity, that the day in our universe could be 50,000 years long as another holy book told us before Einstein came along to explain relativity to us. That man could move beyond the body. We just weren't listening. There was wisdom that had been imparted to us by those who came before us and after us, from beyond the heliosphere, beyond the heliopause, beyond the termination shock, beyond the interstellar, beyond where time and linearity looped over and over, where the visible universe oozed into the invisible universe, a mirror reversed. We couldn't open our minds anymore and we had, bit by bit, closed ourselves to the possibility of infinity. We put our probes out into the universe, sending them off buoyant on the solar winds, scouting the edges of space for a sign that we were not alone, little knowing there were myriads of us, scattered all over, hiding in plain sight.

She sat me down beside her; in our time on this earth she would pass off for a well preserved forty something. In her time, she had crossed a few centuries in earth years. I wondered if they kept time differently in her time, now that the orbit they had was different from the one we had, now that earth no longer existed as the home of humankind, now that we had sprinkled ourselves across and beyond the little corner of the Milky Way that was once our backyard.

'I'm okay. How have you been?'

'Bored. I don't know why we decided to extend our lives so indefinitely. After a point it really becomes a drag to keep on living interminably. And there is so much documentation and process required for getting the permission for termination, it is easier to just keep on living.' She exhaled deeply. The garment she was wearing was a kind that our times had not developed and had no language to describe. It was scaly and mercurial and moved with her, flowed with her, draped her and comforted her, massaged her where it hurt, monitored her vitals, rejuvenated her skin, administered dermal medication as required, warmed her when needed, cooled her when she felt hot. The closest to it I had ever seen were the thermal foil blankets wrapped over those rescued from hazardous situations in news clips, developed first for the space programme on earth back in the 1980s. What she wore was the equivalent of a hospital robe in our times. She had applied for termination and was waiting, had been waiting, for decades. Pure second-generation humans were rare, she was a Federation treasure.

'You look tired.'

I shrugged. Maa had died when she was barely in her late fifties, going from healthy to skeletal within a few months. I often wondered how the breath had left her body, how a person had become a slab of flesh. When we took her to the electric crematorium, I had put a string of mogra on her. She had loved these gajras; they were her mood barometer, her quiet rebellions. Pappa had never allowed her to put flowers in her hair. Only nautch women wear flowers in their hair, he would say. After he died, she began her quiet rebellion with the occasional string of jasmine entwined into her plait. Switching from the respectability of sarees to the convenience of salwar kameez, going to the parlour for the occasional facial, getting her eyebrows done, using nail polish, a soft pink lipstick. All the things Pappa had policed for fear of her becoming even more beautiful than she already was. For years after she had passed away, I would fill bowls in the house with strings of jasmine. It kept Maa close, close enough to have her fragrance fill my nostrils with her absence. I wondered if she would have chosen to live so long if she had the chance.

'She wouldn't have wanted to live so long, Ana,' she said, reading my thoughts. 'It was good she decided to go. It was a release. You know that. And it was a release for you too.'

In a way, I guess that is what it was. A release from the duty that had tied us both together, all those years, with the confining clamps of a biological relationship we both had outgrown. It was rather selfish of me, I realised that now, to have expected her to define herself purely as my mother and resent her for wanting to be a woman first. I realised now, as I grew older, how she must have struggled to constrain herself within the parameters of wife and mother, parameters that left her asphyxiated.

'What has changed since your last visit?' she asked me.

'I shifted her. I put her in a good place. But I'm falling apart and I don't know what to do. I need help.'

She smiled, I smiled. 'What do you mean by falling apart?'

I raised my tunic and unwrapped the waistband around my waist to show her where pinpricks of light emerged through me. She blinked as a bluish brightness spilled out of my mid-section and hit the curved walls, bouncing off them and scattering across the room, as the wall's material did not allow light to travel unbroken. She sighed and closed her eyes for a long while. I wrapped myself up again, put my tunic down. The light strained at the fabric, trying to find its way out.

'It would extract its toll. Things should be allowed to pass. We can't be changing time and all that it unspools. But....' she paused.

'She's safe. As safe as I could keep her. What happens after this I can't control. How many times can I keep going back and changing things around for her?'

'As often as you want to, now that you know how to,' said the woman, a soft smile playing on her lips, her eyes probing and gentle. 'There's no stopping this now that you have mastered how to.'

'I don't really know how to,' I said. 'It happens.'

The woman shifted in her seat and sighed. 'Few of us have the ability to shift ourselves. Your time calls them time travellers. Some books and movies have already caught on to these, but your time can't explain how it is done. Neither can we. All we know is that a few humans can shift between dimensions. You are born with it, no one can teach you how to do it, no one can control it for you. Those before your time called them ghosts, guardian angels, doppelgangers, spirits, but they really are just spirits of the living from another time and world. You can move between times.

She can too. A few of us can. There are others of us doing this right now as we speak. They might just be undoing what you're trying to do.'

She paused, gathering her breath, her thoughts. The windows turned opaque as she shut her thoughts down, focusing inwards, a soft white phosphorescence lit up the room automatically as the light from the outside was shut out.

'You came here first as a five-year-old. The you of You. I knew then what you had, we watched you, we tracked you every single time you crossed. You have crossed thousands of times. Most of them you don't even recall, some of which you remember. You can't control it. You travel universes in a flash.'

Each time I did so, I felt hollower, leaving a bit of myself in the other place, fading around my edges, shimmering molecules of myself leaking away from me, staying back in the other time, bits and pieces of myself now irretrievable.

'How have you been? You look just the same as I saw you last.'

'I'm well. The body is fine, the soul is weary. When you have lived as long as I have, there is nothing one wants to contemplate anymore, you've asked all the questions you want to ask, you've raised all the children you need to raise. It's time to go perhaps.' She paused. 'Ana, I would be 2000 years in Earth time, your time, if we humans still lived there.'

Where we were was no longer a place I recognised. Earth, as I knew it, had long passed into the stuff of history. We had ruined it with our fossil fuels and plastics, making it unliveable for the generations after us. The generations after us had fled to corners of the solar system and beyond, wherever they could find living space, on asteroids, on Mars, going beyond the solar system to galaxies my time had only seen through telescopes in observatories located in cold deserts where the night sky was clear enough.

'Now what do we do about these holes in your body?'

'Isn't there someone who can figure out what is happening?

I mean, if they put in something to track me, they can probably figure out why bits of me are getting left behind when I travel.'

She nodded. It was strange to look at her, in this place, this room, this world, so much after my time, in another time and space, in another universe, where the planet one lived on was all purple skies and no water, and the sun was slowly growing to a red ball of fury, preparing to engulf and devour all its children, and people were slowly and steadily boarding interstellar arks in lottery-determined batches to escape the impending devastation yet again, to transport themselves to zones where they could live in engineered environments that made it easy. Many of them had shed what we called the body, and preferred to live in bioengineered suits they used and discarded as the whim and fancy took them, many did not remotely resemble what we would call human. Some chose not to embody, and stayed disembodied until they finally found a permanent settlement in the chaos of the galaxies they travelled through, and could be placed within forms and settlements, searching for the idea of home in the aridness of time and space when our true address had been left far behind.

She blinked and spoke quietly into her palm, resting her fingertips against her ear, cupping her lips with the inner palm.

'They will take a look at it and patch you up if they can,' she said when she had finished. 'I wish I could go back with you.'

'You know you can't. And it would kill you if you tried.'

'Enough of taking up space for so very long. They've been gracious enough to allow me this space for all these years, but it is time for young blood now. Relics like us must make way. I'm waiting to be allowed to go.'

'What does this mean for me when you go?'

'Nothing. Nothing at all. I'm not the first of us to go. There have been others before me who have gone before, you know that. You made your choice, it was unthinking and selfish but you were young, you were scared, you grabbed your chance.'

'Yes, I know. And I know it now because of you. And how will I know what choices I must make?'

She laughed, her face momentarily lit up by the light filtering in from the giant searchlights outside this mammoth construction that stood higher than the tallest mountain back on earth with infinite eggs and warrens and spaces where we now lived, lights that scanned the periphery every few minutes, checking for vagrants, stragglers, anyone unauthorised who shouldn't be beyond the walls, outside in the air that corroded and killed, in this strange new world that tolerated humankind like a barnacle on a whale.

'You will know. You will just know. I know you won't end up here like me, a forgotten relic waiting for release from this curse of immortality.'

'What if you stepped out?'

'If I was without a body kit, I would get the release I wanted instantly. Well, maybe not instantly. It would take some seconds for oxygen deprivation to set in, for the acidity in the dampness to seep into my skin and burn through the epidermal layer. The toxic gases would reach my lungs and jam them up within seconds. It would be a painful death. But yes, a quick one. The generations bioengineered to withstand these conditions are the ones who can survive on the surface of the planet now for a while without body kits. Not very long though. We have to live in these bubbles, if this can be called living.'

'Perhaps you should try to step out without a body suit sometime,' I said drily. 'It would cut out the paperwork.'

I knew I wouldn't stand a chance if I had landed beyond the walls. What I was wearing was not meant for the temperatures of now, neither on the surface of the long-abandoned mother planet our kind had left behind, nor where we were right now, a distant planet circling a growing-angry sun, as close to what the Earth had been before the tidal shifts, the tsunamis and the poles tumbling over, and getting inverted, magma rising from deep within the core and spilling out through gashes across the land and the seas, leaving nothing but wreckage and destruction. Only a few chosen thousands were lucky enough to flee on the Project ships kept ready and waiting across multiple countries and continents, escaping into the early colonies across the solar system, on Mars, on Ceres, and from there the springboard into the unknown, beyond the heliosphere, into the interstellar. Mankind had not yet escaped the spiralling arms of what we had then called the Milky Way; we sought refuge in our neighbours, we were illegal immigrants. The few who stayed back on Earth, the unlucky few, were tethered to the unliveable surface on their floating platforms, and looked out at their roiling skies and remembered the distant past when their ancestors walked freely on the surface.

'You've had it good, actually. You're here. Alive. Not many are from your time.'

'I know. Not complaining. I'm blessed. But it is wearying. For all we fantasised about immortality, a few hundred years are enough to let us know that extending life wasn't probably the best of ideas.'

The others with her had long since dissipated; she was the only one alive from her batch of survivors. The first batch. Those who had died had been cloned, the clones lived in wary proximity with the trueborn, those who were conceived through the meeting of sperm and egg, an antique ritual now, one that was performed periodically with prime human specimens in order to perpetuate the purity of the race. Embryos and infants who did not meet the standards of the committee were terminated; eugenics we called it then, perpetuating the pure born, now called the trueborn.

'Let's see where her life takes her now, now that she's no longer...'

We fell silent. The unsaid hung uncomfortably between the two of us. Beneath us, the planet was swinging into the dark side, its moons in tow.

She paused and looked at me with eyes that were tired and

drained of all joy. Our eyes mirrored each other's. Soft cobwebbed crinkles at the corner where life had carved its march into her skin, into her soul. Mine still wide and wondering, the anticipation of a loss I was yet to know still dormant and restless within, yet to surge to the surface and create maps on the skin, proof that one had lived and suffered.

The woman sighed. 'I still live with the guilt of my choice. Perhaps I think Pappa had it right. Jump, Nayantara, he said. He still keeps telling me that in my dreams. Perhaps we are all doomed, sooner or later. Perhaps I should have just jumped when I had the chance. It would have ended right then and there.'

She paused. I looked at her. The terrible realisation dawned on her, and on me, infiltrating the space between the two of us like a wall of ice, freezing us into a terror we couldn't express.

'Perhaps it would have not. Perhaps it did not. That's why we are still here, aren't we. Because it didn't end, because it won't ever end. Because we're destined to keep living out versions of ourselves over and over again.'

11

Recalibrating Oneself and One's Selves

'No matter how much suffering you went through, you never wanted to let go of those memories.'

—Haruki Murakami

THE HOUSE ECHOED WITH WHISPERS OF EMPTINESS AFTER Nayna left. Even my breath, which I had never paid any heed to, seemed unusually noisy, occupying space in rooms divested of everything that a home should rightfully have: a child's laughter, a mother's peeved scolding, a father's admonishments. Perhaps they weren't breaths anymore, but an accumulation of sighs. And sighs had no place in a home built of silences.

In the end, it had been rather easy. We had been sitting in front of the television when I caught a glimpse of our reflections together in it. And then, the next second we weren't. She was back where she didn't belong. What about the parents I had taken her from? I would not revisit that time. Had I erased her completely from that time, I didn't know. But she would be happy now. She would be loved by both her parents. She would live with parents who loved one another, she would be safe.

When I crashed back into my time, the city was past the darkness of the long night. I waited, coiled in my solitude, recuperating. It was done now. It was over. I was free to live out my life. Would the patchwork healing they had done, synthesising my cells to regenerate around my torso, start giving away again? Would the gaps in me start expanding, a pinprick at first, then a leaky luminescence that spread and spread until it covered all of me and made me one with the infinite vacuum of the zigzag I kept traversing. Or would the holes regenerate and become skin and flesh, sinew and muscle and tissue again. I didn't know. For now, I wore a stomach binder to keep from imploding and spraying electric blue sequins in all directions.

The sun broke through after two days of rain; the tide went out, taking with it the accumulated rain water, revealing the wreckage of lives, of property, of a city shaken and devastated. A cloudburst, they said. A cloud heavy with rain had decided to empty itself all at once over a city already choked to the gills with garbage and the flotsam-jetsam of human existence. I had escaped the worst. We had escaped the worst.

Aman came over as soon as the roads cleared. He leaned against the door, the sole bulb in the passageway lighting up the nooks and crags in his face, a familiar, loved topography my fingertips had traced and retraced. He drew me into him, an embrace that was aftershave, cigarette smoke, belonging and longing. I pulled him into the house.

'Why have you got this on?' he asked as his fingers bunched against the stomach binder to pull it off, to feel skin against skin.

'Doctor's orders,' I replied, without elaborating.

I moved further down his body and made him forget his question. He picked it up later.

'How long do you have to wear this?'

'Some time.'

If the answer was vague, he didn't give any indication of not being satisfied with it. And the tummy binder was no impediment.

'These past few days it was misery not being able to come here. No one should be alone when the city is collapsing around them.'

'You didn't have to worry, I am happy to be alone,' I rationalised. He shook his head, running a hand over my bare hip, stopping at the tummy binder. 'You definitely need to see a therapist. I'm worried about you. It isn't normal to not want to interact with anyone. How long can you keep yourself cloistered like this?'

I was not normal, I was not something I could explain to him. All I could do now was to take baby steps towards normalising my life, what I had left of it. Or perhaps people like us who went back and forth were not supposed to have a life or fall in love.

'Shut this house and move closer to mine.'

I smiled. We had already had this conversation in another time and place.

I wasn't going to sell this house. This was the house Maa bought by selling her bridal jewellery, the jewellery she had been saving for my dowry, the matar mala, the kangans, the maang tikka inset with uncut rubies and seed pearls fringing it that I pulled out and wore when I dressed up in a saree and pretended to be an adult as a kid. Of course, I had no jewellery as dowry. We had sold it all to buy this, to pay for her treatment.

This house was a cage with box grills put on the windows by Maa who never wanted a space wide enough to jump from, forgetting completely that just a floor above, shut only occasionally by a flimsy lock, was the terrace. And bridges were everywhere, if one was so inclined. Below these bridges, the sea swirled and churned, grey-black and frothy, eager to take all human sacrifice offered to it. I did that a lot these days, stand at the window and look down from within the grill. Stand on a bridge and look down. Stand on the terrace and look down. It took courage to jump, more courage than it took to step back, to retrace one's steps, to go back to what one was trying to escape from. I had seen the images of those who had jumped from the World Trade Center towers in New York after the planes crashed into them, those who trusted gravity more than the flames behind them. It took courage to step off. How did one choose between two forms of death? Perhaps my father was not the coward I had always assumed him to be. Had I been prescient not to jump all those years ago? I would never know the child I could have been. The child I had been would never know me. Perhaps she did, and she called me Ana.

'And we find you something regular to keep you occupied and a good therapist for you to have some sessions with. Talking to someone will help, it always does. There's this great therapist whom Sukanya goes to. I'll ask her if she can fit you into her calendar.'

'Won't that be awkward, same therapist for your wife and mistress?'

'Not for me. Sukanya knows about you and you know about her.'

I was happy for him to take the lead on this, and go along with him. He was high energy, firing on all cylinders, messaging, talking on the phone nonstop, with things to do every moment of the day. Even the minutes he pulled out of his day to be with me.

'I'll schedule an appointment.'

'Okay.'

'We are also going to get you back to work. A proper job, but not so hectic you won't find time for me.'

I laughed.

'Don't worry about that. I'll find myself something to get me out of the house and keep me occupied. There's enough worrying about me and sorting out of my life you've already taken on.'

He shrugged. 'I think this doing your own thing is just a crutch you hold on in order to keep dropping off to wherever it is you go to time and again. If you have something to commit to, you'll stay put.'

I shook my head. 'I can't do something regular anymore. I'm not a regular person, Aman, I thought you would have figured it out by now. You just have to accept that I will never be a regular person. Sukanya is your regular person.'

He kissed my ear.

'It has never been you versus her. You know that. She is important to me. You are important to me.'

I remained resolutely silent. Outside the window I could see Owl, looking in curious and questioning about the conversation we were having, its orange eyes like marmalade. Waiting patiently for me.

Aman hadn't noticed it. He was speaking. I hadn't been paying attention. His words bounced off the walls, I could see the Greyness denting where his voice hit it. I stayed silent. He had no idea that the Greyness had followed me into this house, I had brought it back, I knew, by going back to where it waited for me. It was against the order of the Greyness for me to coexist both in the Grey and the real. It stuck to me like chewing gum on the sole of a shoe, persistent, hovering, waiting for a gap to pass through the layers of my existence here, standing at the foot of my bed in the middle of the night, to take me back to what I thought I had managed to escape, we had escaped. Life yet to be formed colliding with life-defying death.

It had been two days since Nayna had crossed over. She had crossed over relatively undiminished. I had checked her when I deposited her; there was no fading, no missing patches, except perhaps a small space at the tip of her little finger on her right hand that will soon fade into nothing. Emptiness that had once been occupied by spirit and flesh bound together. Nayna hadn't noticed, hadn't realised. Perhaps it would return to her. Perhaps it would grow back after the body realised it would not be flung through space time again. Perhaps it would grow, perhaps she would cross again now that she knew she could. She didn't need me, it came to her instinctively like it had to me. A moment, a thought, a shift in orientation, and a move through what seemed like infinite black and infinite bright. We, the aberrations. We, the ghosts of our past and future selves.

Owl hooted softly.

Aman's phone pinged with a message to reply to. I went to the window, to Owl.

'What is it?' I asked.

'You are not to go back anymore. You were not supposed to pluck her out of her time and shift her to another. You created a situation the last time you did.'

'I can't control it. I just... go. Am I allowed to go ahead?'

He tilted his head to one side and looked at me with those eyes, more questioning than the question I had asked him.

'That is completely up to you, Ana,' he finally replied. 'Going ahead serves no purpose.'

'Neither does going back. Then why...' He didn't wait for me to complete my sentence. He gave a quick short bob, as graceful as a curtsey would have been could he have made it, opened his wings and swooped away into the darkness of the night.

'Whom were you talking to?' Aman asked.

'No one,' I replied. 'You're imagining things.'

He looked around, trying to see if anyone was hidden in any recesses of the room; disbelief scampered into his eyes and was replaced with resignation.

'You need to let me take care of you,' he said. I nodded. He drew me to him like water and I poured all my need for him into his mouth.

I quivered in the knowledge of how my body would respond to his, how his lips would make me unfold myself layer by layer, opening myself up to him, wanting to be all he wanted, living that moment, those moments, when he was with me. We fit together, giving pain, taking pleasure. I closed my eyes for a long moment, then opened them to look back straight into his. There was nothing in my eyes but darkness, acute and complete; his eyes reflected me, I fell through him to where I should not go.

But Owl's words had me worried. I needed to go back to one more of me, to close things once and for all. For the very last time, I told myself.

12

Jumping Across the Pond

'Memories were waiting at the edges of things, beckoning to me.'

—Neil Gaiman, *The Ocean at the End of the Lane*

THERE WAS NO GUESSING SUE'S MOOD. MONSOON IN BOMBAY WAS romantic for the first two days, first showers and the smell of wet earth, and after that the unceasing damp, flooded roads, clothes that don't dry, the stench of rotting garbage and overflowing drains.

She hadn't gone to college that morning. It had been raining too heavily and she was sure the trains would shut down by evening with the tracks getting flooded in. On regular days, she normally left home at 11, much after her mother left for school at around 7.30 a.m. She returned home on a regular day after the sun had set. After classes ended by 5 p.m., she hung out at the canteen, which was a glorified tea stall, for an hour and it took her another hour to reach home. Her mother returned much earlier; the school she taught in closed in the afternoon. The school was across the railway lines that divided the suburbs into east and west. Maa went by BEST bus to the station, crossed at the railway crossing, and then took another bus that dropped her a minute away from the school gates. Sue's college was barely two stations away; she could take a bus, a train, or an auto rickshaw, depending on her mood and how much money she had.

She looked at herself in the mirror and pulled a face. Her face pulled itself back at her. She was ugly. U. G. L. Y. There was no getting around it. Ugly. She was that rather unfortunate creature, the unattractive daughter of a radiantly beautiful mother, a mother who made absolutely no effort to stay beautiful but just was. She had grown up seeing the pity in the eyes of those who looked at her mother and then at her. 'Poor thing, takes after her father, does she?'

Her mother had never loved her father. Her father had always loved her mother. Sue knew she didn't look like the man she called father. And she looked nothing like her mother. Her father had kindly told her once that she took after his mother, someone she had never seen, who had died before she was born and who had never been photographed for her to have evidence of any resemblance. She took his words at face value. Her paternal grandmother, the man she called father told her, was a very sharp woman. After all, she had raised him and his siblings single-handedly after she was widowed at barely twenty-eight and had ensured all her children were educated and settled before she passed away. Sue liked to think she was as strong as the grandmother she had never seen. The man she called father thought so too. He had never thought to count months on his fingers, months between his marrying Sue's mother and her birth. A month or two here and there was normal, wasn't it, he told himself whenever doubt entered his mind. Some children were born early, some late. But they all turned out perfectly, like his Sukanya. She hated being called Sukanya, convent schooling had shortened it to Sue and so she had remained. Sue. When she would get married years later, her husband would call her

Sukanya, rejecting the diminutive version, insisting she was all her name was. A good girl.

She stood in the balcony, waiting for the one she now had a crush on to arrive. A glimpse, even if just for a second, would make her day. Knights these days liked their steeds metallic. He rode a second-hand bike that was always acting up and in the garage most times, but he dressed the part of the biker, in a leather jacket, jeans, white t-shirt and the requisite mullet hair, sending her burgeoning hormones skittering. It was also an act of bravery to wear a leather jacket in this weather, but perhaps his devotion to Travolta in *Grease* was greater than his need to be non-sweaty.

He though had his eye on a placidly curvy beauty called Jenny who was all breasts, hips and a breathy voice that had most of the boys in the neighbourhood follow her around like a pack of mangy curs. Jenny was five feet nothing with her hair in luscious waves, which was the latest style – step-cut – offered at the local Chinese parlour. Sue was sure the formidable chest was nothing but mismatched stocks hastily stuffed into her bra. No one that tiny could have such huge breasts. It would not be farfetched to say that Sue was envious. After all, Sue's best friend had rudely told her that she needed Clearasil instead of a bra when she'd bragged about going bra shopping with her mother. It had seriously imperilled the friendship, but equilibrium had been achieved when Sue had retorted that Shamalee would never need Clearasil because she was never going to hit puberty and would die prepubescent in her white cotton petticoat, never graduating to bras.

She combed her hair out and tied it back in a high ponytail. The weight of her hair gave her a headache and her scalp always felt itchy in Mumbai's heat and humidity, but did her mother care? She had begged and pleaded and whined and sulked to be allowed to chop it but her mother would not be moved.

'You have such lovely, long, thick hair, *beta*,' she would say, smiling her soft smile, bringing to her face an unbearable radiance before it went back to being tired and sad again. 'Why would you want to cut it? So many people would kill to have hair like yours!'

'They can take my hair then and clip it to their scalps and leave me free. This is such a headache. It is heavy and takes forever to dry after a bath.'

What she didn't tell her mother was that it made her look old-fashioned and uncool. Jenny, with all her compact buxomness, was ultracool. She wore dresses that clung to her curves and ended just above her knee. Her eyes were drawn in kohl. She also wore lipstick. Bright pink. Orange. Red. Maroon. Whatever caught her fancy as long as it was bright. Good girls wore lip gloss, Sue had been told.

Jenny's skin was milky pale, the residual traces of some British blood in her genetic pool. Anglo-Indian. A college dropout doing a secretarial course. In a home with over nine siblings, her parents had almost nothing to spare for each one and she was tired of growing up in hand-me-downs, whether books or clothes or make-up. Her maternal uncle, as she told the girls down in the compound, would get her a job as a stenographer and if she was good at her work, she could even rise to become a secretary. That was her ultimate dream, to become an assistant to the head of a firm and to accompany him on all his trips abroad. Or to become an air hostess and travel the world.

Sue wanted to get away too, but she knew that educating herself was her escape ticket. She spent her Saturdays at the USIS library in Churchgate, researching on colleges in the USA and the courses they offered. Or she would do her management at an IIM, she had decided. It would be a way out into a different life, a different world.

When Sue had mentioned Jenny dropping out of college to learn shorthand and typing, her mother had frozen in the midst of rolling out a roti. She turned slowly and when she spoke her voice was a whiplash of ice and fire.

'Here I am struggling to feed you and educate you so you have a better life than this....' she gestured expansively at the walls with their peeling plaster, the doors rotting on their hinges, the wood work peeling. '...And you want to be a *typist*?'

'I don't want to be a typist, Maa,' she protested. 'I was just telling you about J...Jenny.'

She had never seen Maa so annoyed, not since Pappa had passed away. Many years ago, when she argued bitterly with her father, her mother had raised her voice. But she hadn't done so for years. Pappa had killed himself. Maa had driven him to kill himself. Sue had stood by and done nothing, just watched as he climbed on to the ledge of the balcony and jumped over. One smooth graceful movement, a ballet of macabre motion.

It was guilt that would never be erased. She knew that already at fifteen, though she claimed to be sixteen. It had been seven years now and she still relived that moment every single day. Within her she battled with the niggling suspicion that she was, in fact, evil. There was a foul core to her that had allowed this to happen. She had stood calmly in the balcony and watched him plummet like a stone from the fourth floor. It was a Sunday morning. Maa had gone to the market. People rushed out of their homes, gasped over the body, made a complete nuisance of themselves.

She could still remember the blood spreading redly from his head, turning pink in the rain, and the awkward angle of his limbs. There would finally be peace in the house, that had been her first thought. She had stood in the balcony and watched impassively as people below scurried around in confusion around his broken body. She only moved when the doorbell rang. Her eyes were dry, Mrs Pathankar would remark later, when she recounted the incident to the rest of the women who sat every evening on the water tank, catching up on the daily gossip.

'Where's your mother, do you know what has happened?'

'Yes,' she said. 'Pappa jumped from the balcony. Is he dead?'

Some days later Mrs Pathankar would tell those gathered around the water tank, hand on heaving bosom to emphasise disbelief. 'Not one tear. Unnatural it was. Such a small girl and no emoshun! *Deva re.*'

The rest of the cabal around her would cluck in acknowledgement of her observation and it would be dredged up at regular intervals whenever they recalled that morning the man jumped off the balcony, the lack of emotion from the young daughter, and the matter-of-fact manner in which the wife went about the funeral preparations, dry-eyed herself. That was not how widows were supposed to behave, they were supposed to wail, sob, faint, be inconsolable. With each recounting of the incident, the details got embellished, a little at first and then by a whole lot. By the end of it all, Sue was the one who had pushed her father off the balcony and had been laughing hysterically when Mrs Pathankar went to inform her. Soon the people in the colony kept a wary distance from both mother and daughter.

Eventually they were compelled to move out to where no one knew them, where no one knew of the history of the vicious fights between husband and wife that reverberated across all four floors of the building, and no one knew that the beautiful wife had been weighed down by the incessant suspicions of an ugly husband. Maa had been pregnant when Pappa jumped. He knew the child in her belly was not his, that he had been cuckolded twice over, and that a child would emerge from her, bearing the face of yet another man. He had good reason. He hadn't touched her for years. It was a shame he could not bear thinking about.

Maa lost her baby. He was stillborn, destined to never emerge from the Greyness. They moved homes. No one knew them here, no one pointed fingers at her, the girl who pushed her father off the ledge.

'Don't worry,' her mother had assured her. 'I will make sure I get you married to someone good, someone you will love. Or at least like. It is very important to like your husband, I never realised that until I had to live with your father. He disgusted me, I couldn't bear for him to touch me, it felt like snakes crawling over my skin. Wasn't his fault, he was just born with a face like his. Respectable family, secure job, that's all my parents saw before they offloaded me on to him like a parcel...'

'He was my father, Maa.'

Her mother's face softened a bit, her eyes crinkled at the corners with a strange expression that could have either been a smile or a grimace.

'He was not your father,' her mother replied without explanation or elaboration. 'Your father...' Her mother's voice would trail off and then there would be no further conversation. She sometimes wondered why her mother said 'my husband' and 'your father' like they were two different people.

'You're too young to understand,' her mother would tell her when she asked why she and Pappa fought. 'When you are older I'll tell you.' She was almost sixteen now, and Pappa had been dead for seven years, but she still wasn't old enough to be told what her mother had promised her she would tell her when she was older. Her mother eventually would never tell her, it was left to her Lovely maasi to tell her the truth when her mother died.

The man she was married off to when she was few months short of seventeen was on the wrong side of thirty and a widower. 'So educated,' her father preened. 'Such a khandaani boy.'

She was married off to him in a hurry because she was a liability. Her beauty was a liability. The local politician's son had set his eye on her, and had been sending feelers of interest, then outright threats to the family. He already had a couple of rape cases to his roster, and walked around with a katta tucked into his waistband. Her father had three more children, two of them daughters also to be married off. No one in the small town would dare approach them for her hand now that word had got out on the street that Bhaiyyaji's eldest had marked her out.

But she had been in love too, something no one approved of except Lovely maasi. And it had been a love of hasty meets in deserted lanes, trysts on the terrace during hot summer nights, hurried and hot. Then she was married off so quickly she hadn't even had a chance to tell the one she had been in love with that he should stop loving her. Did love ever stop or did it fade away, gradually, lessening an inch daily and then disappearing all at once? She had wondered sometimes, and then stopped. And then she had her daughter, who would never know who her father was. Some days she caught a familiar expression she had almost forgotten when she looked at her daughter, a jawline stubborn and proud. The sharp angled and handsome face she had loved was too square jawed and masculine on her daughter.

She had been a beautiful bride. The wedding portrait in black and white showed a direct gaze at the camera.

The wedding night was the most traumatic experience of her life, and she would spend the rest of her life trying to erase the feel of those reptilian hands on her body, ripping off her lehenga, thrusting clumsily into her, uncaring of her discomfort and pain, her extreme repulsion, visible and evident which made him even angrier and more aggressive with her, and then the loss of the erection, the beatings begun from the frustration. And finally, when he was done and spent, her trembling rage at being violated ignored, she gathered herself and her clothes and slept on the floor to avoid him touching her again in the course of the night. Sue was born a few months later. Mandira never counted the months, her husband did.

Her mother would be home anytime now. She stood at the window and waited for her crush to arrive, as she knew he would, on the battered old Enfield he had inherited from his brother who had emigrated to Saudi Arabia, the Xanadu of the 1980s. There was something about him roaring up the road on a bike. Plus, his eyes. Brown and slightly amused whenever she tried to pick up a conversation.

He thought of her as a child, she knew, and nothing she could do. No padded bras filched from her mother's stash of undergarments, no inexpertly applied lipstick and kohl, no hair left wantonly loose, had served to change his opinion of her. He still looked at her with a benevolent indulgence, like one might look upon an amusing but precocious child. The motorcycle she had been awaiting thundered into the compound and on it was him, the one she had been waiting to spot for the past hour. He wasn't alone today. Perched behind him was a woman in a black saree with a broad red and gold border, her long plait luxurious down her back, a hand placed casually on his shoulder, her body pressed against his. Sue's eyes narrowed. Her mother got off the bike and smiled at him, saying something that was inaudible from four floors up. He gave her a mock salute and drove off to his wing, where he would park his bike just next to the electric meter box and go up to his home on the second floor, in a flat that sadly did not look out on to the common quadrangle between the buildings, and therefore was not visible to Sue. He lived with a bedraggled bunch of siblings that seemed to be ever expanding, his parents living the word of the Lord and eschewing contraception. How did they fit into that little space, Sue wondered; they seemed to be spilling out of every part of the colony, little clones of each other, all light-skinned with the remnants of the stray colonist's gene in their genetic make-up, their eyes a smorgasbord of brown and green. He and Jenny, they came from similar homes. They had a lot more in common than she had previously realised.

Sue went to the dining table and spread out her books in an attempt to show she had been studying and hurriedly wiped off the lipstick she had applied with the back of her palm. Her mother was home early today. It was most unlike her mother to return home early. Was she unwell?

Her mother had gotten off the motorcycle in one elegant step, like she'd done it before, with no fumbling with the saree while clambering on and off unlike a novice pillion rider. The key turned in the door.

'You are home?' her mother said, her expression more flustered than worried. 'Is anything the matter, why are you home? Are you unwell? Did you not go to college?' She put a hand to Sue's forehead. 'There's no fever. Why have you bunked?'

'I had a headache so I decided to stay home.'

Her mom looked her up and down. 'You look okay to me, in fact, more than okay, and is that lipstick? Now, tell me, why are you bunking class?'

'Nothing, Maa, just felt like staying home. And I tried on your lipstick but I wiped it off. All the girls in my class wear lipstick except me.'

'There's all your life to wear lipstick when life wipes the colour off your lips, my darling. Switch on the television. Rajiv Gandhi has been assassinated, apparently. A human bomb, they're saying. Down south, I didn't get the name of the place, somewhere near Madras. Such a quick way to go, in one instant. Boom and it is all over.'

Her mother switched on the television, then threw her handbag on the sofa and went towards the kitchen. It was a distracted move. Normally her mother's handbag would go straight into the Godrej almirah in the bedroom, in the little space between the tiny folded piles of clothes within. They didn't have much between the two of them. One shelf for the mother, one for the daughter, a single rod to hang the sarees. The bottom shelf with the home linen, bedsheets, towels, napkins. The shelves between filled with the handful of clothes they managed with. T-shirts, saree blouses, night dresses, petticoats, undergarments. The monsoon was a reminder of how pitifully little they had when clothes refused to dry and they pulled on damp undergarments because they had no other.

Sue switched on the television set. A grim-faced newsreader spoke about how the former PM had been assassinated, details were sketchy, the place where this had happened was Sriperumbudur in Tamil Nadu. Many others had died, many were injured. The remains of the former prime minister were being airlifted to New Delhi for the funeral rites. Grainy shots showed a sneaker, white, in a blackness of death and destruction. Had he gone into the Greyness too? All who died all of a sudden did, Sue knew. How she knew this, she did not know.

'Why are you home early, Maa?'

'I wasn't feeling too well, why do you ask?'

'No, I just thought they shut school early because Rajiv Gandhi died.'

'He's an ex-prime minister. Violent death follows that family. The brother. The mother. Now him.'

Just then the doorbell rang. Sue rose from her chair and threw the door open. He stood there, her motorcycle-riding crush, one hand on the doorjamb, the other holding a cloth bag out, her mother's bag, one in which she carried her lunch box, and the few vegetables she picked up from the hawkers outside the railway station on the way home.

Sue's heart melted seeing him standing there, all twenty-odd years of him, tempered with the cockiness of 'the world is my oyster' confidence. He smiled, his indulgent half-crooked smile.

'Your mother left this on my bike's handle. I gave her a lift from the station home today.'

How could a person be so gloriously handsome, thought Sue. He had come up to give the bag, in person. He hadn't sent it up with one of the kids loitering around the compound playing seven tiles or hide and seek. Her mind whirred and clicked: surely this was an excuse to meet her. He wanted to woo her. Damn, why had she wiped off that lipstick when she saw Maa get off the bike? Her eyes were still lined with kajal though. She hoped she looked mysterious and dreamy.

'Your eye make-up is on your cheeks.' He pointed at her face. She started to wipe away the smudges when she noticed his gaze go beyond her and into the living room where her mother had just emerged from the kitchen. Sue turned her head; her mother had splashed some water on her face and was mopping it with a hand towel. Her cheeks were flushed and eyes wistful.

'You left your bag behind on my bike, I just came by to drop it.'

'That's so sweet of you.' Her mother took the bag and smiled. It had been a long, long time since she had seen her mother smile like that. She looked like Madhubala. Or Meena Kumari. Or one of those black and white movie heroines, in her high-necked blouse and loosely draped cotton saree, hair untidy around her face, backlit by the sun coming in from the window. He nodded politely and turned to leave when her mother put a hand on his shoulder, a gesture that was uncharacteristic, a familiarity that was disconcerting. On the television set, Lalitaji was exhorting them to be sensible about what they bought and to think hard about why something was cheap. 'Achchi cheez aur sasti cheez mein farak hota hai.' Sue looked at the television blaring its inanities into a moment that was uncertainly loaded. With what, she didn't know or realise yet.

'This is the first time you've visited our home, how can we let you go from the door? Do come in, have some tea.'

Sue nodded in excitement. 'Maa makes fabulous tea. Or if you don't like tea, there's Thums Up. I prefer Thums Up. Or Rasna.'

He smiled. His eyes were on her mother's face, he hadn't even registered what Sue had said. 'Are you sure it won't be any trouble? I'd love some tea.' His voice was hesitant.

'Of course, it is no trouble,' Maa said. 'I was just about to make some for myself.'

He came into the house, suddenly disarmed of the cockiness he had when dealing with Sue. He took his shoes off at the door and placed them neatly outside, before sitting on the sofa, on the edge, as though terrified he would be chased out any moment.

Sue sat opposite him and studied him at close range, a luxury she rarely had when he was down in the compound hanging around

Jenny, or roaring off on his bike. Here, in her living room, or the hall as it was commonly called, a pretentious nomenclature given it was barely a box, attached to two other boxes called bedrooms, he seemed strangely diminished and young, far from the self-assured twenty-two-year-old she'd begged a ride to the bus stop from a couple of times. He also seemed very nervous.

'Sue,' her mother called from the kitchen. 'Come here for a moment.'

'Yes, Maa,' she replied politely because of the company, instead of the surly 'why?' that she would have barked back in normal circumstances.

Her mother was standing in front of the gas stove, looking into an empty canister.

'I was so sure we had tea in the house but, look, the tin is empty. Can you run down to Rajan's store and quickly get a packet of tea and some biscuits. Take the money from my purse. And since you're going down anyway, get some fresh samosas from Chandu's shop. Wait there and see that he fries them fresh in front of you. Don't be in a rush to come back.'

Sue nodded. Anything for him. She put on her slippers and looked at him sitting as purposeless as an extra limb on the sofa. He was handsome. So handsome. But so dense. 'I'll be back soon,' she said; the stepping out merited an explanation. It wouldn't do for him to think she was being rude. 'Wait for me.' Commanding came easily to her, even when it was someone she had a crush on.

He nodded and stood up, something that struck her as strange and gentlemanly, old-fashioned chivalry that had gone completely out of style. As she stepped out through the main door and closed it behind her, turning just a bit despite herself to look through the narrowing gap between the door and the jamb, she saw her mother come to stand in front of him, an undecipherable expression in her eyes. Her mother put out a hand and stroked his cheek with immense tenderness and familiarity. He put out his arms and gathered her mother like a drowning man, burying his face in her hair. She shut the door as gently as she could and fled down the stairs, her heart pounding within like a time bomb that would explode if touched.

At the foot of the stairs an unknown woman stood, waiting, looking up at her as she descended. Hair loose around her face, falling in thick waves to her waist, her eyes red-rimmed, in jeans so tight they fitted her like second skin and a t-shirt that was faded to patches.

'Sue,' she said, glittering like a hologram. 'Let him go. Let Aman go.' And then, in a fire of blue that seared her eyes, she was gone and there was nothing there, no one, just the disquieting sensation that she had no clue who Aman was and why she needed to let him go, and why she had been hallucinating about strange women with wavy hair and sad eyes swollen with sobbing.

13

The Escape Back to the Present

'Memory is the sense of loss, and loss pulls us after it.'
—Marilynne Robinson, *Housekeeping*

I KNEW THAT IT WOULD HAVE TO BE SO. NAYNA WOULD RETURN TO another world, and I would return to mine. Time had passed in the world I plucked her from, events had rippled, altered, bent around the immutable like a brook around stones. How had it changed the course of them unfolding, I didn't know. I hadn't gone there to check. What was past was past. What was present was also past. Untying the knots of the past did not resolve them, I was discovering, the skeins slipped back into Gordian knots that were even firmer in their complexity the moment one came loose.

I had dared play God, when all I'd been instructed to do was to be a guiding angel. There were always repercussions to going above one's station. The changes had accumulated, spilt over, like a snaking river changing its course, events had then unfolded, cutting paths through new destinies, gathering new debris along the way, depositing loam and alluvium on newly formed banks, steering themselves through rift valleys, through turgid plains, through dry rocky terrain, questing slowly and steadily towards the sea of forever, where it would merge with all the waters pouring in from all the lands.

When Nayna grew up and looked at herself in the mirror, would she see the face she had seen many years ago? Had she changed for her new knowledge about how we could move across times? Would she figure out that she can do so on her own now, that she didn't need me? Will she be able to control it, manipulate it? Would our paths cross again in some remote vortex, or do we continue to singly hurtle down individual paths until spun into a collective existence by the extraordinary loom of time space?

I didn't know what to call them who watched over us, versions of us that had transcended the physical body, shrugged off the carbon-based, but yet kept tinkering with their primitive versions still locked in physical dimensions of time, space and matter, like gods playing with dolls. Would I go so far ahead so as to meet a version of myself who was only thought and no form, or only consciousness encased in a synthetic bioengineered body? There was no one to ask. Nothing for me to do but recalibrate the decisions I had taken so impetuously in the past couple of days. There was a bereftness, a jagged edge within me that hurt when I traced any memory. People hurt. More than wounds and cuts and stabs. People hurt when they were around you, they hurt when they were not around you, and all you can do is draw a bubble around yourself so they never reach close enough to hurt. It was lonely in the bubble, but that was a choice you made, to hurt alone or by others.

The new mirror that had replaced the smashed one was clear and clean, the sun shining in it. Glass that reflected as glass must, not absorbed. I looked at myself in it. I looked pretty much unchanged, even thinner if that were possible. My clavicles, the semicircles under my eyes... My ribs were visble under my t-shirt and my hip bones jutted out of my jeans. I lifted my t-shirt and touched the waistband around my torso, it felt icy and scalding. With trembling fingers, I ripped the Velcro open and dropped it to the floor. Streaks of blinding blue light splashed out of me and hit the mirror, making it vibrate with a curious monotonous hum that I had never heard before, the song of the vacuum. The blue clawed into the room, creeping up wall and wood, the hum sawing my skull. I touched the pinholes of light on me, where flesh had given way to the ether. Those who had tended to them had put me under a machine that had caressed me gently and regenerated flesh, tissue and organ. The gaps would continue to fill, they told me, I would become whole again. But I could not cross anymore.

I would live my life here, on this side, in this time, continue as I was. Find myself a job perhaps, continue being the mistress of a married man. Nothing good came out of being the other woman, Maa had told me that. She'd always been prosaic about divorce and extramarital relationships. She'd been calm through my divorce, sanguine through my dalliances post-divorce.

From the perspective of one in her thirties I now looked back upon the marriage of my parents, a marriage of unequals if ever there was one. My mother young and stunning, animated and articulate. My father stolid, middle-aged, conservative, diminished, undistinguished. To be honest, he looked more her father than her husband. With his thick spectacles that gave him two faces, one outside the frame, his own, and the second the minimised image of his face within the lenses of his spectacles that onlookers saw when they looked at him. It had been disconcerting to look at him sometimes. His insistence on Brylcreeming his hair down flat across his scalp in the faint hope that it fooled people that he wasn't going bald. His shirts with the starch out of the collars, and the pants shining at the seat from too much use.

I should have jumped with him. In another world, in another time, I had and lived with the consequences. In this world and time, I hadn't and lived with the consequences. I wondered what my father would have had to say, had he been alive, about me being the lover of a married man. I wouldn't have been divorced and single in my thirties to begin with. That I owed to my mother, her ability to walk on the side that society didn't always allow women, single, without a father or a brother to lend her credence, and then not even a husband to validate her. My mother had taught me that all I needed was financial independence, a house of my own and a skin so thick taunts would bounce off it. Nothing else mattered. Society moved on around you, like a brook, if you remained a boulder, unchanging and fixed.

I had been lucky to have neighbours who watched out for me. Not many people did, and not in a city like Mumbai, where one often didn't even know who one's neighbour was. But this was a different kind of apartment complex I lived in; everyone knew everyone and everything about everyone. Every annual society meeting was the stuff of loud and irate arguments that somehow stayed clear of fistfights by some miracle. Occasionally builders popped up to offer gilded promises of redevelopment with an extra room, and the added temptations of a swimming pool, club house and jogging track thrown in. I had been holding off on the paint and furniture for the simple reason that the building was on the verge of signing a redevelopment offer every single time I had moaned at how decrepit it had all become and then Maa had fallen ill, and the house and the peeling plaster had gone on the backburner. After she passed away, it didn't matter.

If there had been talk about Aman visiting me at odd hours, it hadn't reached me, and for that I was grateful. We had moved out of our earlier home because of the gossip when Pappa jumped. There is no kindness in words spoken about one in one's absence, even if dressed as concern.

Initially, after I was found, there was an overwhelming curiosity about me. They came at odd hours to gawp at me, folks from the building complex, from down the lane, others from the neighbourhood, parents of the children from my school. I was the girl who had gone to the land of death, stayed there for three months and then returned, one morning, out of the blue. It was a blackout, a coma, it was something the doctors couldn't explain and I couldn't explain it to them. I had detached when it had happened to me, the hands, the bodies, the violations. I had thought I had died, but I hadn't. I'd shifted into the Greyness, the limbo, the space of eternal waiting. The Greyness was a place I still half inhabited, it drew me in sometimes, and then always sent me back to the lights and colours of the living. It was waiting, waiting, biding its time.

Aman called sometime between tea and dinner. The evening was a drabness that made telling time impossible. The day had gone by, and I was still at the dining table, deep down the rabbit hole of social media.

'I'm checking you into the serviced apartment that our partners use. We'll have the lease on a permanent apartment within the week. Not too far from my home, but I can't have Sukanya bumping into you or you bumping into her.'

'Sure,' I replied. I would not bump into Sukanya and she would not bump into me. We were his two parallel lives, and it remained to be seen how long he could have us run this way without us intersecting.

'Pack what you need for a few days,' he told me. 'I'll get the movers to pack the rest of your stuff and shift it out as soon as the paperwork on the apartment is done. I don't want you staying there alone anymore. It just isn't safe. I'm reaching there in an hour.'

It was easier to go along with him, to be gratified that there was someone to whom my safety mattered, my presence mattered, I mattered.

It didn't take me long to pack. Aman arrived while I was doing so and waited while I did. After all, what did I need to throw into the suitcase? Clothes, of which I had a limited number – I barely shopped for myself anymore, most of my clothes were from a time when I took pleasure in dressing up; a photograph of Maa, one in which she was still young and laughing, wearing a floral georgette saree, the pallu of which she had wrapped around her shoulders for some strange reason in that studio shot. I still remembered that saree, she had gone all the way to the Garden Vareli annual sale and bought it for herself from money she had saved up for this one indulgence. It was white with soft billowing roses in soft hues of pink spreading across it, a garden of unfulfilled desires that I, at six, was too young to comprehend. She wore it on her birthday, a birthday we never celebrated because Pappa didn't believe in celebrating birthdays. To be fair, he didn't celebrate his own too. She wore it when he was away at office, when she came to pick me up from school on her birthday and walked down the road looking like she had rose petals falling off her. Everyone stopped and stared at her, men and women alike. She was magnificent when she deigned to unshrink herself. She made me believe that gloriousness could be shut on and off, as per one's will, like a light switch. Perhaps it was camouflage, a survival instinct; too much gloriousness made one a target, and she had already paid the price for it.

I packed my easel, folding it down, wrapping it in cloth, and coddling the canvases like the children I never had, lingering tenderly over each, savouring the brush strokes, reliving the painting.

'Leave these here. I'll get them picked up along with your other things once we've found an apartment. Just take your clothes.'

So I zipped up two suitcases, my life condensed into the few clothes I needed.

'I'm done,' I said, standing up from the bed and looking at the pitiful suitcases that made up all my possessions. This was it. This was my life, folded and packed into old, soft top zip-ups bought years ago when I got married and went off to Delhi. They returned from Delhi with me, the contents relatively unused, me the one who returned sullied and crumpled.

The crumpling would get ironed out, Maa would soothe my brow and inject steel back into my spine, cleanse my soul of all the darkness that had taken up space in my soul. The Greyness though would never leave me.

Aman would never know, he must never know, he wouldn't understand what it meant, a sweeping marauder across the plains of my consciousness. It swooped in as soon I thought back to it, recognising itself in my thoughts, a reaching out, a summoning I did inadvertently, sweeping down on me, fogging my eyes, freezing my brain. The icicles pierced my thoughts, the voices of those suspended in the emptiness spoke to me, calling me back, promising me the bliss of oblivion and nothingness. The Greyness was soothing, all encompassing, all forgiving. When I came back, I was lying on the bed and Aman was sprinkling water on my face.

'Whatever is happening with you?'

'Probably just my blood pressure falling.'

'You had gone rigid, you were here and not here. And you were speaking with someone.'

'You're reading too much into it.'

He sighed. 'It's been almost fifteen minutes that you were out of it. If this happens when you're alone, there's no telling what could happen. There is something really wrong with you! There's something you're not telling me. You need to get a complete check-up done.'

What could I tell him? That I inhabited many worlds and had wrested him from an alternate self, to make him mine, little realising I would fray him and myself trying to reconcile the varying planes we inhabited.

The room was still spinning around me as I tried to sit up. He gave me the glass he was holding, the chilled water warming itself as it made its way down my throat. I could move my limbs, wiggle my toes; I was coming back from the rigor mortis of the land of the undead I had visited.

I began, uncertain how to tell him the part of the story that I myself didn't understand, 'When I was a child, I had an accident and I went into what they told me was a coma. It was a stasis that put me into a greyness where I could see, feel, move and be, but no one on the other side could feel my presence. It still pulls me back sometimes. For a moment or two. And then releases me.'

'What accident? You've never told me about this. I need to know.'

I looked into his eyes, uncertain of how much of myself I could share, how much of my truth he would be able to bear. It was a burden, someone's secret. No one deserved that burden, especially not this beautiful man who was too burdened already with all that he had in his life. He sat there, an Atlas in the waiting, his broad shoulders weighed down by the invisible globe of the worries he needed to deal with, at work, at home, his hair dishevelled, his tie knot loosened. Here he was, having cancelled his meetings, all his work for the day, to take me away from my home, which was no longer home. Here he was, his heart in my hand and my life in his, and I owed him the truth I dared not tell. Would it change how he felt about me if he knew? It had ended my marriage when I had told my husband about it. But perhaps Aman was a better man, a stronger man than the one who could not handle the ugliness of what life had thrown decades ago at the woman who was now his bride.

'No. You don't need to know. It's all in the past. What matters now is that I make sure I don't fall into the Greyness again. No matter what the temptation.'

'Temptation? I don't understand...' He rubbed a weary hand over his forehead. 'You may have your reasons for not telling me, but I do need to know. I'm not pressuring you. Tell me what you think you can share, whenever you're ready.'

There would be a time for the telling, it was not now. The sun was bright today, the day fell in hard bricks of light through the windows on the walls, shimmying up the asphalted roads. The walls shifted temptingly, the mirror called. I avoided looking at both, as though ignoring them could make what they did go away.

'I can't talk about it,' I said, looking down at my hands. 'Not right now. I'm not ready.'

'I must also check about fixing that appointment to begin your therapy sessions. That will definitely help. Now, are you ready to leave?'

I looked around one last time and nodded. The bare rectangle on the wall where Maa's pic had hung stared at me accusingly. I was abandoning her here. But I was also taking her with me, in my suitcase, wrapped carefully in newspaper and tied with a string, a picture of her, when she was in her late thirties, laughing into the camera, her gaze imperious and defiant, challenging the one behind the lens to capture her in all her glory.

Changing the time and place hadn't mattered. Death would seek me out, I didn't know that then. I knew it now, but it hadn't stopped me from trying incessantly to shift things around. I'd gone back to the Grey. Then I'd taken what wasn't mine to take. I didn't know what I was anymore, who I was.

'Don't revisit it,' I heard my mother say from behind me. 'It happened, it's over, we moved past it.'

'Did we, Maa?' I replied, without turning back. 'You are lucky you're dead now. Stay dead.'

'It's boring to be dead. And your father is right here in the dead space, hellbent on listing out my sins for me to repent.' There was a slight pause and what sounded like a laugh. 'I'd rather be alive than get bored by him again.'

I shook my head. Maa was irrepressible, both when she was alive and now when she was dead. I knew that if I turned around, I would see nothing, no Maa frail and withered in her spot on the divan in the living room, lying there all day to watch television. The only way to see Maa again was to go back through time. Perhaps I should see Maa one last time. Maybe she was stuck in the Greyness as I had been, a world heavy as molasses, with no ground, no sky, just an expanse that wrapped itself around me and went wherever I went.

'Pappa,' I called.

He continued sleeping. His face was tired, there were dark circles under his eyes. He turned in his sleep and moaned a bit. He couldn't hear me. He couldn't see me. I was here. Trapped. Perhaps the Greyness was better, I thought to myself. This was excruciating. Being right here, and not being able to make my presence felt. I looked around: it was a hospital room I was in I knew, but I didn't know where.

'Pappa,' I tried again. He stirred a bit and then jumped up.

'Naynu...'

He stood up, wiping the sleep from his eyes and came towards me. The night lamp was on.

'Her eyes are open!' he said, softly first and then loudly, causing a ward boy to run in. And then a nurse.

'Look, look, her eyes are open!'

There was a flurry of activity after that, the doctors were called, first the residents, and then a couple of hours later, the senior doctor. They shone torches into my eyes, moved objects in my line of vision, checked my vitals, rechecked my vitals.

It had taken months, but I had come back slowly. Learning to use each part of this body bit by bit, training myself to inhabit this body, to move it to my command, to make it work. They'd sent me home when I had regained full control of this body. It was not mine, it took time getting used to. The Grey never really left me though. For a moment, a micro second, it would invade me, step in to look around and check the premises so to speak, and then vacate it as quickly. A reminder administered periodically that my residence here was temporary and makeshift. This body was on loan. It wasn't my permanent one.

I couldn't tell Aman all this. I couldn't tell him when I became Ana from Nayna, and why I kept revisiting the child I was. He picked up my suitcase and went out of the main door – he had four flights of stairs to take it down, it was heavy. He carried it like it was an empty cardboard box with a handle.

'I'll wait for you in the car,' he said.

I shut the windows, turned off the gas, bolted the door to the balcony, switched the electricity mains off. I'd kept all the papers I needed, the deed to the house, the ration card, my certificates, all in a single box file, a pitiful accumulation of one's entire life condensed into sheets of paper to prove one existed and one had the right over this little box of brick and mortar.

'I'm going away,' I said to Maa, who was lying and not lying on the divan. 'I'm locking up the house and going to stay in a service apartment till Aman finds me another house. I can't live here anymore.'

'Go then. You know where to find me. Lock the door from the inside when you do go there. You don't want anyone coming in and waking you up when you travel. Remember, you'll be stuck there forever if they do.'

How did Maa know? I had never told her about it. How did she know?

I turned around. There was only the curtain fluttering, and nothing in the house to denote anyone else was in the room except me. Had I really expected to see her?

Perhaps, I told myself, it was time to live the life I had so yearned to live elsewhere, in the spaces between the here and the there, where I had left bits and bobs of me behind. Perhaps that was all I was supposed to do, live in the spaces between all my lives.

14

Where Worlds Collide and Recoil

'The happening and telling are very different things. This doesn't mean that the story isn't true.'

—Karen Joy Fowler, *We Are All Completely Beside Ourselves*

WHEN SUE RETURNED HOLDING THE PARCEL OF FRESHLY fried samosas wrapped in newspapers, the tea powder and biscuits, she made a short detour to the spot where she knew his motorbike would be parked, just inside the entrance to his building, next to the electrical meter box. He kept it safe from the rain and the pigeons, and by doing so put it at the mercy of every little boy who could clamber on. It was also out of sight and vulnerable to vandalism, exactly what Sue had in mind. She pulled out from her skirt pocket a penknife from the Swiss knife set gifted to her late father by a Gulf-returned relative. She poked the knife into both tyres with all her strength. She looked around to see if anyone had spotted her act of delinquency, and satisfied that she had no witnesses, went up home with the samosas getting rapidly colder, composing her face as she rang the bell.

The door took just a bit longer than it should have to open. Her mother was seated on the sofa while James returned to the chair next to the door. There was a coffee table between them, but it did not diminish an unstated intimacy that Sue was suddenly and keenly aware of.

Her mother got up and took the bag from her. 'There you are.' Sue looked at the clock. She'd been gone for almost an hour. Long enough. Her mother deserved some joy in her airless life too, didn't she?

Her mother was happy. It was there in her voice, eyes and animated hand movements. James, on the other hand, was subdued, almost embarrassed, and seemed eager to get away. 'Sue, chat with our guest… Always with her nose in her books, this girl!' And turning to Sue again, 'Be polite, okay.'

'Yes, Maa.' She sat opposite him and observed him at close range. He had just barely graduated, going by his younger sister's reports about his marksheet, and was working part-time so he could become more responsible. For the most part of the day, he roared around the premises, picking up and dropping people to and from the railway station, loitering at the cigarette store down the road and sending job applications.

'Where's your office?' she asked him, seeing as he was sitting with a stupid grin on his face.

'Andheri East, Saki Naka, just temporary. I've applied for jobs in the Gulf,' he replied confidently. A confidence, she realised with a shock, that came from being the cynosure of every eye whenever he walked into a room. He was a golden child, he believed, his good looks would see him through life. The conversation had now run its natural course and Sue had nothing more to say to him. She felt that with most people and most conversations. She sat back and looked at the book she had left half read on the table, wondering if it would be in good form to pick it up. It was an interesting one, *Hollywood Wives* by Jackie Collins. She had got it from the local library where the staid bespectacled gentleman who ran it had prudently covered it with brown paper, while the less scandalous books in his collection had been purely protected by a transparent plastic cover. He had frowned when she had picked it up and asked if her mother knew the kind of books she was reading.

'Which class are you in now? Ninth?' James asked.

She bristled. 'I'm in college.'

He raised his eyebrows in mock surprise. 'You don't look it! I would have thought you are twelve.'

'Is it because I don't have breasts?'

He laughed. Sue was known for speaking her mind, uncaring of what was considered nice and proper for a young girl to speak.

'That too, among other things.'

'What other things?'

'You are childish. It's good to be childish. It is charming. You are charming.'

'You are not making sense,' she said. And because she felt she had to snub him too, added not too wisely, 'And I wouldn't have put you down for a man with a job, you still look like a college kid.'

He laughed again. His laughter was open and ringing, and rolled like a ball into the corners of the barely furnished living room. 'You are very handsome.' She looked at him straight in the eye when she said that. 'Didn't you think of getting into the movies?' she asked. He shrugged, the air in the room shifted a bit.

'Not my cup of tea. Folks have told me I should try acting, but it isn't something I enjoyed even in college plays. Modelling is okay for pocket money.'

He was matter of fact about his capabilities, she liked that. In middle class suburbia, acting was something that no one aspired to; it did not denote respectability for women or stability for men. Men aspired to government jobs.

'I'm going to become a businessman, with a bungalow and a car and more black money than you could ever imagine.'

'And what business will you do?' Her mother came into the room, her voice warm and teasing. She had never spoken with her father like that, Sue thought. When she spoke with Pappa, her voice had always been broken glass drawing blood.

'Import-export,' he replied. Her mother laughed, handing him a cup of tea, her eyes teasing and gentle. This was a strangely intimate expression. Sue felt like an intruder in her own home.

'What do you know about import-export?' her mother said, holding out the plate with the samosas. 'Do you have contacts in the business?'

Theirs was not the world of businessmen. This was the world of those who got into government jobs and stayed in them till they retired with a modest pension and the lumpsum provident fund, which got them through old age unto death. The ups and downs of the world of entrepreneurship were not for those who clung to security.

'I'll make contacts,' he replied smoothly, unshakeable in his determination to go beyond what middle class India demarcated as their parameters.

'And what will you import and export?'

'I don't know yet.'

Sue snorted in disbelief. He was as inversely sharp as he was handsome.

'What will you learn when all day you are hanging around at the cigarette shop, looking for the next person to give a ride?'

He started at the life advice being hurled at him by this chit of a girl.

'Don't get on the poor boy's case,' said her mother, picking up a samosa languidly, putting it on a quarter plate, next to which was a small bowl with chutney. Maa handed him the plate with a familiarity that was disconcerting. 'What kind of a job are you looking at, perhaps I can help you,' her mother said, moving to sit next to him like she owned that spot, an unbecoming proximity between an older woman and a younger man, a widow and a boy. 'I have a friend who works in an import and export firm.'

Eyes shining, he turned to look at her mother with abject devotion in his eyes. 'I would be so grateful, thank you... just until my job in the Gulf comes through, that would be a big help. I'm giving my probationary bank officer exams too, and civil services exams.'

'Make up your mind,' Sue interjected. 'Do you want to go to Dubai, start a business, get into a bank or model? You can't do everything – you have to focus.'

'Arrey, Sue, he'll have to try everything, na, until something works out?' Maa was forgiving of his inadequacies.

'Thank you for offering to help.'

Her mother ferreted around for a notepad and pen, and began scribbling something down. Her writing was quick and definite, like she was.

'This is my friend's name and office address. Go there at around lunchtime tomorrow. I'll call and tell her you will be coming to meet her. Take your biodata.'

Sue got up and went into the bedroom, the bed was unmade. She put her penknife into the drawer and went back into the living room, where James appeared besotted by her mother. She didn't blame him. Her mother was beautiful. It had been she who had never realised just how beautiful her mother really was. It was like living with an exquisite work of art, seeing it in the humdrum of everyday living, and losing reverence for its beauty because it was now your mundane.

Sue went out into the balcony and stared down. Jenny walked in through the gate and looked at James's bike sitting there with flat tyres, before turning into her building.

'James,' Sue said sweetly as she returned to the hall. 'Jenny's just come in. Jenny is his girlfriend, Maa.'

She looked at her mother to check the effect of her words

on her. There seemed to be none. Maa nonchalantly bit into the samosa she had in her hand and looked at James with a questioning, open gaze.

'A girlfriend? Tell us more about this Jenny. Is it serious? Are you going to get married?'

James seemed a trifle flustered. 'No, not my girlfriend. I'm not sure if I want a girlfriend.'

Her mother nodded. 'Yes, how can one ever be sure about what and whom one wants in life? Forever is a long time. How can anyone be with the same person for the rest of one's life. They have it good abroad, you can get divorced if you don't get along. Here, you just wait for the other person to die before you, or you kill them.' She smiled, a smile laced with arsenic. 'Or better still, you make them kill themselves.'

James frowned at the turn of the conversation. Maa stood up briskly, ending the visit with a firmness that Sue had never seen before.

'Yes, we have kept you for far too long, James. Do keep dropping by, it was good to have you over. Bring Jenny over sometime too.'

He looked confused and disoriented. He put his empty cup down. The crumbs of the devoured samosas formed a bereft pattern on the white ceramic plate. Sue looked at him with something close to pity.

'Thanks for the chai, I'll see you around,' he said, awkward and unwilling to leave. Her mother stood up, walked towards the door, waiting politely for him to exit the house. Sue waved at him and went back into the balcony. She heard her mother go into the bedroom, from where the wardrobe was banged shut uncharacteristically loud. Sue knew, without going in to check, that her mother was looking out of the window too. James stepped out of their building, walked across to his own, and then looked up quickly. His gaze not at the balcony where she was, but at the bedroom window where her mother often was. Sue realised, with a sudden sharp pang, that she had been mistaken, that he had not been looking up to see if she was standing there. He had never been looking up for her. What a fool she had been! She went into the kitchen and grabbed a samosa, chomping through it unthinkingly. One dozen samosas in the house at a single time were an indulgence. They were also a delaying tactic, she realised. The shop rarely had one dozen fresh samosas available, they sold out as soon as they were made. She picked up a second samosa and ate it too. Hot tears trickled into the sides of her mouth and mingled with the taste of samosa.

Her mother emerged after a little while and went straight to the kitchen to begin preparing dinner. She would call out for Sue any moment now, to come into the kitchen to roll out the rotis or chop the vegetables. Right on cue, her mother called out.

Sue said, 'I have homework.'

'Then go do that.' Her mother was always clear that studies took priority over everything else, even learning how to be a good housewife.

When her father came to call her to the balcony late at night, so late that the bats had gone to their caves, others hung upside down on branches and the night sounds themselves had stilled, she didn't waver. She stood up and followed him into the little balcony, took his hand as he held it out to her to lift her up to the ledge. When he whispered to her to jump, to not look down, just jump, she did exactly that. Next thing, she was looking at herself, lying crumpled on the ground. No rain to make the red blood pink, as it had made Pappa's. Her blood was dark and smelt metallic. Pappa stood next to her, a small smile playing on his lips. She had finally made him proud, the girl he was perpetually dissatisfied with.

From above her the wails began, as her mother realised what had happened; the lights came on in the windows around, popping bright squares on to the ground. The watchman came running across with a torch and flashed it on her body. The eyes were semi-open, the head tilted at an angle that made it clear that her neck had snapped. Someone called for another to call for an ambulance, horrified gasps filled the air, a child began crying somewhere in the distance, an elderly male voice said quite prosaically that there was no need to spend extra on an ambulance since she was quite dead and a taxi would do to take her to the hospital. Someone else wondered if they should call the local doctor and get a death certificate, so she could be taken directly to the cremation ground. And the Greyness circled her, before swallowing her whole, taking her where there was no thought, no feeling, no sensations, nothing except the Greyness.

When she woke up from the dream, for long moments she was unsure if she was flesh or spirit.

15

If It Were Only Just a Dream

'Dreams are composed of many things, my son.
Of images and hopes, of fears and memories.
Memories of the past, and memories of the future...'

—Neil Gaiman, *Fables & Reflections*

DAYS PASSED. WEEKS PASSED. MONTHS AND THE YEARS. TIME passed without waiting for a by-your-leave. It snaked past fast-forward. Nayna knew as she grew that she had crossed something so immense that words weren't enough to explain the inexplicable. She also knew she was not the she she'd left behind, her parents weren't the parents she'd left behind...

Ana never returned. The windows to A-302 were always open, a family lived there, a spilling of children and noise. The questions behind the shuttered windows remained unanswered. She would grow in height and years, and go on to the next grade in school, and the next, and then the next. She stood at the balcony, looking down, looking across, knowing she was not home. Here she was loved, and she wore that love that was not hers like a hairshirt of penance. Maa here was different. Maa was soft, pretty and loving now, whereas Maa there had been sharp, pretty and scathing. The Maa who never ever wanted to be touched or hugged now hovered over Nayna like an unasked benediction, taking her to school herself, waiting outside school for all those hours while school was on, then picking her up and getting her home. Watching her from the balcony when she played downstairs, a love that refused to let her be, terrified to let her out of sight, a love that she had always longed for from her mother but which suffocated her now that she had it.

Mandira did not realise the cruelty of girls who would not let up on Nayna as the new girl in class and one with a bodyguard of a mother who wouldn't leave her alone for even a moment. She couldn't dawdle at the ber waalah and get a pack of the sour bers sprinkled with salt and chilli powder like the other girls did, or the golla wala who added psychedelic sweeteners on the crushed ice he packed on to a stick that all the girls ate on the way home, or the candyfloss man with his spools of sugary pink candyfloss. Her mother allowed no street food, no dallying. She followed her mother for years, dragging her feet in protest.

'I will go to school and come home on my own, Maa,' she dared say again after a couple of years. She was in the eighth standard now and the red stain had begun blooming between her thighs once every month like clockwork. Her breasts had begun budding, little sprouts pale and tentative on her chest. She covered them proudly with the training bra her mother had bought for her from the market. She'd spend the entire day showing off her bra strap to classmates, being one of the earliest to be awarded the honour.

She began learning and observing these new parents she had, still draped in the skins of her real parents, like they were specimens in a lab. They felt unreal; she still shrank away when this mother reached out to embrace her, unsure whether it would be a hug or a cuff to the ear. At first, she told them that this was not her real home and they were not her real parents. They were indulgent about it, a child's overactive imagination. Then they consulted the family physician who had seen her grow from a baby to a young girl. He laughed her fears away and assured her that she and her parents were the same as they always were. Dr Shanbag – he of the tufts of hair in his ears, the phenyl swabbed clinic and the coloured glass bottles filled with syrups he prescribed to every patient – gently suggested a consultation with a psychiatrist if this insistence to be returned to her 'real' home persisted.

Her father had nodded, and paid the doctor's fee. The insolent Subhash from C Wing, all of twelve, kept teasing her. 'Dead girl, dead girl, you're a zombie.'

She had thrashed him to within an inch of his life. The injured Subhash had gone yelping to his mother. Sundari – she of the mammary that defied gravity – had dragged a squealing and embarrassed Subhash to Nayna's home to apologise for having picked on a younger kid and that too a girl.

He had tendered the requested apology and then demanded to see Nayna's latest Archie comics, which she promptly brought out and demanded his Phantom comics in exchange.

When these pleasantries were dispensed with, Sundari put forward her own theory of Nayna's disappearance. 'I think, Mandira, that Nayna was put on ice, it froze her, and then when this Ana remembered she was inside the ice box, she took her out and defrosted her and that's why she can't remember anything that happened in those two days. I've read about it.' Sundari was, as she was proud of saying, a centum student from Madras College as it was then known. 'I read about it in a book, science fiction.' She pushed her glasses up her nose and stared determinedly at Mandira, who smiled and nodded.

'Nayna says she went into the future – can you believe that? It fits right in with your science fiction theory. But Dr Shanbag feels she fainted and then probably dreamt it up.'

When the last biscuit on the plate was eaten, Mandira stood up politely but firmly. 'It was so nice chatting with you, Sundari, you must drop in more often.'

'I will,' promised Sundari, lumbering to her feet, her skin shining ebony with oil and humidity, her eyes shining with morbid curiosity, a potent combination if any. 'Now you take care of your girl,' she whispered. 'Not everyone gets their child back from a disappearance like that completely unharmed.'

Sundari moved her corpulence to the door and exited quickly, eager to discuss this little bit of information with her husband. Mandira was one of those strange women who rarely chatted with the other women in the colony, not before Nayna had disappeared, not during her disappearance, not after. Nor did she stop and chat when she bumped into them on stairways or at the gate or in the market. So much beauty, and so much sorrow in her eyes, Sundari thought.

The shift began with the kids subtly keeping Nayna out of the games some days after the fight with Subhash. 'You're a bhoot, you died and came back from the dead,' they told her. 'We can't play with you! You will kill us too.' The real dead who hung around in the trees around the compound sighed and told Nayna to ignore them. She smiled, knowing that if the kids ever saw the true dead they wouldn't be coherent enough to even be mean to her.

At the society Independence Day function, the chairs around Nayna and Mr and Mrs Khosla stayed vacant. What people don't understand they fear, and what they fear they stay away from. They had moved homes soon after and she moved schools. Another GP now looked at Nayna when she seemed peaky or feverish. The new home was bigger than the previous one as Mr Khosla had been promoted to manager level from a mere officer. They now had two bedrooms and a pantry, they also had house-help supplied by the company: a Man Friday who was her father's shadow, and his wife who helped with the household chores. They had their own room at the back of the house. The additional room gave Nayna her privacy, her own study table. She covered the wall in her room with posters of film stars and pop stars she tore out from magazines. As she grew, the posters changed from Cyndi Lauper to Boy George to George Michael to Bryan Adams. She moved from Rahul Roy to Salman Khan in her devotion.

She was the new girl in the new school, an outsider, a creature to be wary of. Cliques had already been formed and breaking into one was difficult. Girls are closed creatures; they bait, they test, they gang up…

'New girl.' 'New girl.' The whispers followed her in the corridors, at assembly, at lunchbreak. No one invited her to sit with them, so she found the furthest spot in the grounds, beyond where all the girls sat in circular bunches of giggles and squeals, to eat her lunch alone. Beyond the tree behind which she sat was the compound wall, and beyond that a slum that lived its own life, within and apart from the city that contained it. There was a certain solace in being alone for those few minutes when she had her lunch—there was no one asking her questions, trying to show her down or being condescending to her in the manner pre-adolescent girls secure in their insular cliques are. She would sit under the spreading peepal tree, nestled in a crook within its trunk that ensured she was hidden from view, the deep shade cradling her.

It was sometime in the second week of her new school and sitting in her hiding place for lunch that she saw an eye looking at her through a small hole in the wall. She blinked at first – maybe she was imagining it. She looked again. It was definitely an eye. A human eye. She ignored it at first. It was difficult though to continue eating when an eye was staring at you through a hole in the wall.

She put her eye to the hole and saw nothing, just the grey cement concrete wall of a tenement that faced that particular spot in the wall. She went back to her spot and finished her lunch with a growing sense of unease. It felt like an invasion, having someone stare at her while she was trying to eat in peace. The next day, the eye was there again and disappeared when she went towards it.

The next day was a Saturday and then a Sunday, and on Monday she went back to school determined to find out who was staring at her through the little hole. The lunch bell rang, Nayna slipped out from the backdoor right next to her bench and ran down the corridor, her feet flying swiftly over the old stone stairs. She dashed down to the compound but didn't go directly to her tree. The other girls watched her curiously, this new girl who hadn't bothered to try ingratiating herself with the rest of them when they had made it clear that they wouldn't be easily befriended. Who did she think she was, and which royalty did she think she descended from? They sniggered among themselves, mocking her too-long legs, too-little bosom, too-white skin, too-big grey eyes, too-quiet self. She was a too-much and a three-much, they concluded. 'Where is she going today?' Christine Pereira, leader of the pack, hissed. 'Not to the peepal tree? Let's go see.'

Nayna was almost sprinting to the other end of the ground where she knew a ladder was propped up against the wall. She hauled the ladder over her shoulder and went swiftly to where the hole in the wall was, propped it over the wall and clambered up, to peer over it. The eye peering at her through that little hole belonged to another girl standing, hunched down, looking into the building compound.

'Hey,' Nayna called from her perch up on the ladder, swinging her feet easily over to the other side of the wall and dropping down in one smooth jump. The girl looked up with a fright, and fled through the narrow lanes. Nayna, who gave chase, lost her. And, she realised, she was lost herself now. The slum colony she had entered twisted into narrow lanes; she had entered a maze. The doors were curtained and the windows had plants in old Dalda tins, the regulatory tulsi sapling to bless the premises, and red rose shrubs stunted by the lack of space. Within the miserliness of the surroundings, hope unfurled itself through the vibrant prints on the sarees converted into curtains, the TV antennae that stuck out on the roofs, catching the broadcast from Doordarshan that had just about gone colour a few years ago, and added an additional metro channel for the city which had serials that the young saw as a life they could aspire to, and the old saw as a life they could never touch. Curious faces looked at her as she ran past, trying to find her way out of the warren of lanes, slick with water and refuse, a stench she wasn't familiar with flooding her nose, the stench of life decaying. Women cleaning grain on the stoops of their homes, children running snot-nosed, and a group of young men, charged with testosterone and joblessness, standing at the corners, wondering how best to while their day away. They stared at her, gazes that sent shivers down her spine, though she didn't quite understand why. One of the group detached himself from the lot and sauntered towards her, a twisted smile on his face as his eyes raked her up and down.

'A convent school girl in our jhopad-patti,' he said in a language she didn't quite understand because she didn't speak it. 'How can we help this little princess?'

'No, nothing,' she stuttered and turned around, beginning to run in the opposite direction. He planted a determined hand on her shoulder. In that moment Nayna knew fear, knew what it meant to be a girl in a world where men still laid down the rules. 'Arrey, what is the hurry, come talk to us for a while.'

A fetid, stale smell enveloped the air: it was the smell of unwashed bodies surrounding her purposefully. The shopkeeper of the paan shop watched the unfolding drama in front of his ramshackle little store and hoped that he wouldn't be called in by the police again as a witness in case there was an incident; the last time that had happened, he had been beaten up by both the police who thought he wasn't telling them the truth and by the goondas who thought he'd told them the truth. There was no winning this.

The girl was swift. She dodged the chap blocking her path and ran, dodging lines of washing and pots of ad hoc greenery, running until she could no longer see the men behind her, and had reached a strip of road. An auto rickshaw approached from a distance and slowed down as it came nearer, a speck of yellow and black that brought with it hope and the possibility of rescue.

'There she is, on the road, catch her.' The footsteps behind her caught up with her. She ran towards the auto, waving at it in desperation to slow down and stop for her, which it did. She hopped into it.

'Take me home,' she shouted in a panic, rattling off the names of the colony and the road she lived in, which was only a ten-minute walk from where they were if only she knew the route. 'Start the auto quickly, those men are chasing me.'

The auto zoomed off, leaving the chasing men behind.

'Thank you,' she told the auto driver, her voice still shaking from the running and the fear. 'They were trying to kidnap me.'

'Why would they do that?' His voice was old and tired and there was a bald spot at the back of his head that she was staring at. He was looking at her from the rear-view mirror.

'I don't know. Can you take me home?'

'Yes, bachcha, I will take you home, don't worry.'

She settled down in the seat, worried because she had no money to pay the auto, and didn't know how to explain her arrival back home at an odd hour to her mother, divested of her school bag. She shuddered. She would ask her parents to shift her to another school, she decided, and she would borrow some money off Mhatre kaku on the ground floor and return it when Pappa gave her weekly pocket money.

'Did they know you?' the driver asked, negotiating the narrow roads with a grace that was beyond the repertoire of the regular auto driver. The vehicle moved sinuously, like it hovered an inch or so above the rough and pitted road and thereby avoided all the bumps and lurches that were inevitable in any drive down the city's roads.

'No, as I told you, I lost my way and they began chasing me.'

He was silent for a while. An errant cyclist crossing the road had him brake really hard so that she was almost flung out of the auto.

'Sorry, *beta*,' he said kindly. 'You aren't hurt, are you?'

A crow flew alongside the auto, cawing frantically. Crow! She gasped.

'Crow!' she called, 'Why are you here?'

'Get out,' he told her. 'Run away.'

'Stop the auto,' she cried, panicking, realising that she was in a completely unfamiliar area, one quite deserted.

He picked up speed and turned into a narrow alley. She realised she could not see anyone around; the area was completely bereft of human or animal. Even Crow had flown away.

'Stop, please, stop!'

He did not reply, just continued at a speed that churned her stomach. The auto came to a shuddering halt at the end of a disused alley. The driver got out of his seat swiftly before she could even ask him where she was and hit her hard on the back of her head with a little truncheon he had pulled out from his waistband. He caught her swiftly before she hit the ground and carried her into the empty building. The men she had run away from joined him in a short while. It was a pre-decided spot, one that had seen such horror before, horror that no child should have to undergo, horror that no power intervened to stop, not human, not divine.

They would find her days later, naked, violated so brutally that her body was ripped apart. And hovering over the body, unseen to all, encased in a little grey bubble, she watched as they moved her to the hospital. They abandoned her when they thought she had died. If she had shown any signs of life, they would have taken her to the red-light area and sold her to the first taker. Perhaps there was a darker fate that had befallen another Nayna.

There was no escaping, no matter what oceans of time and space one crossed. Pulling Nayna out and putting her in another place, another time, had only been a momentary diversion for the three fates with their intertwining silken skeins. In this time or another, they would inflict the horror they promised; a soul could never escape the pain that had been pre-ordained for it, in this world or the other.

16

They Waited, Ghosts of the Past

'Sharing tales of those we've lost is how we keep from really losing them.'

—Mitch Albom, *For One More Day*

THE GIRL DIDN'T COME AGAIN TO THE OTHER SIDE OF THE WALL. The other girl didn't come again to class before the other children did. Sue went away. The Sue of the early mornings. The Sue who let air out of motorcycle tyres with a Swiss knife. Pappa didn't come again into my dreams asking me to jump. No one took me to a deserted building. No hands crawled over my body. No one violated me. There was a silence in my head that was absolute. The ghosts had been put to rest but other ghosts were rising, and they weren't from the dead, nor were they from the living.

Changing pasts had speckled me, punched holes that shone with darkness and iridescent light from whichever time I'd left parts of myself behind. I ordered corsets off the internet, meant for women to hold their stomach muscles in after pregnancy, to hold in my light. I wore them out, the vacuum within me sought release and strained at their elasticised restraint, too pitiful to contain its infiniteness. The holes were healing, but they still sparkled through me. All creation involved destruction; I knew that all that you changed would change you too. There was a price to be paid for every little bit of meddling you did with what was the order of things.

I rarely stepped out. Everything I needed was home-delivered now: food, clothes, books, appliances, medicines. Everything except human company. Sometimes I forced myself to step out of this anonymous, glitteringly gilded gated complex I had shifted into, just to feel the air part to let me pass in a way that the vacuum I slithered through did not. When I got back from these occasional walks, the door let me into the dissimulated silence that I now associated as home. This house was occupied, not lived in. It existed as a covering that I shed when I stepped out and pulled on when I entered, shifting and expanding to accommodate me, wrapping its walls around me like a blanket, comforting, keeping me insulated from what the world might bring. Perhaps that was all one wanted from a home. When we had shifted to the house I had now locked up and left behind, all those years ago, Maa and me, the world still believed in neighbours and the warmth of open doors. The doors to most flats were open all day and the children ran up and down the stairs and into houses. Chor Police was played not just in the building compound but in the staircase, in homes; water was asked of freely from any home. Glass windows sacrificed to the shots of budding batsmen were grumbled about and compensation sought good-naturedly.

I had played with them – the children didn't ask too many questions. Where is your father, they had asked. He died, I told them. How, they asked. He fell down from the balcony, I replied. That was darned careless of him, another replied. I laughed. They clucked in commiseration for a while, one grumbled that he wished his miserable father would fall from the balcony and spare him from the everyday beatings, and then they were all nice to me, the girl with no father and a mother who didn't seem to care too much, given I came to play in dresses that were worn out and torn. What they didn't know was that Maa lived in a world of her own ever since Pappa jumped, and she rarely emerged to see if I needed her, and when she did sometimes, it was so terrifying that I wished she had stayed within her uncaring shell.

We played Dabba Ice Spice and Seven Tiles and Chor Police when the weather was fair and when the weather was foul, we took out our bedsheets and played house-house under carefully draped dining tables, or antakshari in the staircases, which echoed with raucous singing. They had all grown up, the friends of my childhood. Most had moved away. Some through marriage, others through jobs, a couple through death. Those who remained were the ones who didn't have much expected of them, the ones who were a tad slow in school, the ones who marched to a different drummer. Perhaps I was one of them too, I realised.

'Be pleasant with the neighbours. You have to live here,' Maa had told me. 'I will be gone.'

'There's a long time for you to be gone,' I had replied.

'Not so long as you imagine. It will be a relief for you too. You will be happy when I die. You will celebrate, distribute mithai. You will be free from me.'

I didn't argue with that. She knew exactly what she was, and I was not going to pretend otherwise. A few months later she was dead. All that remained of her was her voice that called out to me from the spaces between thoughts.

'Ana....'

'*Haan*, Maa...'

Death is always and never final. Not until you decide to forget the one who has passed away. Not until the one who has passed away decides to forget you. Maa hadn't. She was still around. In my head. In the room. In the silences. In the noise.

I did not run up and down the stairs anymore. The front door would now remain closed, the doorbell would no longer ring as it had done in the past. A cup of sugar? Manjari kaku was just making some kheer and realised she had run out of sugar. The cup of sugar would be handed across in the anticipation of it being returned filled with the promised kheer in the evening. A couple of limes? A functional pressure cooker? Could Mrs Iyer borrow the mixer for an hour, she wanted to make dosa batter, she would send some back for Mandira and Ana too. Would they, by any chance, have some cornflour in the fridge, Fonseca aunty was making Chinese tonight. Mrs Mhatre had just made some thalipeeth, here was some for them. Relationships were built with food back then. I was perhaps the only one from my generation who had still continued living there, in the same house, with the same furniture, walking up and down the stairs and realising how difficult it was to negotiate the staircase with no lift only when Maa fell ill and needed to be carried up and down every time she had to be taken to the hospital and back. These were flats that didn't get sold, the buildings were too decrepit and everyone was waiting for the redevelopment sharks to come sniffing around. Other buildings down the lane were already being crumbled to dust, notices put up to inform passers-by that so and so builder had taken over the property and was now intending to build something of value here that would overtake the corroded value of what had existed in those spaces earlier. The residents who chose the redevelopment waited in rented homes until the projects crawled up plinth by plinth. There was always hope and waiting. It defined most lives, hope and waiting. It was the mainstay of most lives. Human beings could endure almost anything if they were living under the canopy of hope.

This new home was antiseptic and sterile. It was fully furnished, with the dispassionate stamp of an interior design agency, which had been commissioned to make it liveable at minimum cost. The builder had sold these pre-furnished. Neutral shades and clean lines. Standard aesthetically pleasing botanical prints on the wall, in gilt-edged framing. Textured wallpaper on accent walls. Curtains double layered, to let in the light, to keep things private, to make it dark, and to keep out the world and its prurient gaze. These were choices I hadn't had in the previous home. This was a luxury. It was convenient. Barely fifteen minutes from Aman's office, fifteen minutes from his home, both in opposite directions. A convenient circular circumference that meant he had been planning this shift for a while and had given this place a fair amount of thought.

What I left behind in the house I locked up I did not want to think about. It would come, boiling with rage, wanting to tear me to pieces, drag me back with it. The Greyness. I had broken through and emerged without its consent. I would never be forgiven for coming back, back to being Nayna. The undead should remain undead. There was a reason for purgatory, souls were not supposed to wander back and take up residence in available bodies, and then live out their lives for them.

The air in the house heavy with my exhalations and inhalations. Aman came and went as he pleased, his presence an absence and his absence underlining the heft of his presence.

The week was an absence. Aman was in a country so far in the Northern latitudes that he hoped a day trip could take him where he could see the Northern lights. Aurora Borealis. Plasma hurled through space at us, solar winds blazing through 150 million kilometres, passing through our magnetic poles, through our magnetic shield, making love to atoms and molecules in our atmosphere, orgasming in resplendent blue, green, violet streaks through the skies. Everything had a scientific explanation. Someday I would find one for the aberration that was me.

'Are you okay? Have you settled in well?' he asked, calling from the hotel room after his day was done, before going off for drinks with his hosts. It was a cold European country, one of those which had splintered away when the Soviet Union had broken up in the aftermath of the cold war, at the time India gingerly stepped into the economic wonderland called liberalisation. He was miserable, he claimed, and couldn't wait to come back to saner temperatures. The weather, he said perfunctorily, not that I had enquired, was lousy. Grey and rainy, with a chill wind that pierced the bones when one was outside. Sleet so slippery under feet, and food bland and unsatisfying.

'Find an Indian restaurant,' I had laughed.

'I think that's what I'll do,' he'd concurred in all seriousness. 'I miss you.'

'I don't,' I replied. 'This soppy stuff doesn't suit you. Who are you screwing?'

He laughed. Liquid warmth flowing down the ethers.

'You know me too well. No one you know.'

'Make sure you use condoms, don't get any diseases back.' I disconnected the call without a goodbye. Goodbyes were unnecessary, as were hellos. Infidelity was nothing to be upset about. I would do the same if I came across someone who attracted me and he knew that. We were kindred souls who wanted to be together and understood that the body also demanded other bodies. I could not demand fidelity when I could not promise it myself.

I'd moved here over a month now in this time. The anonymity this space provided suited me. Everyone one encountered was face deep into their phones. It was liberating to not be looked at, not to be smiled at, not to be compelled into the thrust and parry of polite conversation. I perversely missed that about the old home, the pleasantries that didn't care about boundaries, neighbours who had known you for decades hauling you up for not being more neighbourly.

This was completely unlike my previous home. For one, it was in a better part of the city, the newly developed, with old constructions razed over, the residents settled elsewhere and the spiffy new condominiums sold to professionals who had come in from other cities and were looking to grab the life of high-flyers that Mumbai had promised them, glittering from afar with its seedy glamour. It looked out on greenery and squatness; not too far to the East the flamingos would gather after their long flight from Siberia, creating a sea of fluttering pink. There was beauty, waiting, in the mundane, ready to take your breath away if you paid attention.

Saachi called as I stepped out of the lift. I planned to walk around the complex, and out of it, and from there to the driveways and the many gates that allowed entry and exit from the main roads surrounding it.

'Where are you?' she asked without preamble.

'Down for a walk, why?'

'I'm coming over and I'm bringing wine with me. Let's order some food. Go back home and tell your boyfriend you are booked this evening.'

'Oh, he's out of town, fucking someone else.'

'Good for him. I'll be there in half an hour. Send me directions.'

I did so, turned around and went back into the building. A man in jogging shorts who gave me a curious look and a half-interested smile in the lift went back to his phone when I refused to smile in return. I saw no utility in being social with strangers.

Saachi came in hauling two bags. One contained a huge Ganesh statue as a housewarming gift, the other contained an assortment of wine bottles. I ordered some Chinese food. We drank the wine in celebration of my moving out or moving in, I wasn't sure. I placed the statue on a shelf, uncertain about the correct direction to keep it. I would need to ask someone. Maa had, in her later years, completely given up religion, though not vegetarianism.

'I was so terrified that building was going to collapse after one heavy rain. So glad you moved out!'

'It was long overdue,' I agreed.

'What now? I hope you're planning to get back to fulltime work?' She paused, weighing her words, and then continued. 'He is no good for you. It is so predictable. He isolates you from everyone you knew and keeps you like a...'

'...A keep? Is that the word you're looking for, Saachi?' I shook my head. 'It isn't like that, and this is not Stockholm syndrome. I allow myself to be isolated and used. And perhaps I use him too. It was a parasitical relationship.'

Saachi laughed. 'It is strange you say *was*. And that holds good for all relationships, doesn't it? We're all parasites in some way, feeding off each other.'

'You aren't feeding off me, Saachi. If anything, you give me a glimpse of what regular life could be.'

'And you give me a window into how things could be had I chosen not to get married and domesticated. But these are choices one makes and lives with.'

'Nothing is written in stone, Saachi. I can still get married, and you can decide you don't want to remain married. Things change, that's the flux of life and the beauty of it.'

Saachi smiled, and put her hand on mine. Her other went to her stomach, rotund with child, unconsciously telling me all I needed to know. 'There are always choices. Yes. Some we can't undo. Like having a child. It changes everything permanently.'

'Yes, having a child is pretty unchangeable a decision. It is a brave one.'

Her eyes shone with hope and life. Another chain of events being set into motion, another splinter of consciousness finding itself through the cosmic dust and chaos hurled into this womb and all that would ensue. Right now, the only thing to do was to hug her and wish her luck. I wondered what destiny her child would bring, and what wool of existence would unravel and ravel in his or her lifetimes.

'But you haven't told me what your plans are now.'

'I've sent out feelers for work opportunities to ex-colleagues and applied for positions advertised. Something should crop up soon.'

'You're doing it half-heartedly. If you were serious, you would have found a job by now. You have got comfortable with this piecemeal project-based work from home business.'

'Perhaps you're right. Perhaps I really haven't been trying too hard. I think it scares me, to be honest. Stepping out of the house terrifies me. I must see a counsellor, it could be this thing, agoraphobia they call it, I've researched it. Every time I need to step out, I have anxiety attacks. Even today when you called, I'd stepped out alone for the first time since I moved in. Had to psyche myself for an hour before I could bring myself to step out! I had cold sweats, my heart was pounding… I was actually relieved when you called and I had a reason to rush back home.' I paused, then continued. 'Aman is booking me into therapy when he gets back.'

It was easier for me to cross the vortexes of space time than to gather the nerve to cross the road, I admitted to myself. It was less stressful to interact with the girl I'd left behind and the woman I would go on to be than to interact with regular people in the here and now.

The day sank quickly as we chatted, and dusk was dark and overwhelming. The lamp cast strange spirals of light across the room.

The glasses were empty, so I refilled them. Wine went through me like water; no longer was the head light after a few glasses, nothing gave me a high anymore, no wine, no alcohol and I'd never tried anything harder than weed back during college. I was not about to start now.

'And you think a new job would be the solution to my shutting myself in? Seriously, Saachi, I need help before I commit myself to professional work or I will just end up making a damned fool of myself. I'm too messed up in the head right now.'

'You can be messed up in the head and step out into the world. Look at me. Happily married. Pregnant. Wanting to complete my family. And messed up and depressed most days.' I hugged her. I knew of her battles with her weight and eating disorders.

Saachi laughed. 'What was that first line from Anna Karenina? All happy families are the same but every unhappy family is unhappy in their own way, I think. Tolstoy got it right.'

I sighed. 'We didn't recognise it then, but Pappa was probably depressive. He should have got help. Back then, no one spoke about these things, and seeing a counsellor meant you were mad. This held true especially for men. Men had to hold the home together. They had to run the house. It was tougher for men...'

Saachi nodded. 'Maasi could be mean. She would say terribly mean things, her tongue was like a knife, and then laugh like she didn't mean it and you were overreacting if you took offence. But her words left gashes on your soul. She would always call me *moti*, and then say she was saying it for my own good because who would marry a fatso like me.'

'She was mean to us too. She would say such hurtful things to me, like, I wish you had never been born, because of you I was forced to marry this ugly creature... My dad would never retaliate. He always kept quiet. And then one fine day he just jumped. She drove him to it.'

'I'm so sorry, Ana, you shouldn't have had to hear all that. Parents can be cruel. At least your father was kind, I mean Maasi's husband was kind to you....'

Saachi looked at me, and the unsaid hung in the silence, what I had never asked and never been told, what I had no courage to hear. I stopped, the words I had uttered hung in the air and it dawned on me why everything about my childhood was so very wrong.

'Whose daughter am I, Saachi? Who was my father?'

'I can't answer that, Ana. Only Maasi could.'

She had taken the answers with her to where I dared not follow her, the Greyness. To get the answers I wanted, I would have to go there again and if I dared go there, the Greyness would not let me come back to the here and now.

17

And the Mirror Cracked

'It's a poor sort of memory that only works backwards,' says the White Queen to Alice.

—Lewis Carroll, *Alice's Adventures in Wonderland / Through the Looking-Glass*

WHEN NAYNA STOOD IN THE BALCONY AND LOOKED DOWN, THE world no longer swirled. The people below were like ants. The world hadn't shrunk, she had grown. She had grown tall. She was growing taller. Something was stretching her to a preternatural height that made her taller than her parents already.

'When will she stop growing?' her worried mother asked the doctor.

'Once she hits puberty. Not more than an inch or two after that I would think.'

Her mother was not assuaged, every morning visually measuring her limbs and gauging whether they had lengthened in the night.

'It will be difficult to find her a decent boy if she gets too tall. No one wants a wife taller than them.'

Her father was more prosaic. 'She'll find herself a tall husband, don't worry, Mandira. And if she doesn't get a tall husband, it won't be the end of the world.'

Mandira fretted about how Nayna was stretching out, all long fluid limbs, golden skin and soft downy golden hair on them that shone when the light caught them. Her hair, which had been growing at the same preternatural pace as her body, had now crossed her hips, black waves that Mandira determinedly tamed into two tight plaits, in keeping with the schoolgirl she still was. Her face, delicately featured, had a soft smile playing on her lips like she was listening in to an inside joke that no one else could hear. Less charitable amongst those in the neighbourhood called her 'half mind', a beauty no doubt, but with the mind of a five-year-old, given she wandered around lost in her own thoughts. Little did they know that her mind was a froth of activity, and she found it tiresome to make casual conversation with them.

'She could be a model,' said Ruby Pardiwala, from the old bungalow down the lane. Ruby was an airhostess with Air India and the most glamorous person in the neighbourhood, no, the entire suburb. She wore her hair in a sharp bob with a fringe, cut at salons abroad, applied eye make-up with professional expertise, dressed in sharply tailored dresses and wore high heels whenever she stepped out.

'They look for really tall girls for the catwalk, and she has such a beautiful face. She reminds me of one those Renaissance paintings, of a goddess, Venus, I think, standing in a clam shell, emerging from the sea naked. I saw it in a magazine, some Italian chap had painted it, hundreds of years ago. Can you imagine painting a naked goddess, even if she was the Goddess of Love?'

Her mother froze. Goddess or otherwise, her daughter was not going to be compared with anything that was unclothed. She'd heard terrible things about the modelling circuit, and her child was not going to step anywhere near it. Nayna found the prospect exciting. She waylaid Ruby one evening as she stepped out of her overgrown garden, startling her as she was opening her rusting rickety gate by springing out from behind the old spreading mango tree that shaded most of the lane. 'What do I need to do to become a model?'

Ruby looked up at her, this tall child with the face of a Botticelli angel, and an innocence that was almost otherworldly. There was something about her that made one want to protect her, and keep her away from the world and its evilness. Ruby looked at her, seeing a softness that she couldn't quite put her finger on; perhaps this child was not meant to be put out into a world that devoured beauty. Blood had not yet begun staining her thighs every month, a reminder of her body being flesh and blood rather than light and space.

'You told Maa the other day that I could become a model. Do you know how?' she asked. She had a Pepsi Cola in her hand – not fizzy cola in a slender bottle but a frozen cola-flavoured mixture in a plastic tube, bought for fifty paise. It was an occasional treat, for which her mother allowed her to go down unsupervised to the store right outside their gate. Her mother had already removed her from school after men began following her back home and standing outside the gate staring at her besotted. The school called them in to insist that her parents bring her to school and pick her up after school because they would not be responsible for her safety after a youth scaled the walls of the convent and went hunting for her in the corridors, a knife in his hands ostensibly to end his life and hers if she didn't accept his marriage proposal. She was thirteen. Marriage proposals didn't even figure in her lexicon. Right now, she was wearing a dress that had a frilly yoke and ribbons in a sunflower yellow and white check pattern. She was a child. She was almost a woman.

Mandira had lost the baby she had been carrying; he'd been born early and died a day later, too weak to survive out of the womb. It had made her even more feral and protective of Nayna. Perhaps it was for the best, she rationalised as the years passed and Nayna became gloriously luminous in her beauty. Perhaps the loss of that child was needed so Mandira could put all her energy into keeping Nayna safe.

'How long will you keep her confined within the house?' Pawan argued. 'Sooner or later, she will have to step out. She will have to learn to deal with the attention.'

'We can't keep her safe,' Mandira declared flatly. 'The world is evil. It's better she stays home.'

Nayna didn't understand what they worried about, as she floated through her day lost in her head, having conversations no one could hear with animals and birds. They were all the conversation she needed, since the conversations she had with humans were proving to be sadly inadequate. She didn't mention these conversations to her parents – it would only worry them more. It was a burden, a daughter who glittered like an island in a sea of ordinariness. She glowed, she shone, and some swore that when she walked past, they saw her enveloped in a pulsating column of light. The strange pull that everyone who came in contact with her felt towards her, they translated as romantic love if they were young and male, and a curious protectiveness towards her if they were older or female. She barely noticed it; all she wanted to do was get out of this, which was not her life and find that which had been her life before she came here, one in which her parents, flawed and squabbling as they were, were hers. One in which she had been ordinary, not touched by the vacuum of the beyond.

'Great beauty is a curse,' her mother told her. 'You will learn soon enough. There is only so much I can do to protect you.' Her mother had been a great beauty too, but she would outshine her mother, and her mother knew it, and worried for her.

'Till the time I'm alive,' she told her husband, her voice soft and firm, 'I will protect her from the world.'

'What happens when you die? When I die?' he asked.

'I don't want to think about that. I will kill her before that,' she thought to herself. It was stupidity, she knew, as if death came with an advance warning. It descended unannounced, always. She should know. The one she loved had been killed for the crime of loving her. There was no advance warning, just a message from a classmate of his death and the sudden realisation of the grim faces of her father and older brothers when they'd returned home late the previous night, with bloodstained clothes her mother quietly burned in the backyard with a pile of October leaves.

Her parents had not thought it important to ask her what she wanted, and she was doing the same with Nayna. Nayna did not wish to stay confined to the house. If anything, Nayna was suffocating in the house, a house too tight for her as she grew. The ceiling too low and the rooms too boxy, with a balcony that looked out into the walls of the next building. And she, who had traversed through the vastness of never-ending eternity, couldn't explain why she found herself gasping for breath when the walls of the home closed in on her. Her parents took her to the doctor who diagnosed asthma and prescribed inhalers and fresh air.

Nayna slipped out when her mother was busy in the kitchen or having a bath. She walked out into the lane and went to where she was not allowed, turning at the main road and walking into the little unpaved street alongside the marshes, where no one went. She liked the aloneness of going where the only sounds were those of the birds who flew overhead or parked themselves on the stumpy trees that fringed the border of the creek and the land. Noisy pink and black starlings moving in clumps towards the thickets. Ducks quacking from within the waters. The egrets and gulls imperious in their ownership of the territory. And in the midst of all this beauty, the occasional cawing of the humble crow. The other birds were not why Nayna came here. She came here to meet Crow. If you sat strategically on a huge boulder marking the end of the lane, you could see where the creek went out into the sea, a silvering where the sun hit the infinite expanse of water, and across it, she knew because she had studied the map, the Gulf states, where the Arabian Sea ended and land began again, and beyond even that, the Horn of Africa. How would it be, she wondered, if she cast herself adrift on the tide and floated out on the ocean, washing up on some distant shore where no one knew her. Wouldn't it be much the same as what had happened to her, after Ana had taken her away from her home, depositing her back on a shore that was not the one she left? Where she knew no one, except perhaps Crow. Not even her parents, who thought they knew her but were strangers to her, familiar faces, and just that bit dissonant, to make her realise that nothing was as she had left it, and yet everything was the same.

'Why did she do that, Crow? Why would she do that? Whatever it was, they were my parents. These are strangers who just look like my parents. I miss Maa, even though she didn't like me too much. Do they have another Nayna in my place?'

Crow bobbed his head, and turned his face to one side. 'Yes, they have another you in your place. Parts of the story need to be fitted back together even if they get shifted. Another Nayna got into your story. It must be tougher on her, think about it. Her parents don't love her anymore and are constantly quarrelling. She will remain ordinary all her life. Whereas you now have been touched by infinity, tinged by the divine.'

'Tinged by the divine?' Sometimes Crow said things she could not quite comprehend. But he was the only one who made sense to her in a world that had stopped making sense.

'The eternity of the vacuum you travelled through has made you what the earlier generations called gods, beings much more splendid than normal humans. Tell me, have you hurt yourself recently?'

Nayna thought long and hard, but couldn't think of any cuts, burns, falls, stumbling or bleeding. She was suddenly immune to all affronts to her person and it hadn't even occurred to her that this had been one of the benedictions that traversing across space time had bestowed upon her.

'You have,' said Crow, 'become invulnerable. A little miracle. Ana doesn't know that, of course. All she was trying to do was to take you away from harm's way. Now, she has with her insistence on taking you through a different path made you something you weren't. And you have no option but to live with this. Unless you can find your way back.'

'How can I do that, Crow?' she asked, flinging pebbles at the tide coming into the marshes.

'You know how to.'

He would fly away just when the conversation came to these points, leaving Nayna even more perplexed and sad. Slowly and steadily, Nayna withdrew into the house. Her father, worried for her, brought the world home to her. A leaf from a tree that had grown from the mango seed she had planted in the playground. A shell from the beach they used to visit before it got run over with sightseeing buses and the throngs that spilled over every weekend, snacks from the halwai down the road, hot and aromatic jalebis just out of the boiling oil, warm and crunchy just the way she liked them, a brick from the construction site down the road, where an old crumbling one-storey bungalow had been demolished to make way for a multi-storeyed tower to come up, with high-speed lifts and glass-front balconies. Tinkle comic books from the circulating library down the lane, Archie comics from the bookstore near his office. Succulent targolas from the vendor outside the railway station. Tooth-rottingly sweet Phantom cigarettes that she chewed ferociously down to the knub and swallowed or the Kwality orange ice lolly on a stick that turned her tongue orange. Cake batter she would beat up till her hand went numb for her mother to make her famed pressure cooker cakes. Tall mugs of Rasna served in the lemonade set, orange flavour, to beat the summer heat. Or if

Pappa was feeling generous, Rooh Afza, with its wafting promise of roses and all the indolent luxury it conjured. She had all the world she wanted within the walls of her home. And so she grew. The only ones who saw her were her parents, her two tutors, Owl and Crow. The same crow who flew around the universes checking up on all versions of her. The same owl who landed up, dispensing unasked for advice.

As the circumference of her living decreased, her senses heightened. Her hearing became painfully acute, her vision was almost telescopic, her skin became so sensitive to touch that she wore clothes stitched out of the softest mul that was used to stitch infants' clothes. Her mother stayed up late, stitching dresses for her on her sewing machine, the one with the foot pedal that she loved to play with until she got scolded. Evenings were spent in front of the television. The television set, the Cyclops of the living room, took her around the world, to the home of a middleclass everyday family in Delhi, to the fires of the Partition, *Surabhi* that visited the corners of the country, *Vikram aur Betaal* that made her wonder about the face powder that Betaal used and the Sisyphean task that King Vikram had before him, the spats of families living in a Bombay apartment complex in *Yeh Jo Hai Zindagi* and more.

Sleep didn't come easy to one with heightened hearing in a metropolis, as there was always some sound, some noise, some disturbance to disturb one's rest. A dog barking, police sirens screeching, bikes speeding, a rowdy drunk on the street, a domestic fight in the building opposite, a radio on at full volume in the flat below – there was no hushed respect for the night. Even when man-made noises muted, nature made its own noises: the wind that whistled through the window, the slats bringing the breeze in on humid days becoming nature's mouth organ, warbling a sibilant melody that was both a warning and a wish. Sleep was a long time coming for her most days; she tossed and turned on the mattress on the floor, specially made to contain all of her, now that she had grown out of the trundle bed that had seen her through most of her childhood. When sleep finally came, she fell through a spinning void and went places she was yet to visit in this lifetime.

As she grew taller, she retained the fineness of the features she had inherited from her mother. The paleness of her skin, the black waves of her hair and the grey eyes created an unusual palette that set her apart from the others around. Her father had lost the original black of his own hair and owed his borrowed youthfulness now to a bi-monthly application of hair dye, generally on a Sunday morning which was conducted to much joyous humming of romantic songs and leaving a residue of black patches in the little white Parryware basin, causing her mother to ask whether her dear departed mother-in-law would come back to earth to clean the mess he had left behind. Nayna would listen in to their mock enraged bantering, an essential part of her Sunday morning, like the aloo puri breakfast or the kheer or sooji halwa that made its way to their plates mid-week to keep their cheer up. Indulgences were few and far between in the household run on a limited income, but it had been a happy house. Living in these old government quarters had its advantages and disadvantages. 'Say all you can about a boring government job with no growth prospects,' her father told her one day. 'But you get a house to stay rent-free in a city like Bombay. And then you get pension after you retire till you die. Or if you die in service, your widow gets a pension. What more does one need?'

It scared her, her father's complete contentment with a life that confined itself to no rent and assured pension. Wasn't there more to desire? She asked Crow the next time he landed on her balcony, 'Will I never get out of this prison?'

'You can't blame them. They're trying to keep you safe.'

The neighbourhood gathered to watch her as she stood at the balcony, the faint halo around her changing shades as late evening turned to night. Her mother returned from the market and saw the heads turned up towards their balcony, and Nayna standing there, unaware of the eyes on her, seemingly deep in conversation with a crow.

She rushed up and charged into the house. Crow flew off, startled, Nayna looked at her with dreamy eyes, not registering the annoyance on Mandira's face.

'You are not to stand out in the balcony like that when I'm not home,' Mandira thundered, dragging her inside.

'But why, Maa? What's wrong with standing in the balcony?'

'Everyone was looking at you,' Mandira hissed accusingly, an accusation that Nayna did not understand. She had aged while Nayna was growing, Mandira's radiance transferring itself to her daughter. Her face was sallow and jowly, lines etched down the nose to her lips. Her eyes refused to un-crinkle their corners long after her smile had faded. A short line shot up the middle of her brows, and her neck was tumbling down itself. She was not even forty, but her face and her body seemed to have signed up for some accelerated ageing programme. She had also hit menopause, strangely enough, much earlier than mandated.

Nayna's father was transferred to a new town, a long train ride and then a bus ride away.

'How will you find me now?' she asked Crow.

He laughed. 'I will find you.'

The train ride, in a reserved coupe, was two long days and when they finally reached their new home, Nayna marvelled at how open and green it was, the trees spreading themselves generously, bestowing cool shade and hesitating to touch each other, maintaining a respectable distance between their canopies. Canopy shyness, it was called, Nayna had read somewhere.

'The bungalow is barely ten minutes from office,' her father said, a tinge of pomposity entering his tone. 'All the important personnel stay close to the centre of the town, so they can reach work easily. Of course, I will have an office car and driver now.

And a secretary and a P.A.' These were perks of the job that didn't matter to Nayna, all that did was the fact that she would now live in a quaint double-storeyed bungalow, a palace to a child born and brought up in a city like Bombay. The ground-plus-one quarters had a small patch of personal garden in the front and at the back, which the previous tenants had let go to seed. Mandira looked at it and swore she would have a thriving herb garden for the kitchen and a patch of lawn with rose bushes with a sit-out up front within a couple of months. Nayna revelled at the full-length mirror in her bedroom for she had never seen herself in a full-length mirror yet. The mirror attached to the Godrej cupboard in their Bombay home cut her off at the knee and, as she grew, part of her head as well. She had to bend to see her face. This felt like a luxury. She looked at herself, befuddled, like she was looking at a stranger.

'I love it, Maa, its lovely. And if I stand far back enough I can almost see all of me in it.'

'Okay,' Mandira called up the stairs. 'Wash up and come down to eat.'

'Yes, Maa,' she called back, still looking at herself in the mirror, admiring herself much in the way Narcissus would have stared at his reflection in the pond, seeing herself as a complete person for the first time and realising, to her surprise, that she was no longer the girl she had been in her head but was now almost a woman.

She touched the surface of the mirror, feeling the familiar emptiness ripple through it. And then she saw her in it, through it, a face she'd almost forgotten, in a different room, in a different world. Ana. And Ana turned towards her and smiled, reaching out her hand. It was the most natural thing to do, to put hers out and take it. Then the winds of the stars rushed through her ears and the lights of the nebulas danced through her eyes as she fell through a hurricane of lights and emptiness and then there was a darkness so deep she could see nothing and hear nothing and didn't know if her eyes were open or shut, and she was falling falling falling. Just like she had all those years ago.

She landed lightly. And standing in front of her, like she had all those years ago, was Ana.

18

To Let Go, To Never Return

'Time is the longest distance between two places.'

—Tennessee Williams, *The Glass Menagerie*

HE LAY IN A TENT OF TUBES THAT WENT IN AND OUT OF HIM, EYES unmoving beneath the lids. He was in a sleep so deep that he had disappeared from where I sought him out. It had been days, I had lost count. They had gone by in hopeful wait for a blink, a groan, a movement, for something, anything, that would tell me he was there within that body, the body that had held me, comforted me, given me ecstasy. That the heart within was beating because he was telling it to from somewhere deep within to where he had retreated, not because a machine was ensuring it did. I waited. My breath on edge every moment. He wasn't in there. I knew, but refused to accept it.

Beeps sounded with reassuring regularity from the equipment hooked up to him. The standard issue blue bedsheet he was covered with could not diminish him. He dominated the room just by his presence, still and unmoving as it was. Through the glass that separated us, I could see his chest rise and fall, rise and fall, a rhythm that gave me a tenuous solace. He breathed. He was still in the here and now, at least his body was. His soul would return from wherever it was it had gone off to in the shock of the impact, I could hope. I knew what it was, the sudden detachment of soul from body when the pain was unbearable. I had been there, I had detached, I had gone into the Grey. I had come back. Perhaps I could find him there and bring him back. But I had stopped crossing, I hadn't crossed for years now, I had healed and forgotten how to. The holes in my torso had closed over, the body had swollen and given birth. I was that horrifying thing again, a normal person. A woman, a lover, a mother.

A tiny, sweaty hand in my hand tugged insistently, I'd forgotten about Myra. She looked up at me, her eyes his eyes, thick-lashed and deep brown, her brows straight and thick, with the promise of getting thicker as she grew. She was three. It was no age to see her father perched precariously on the brink of death. I had been eight. There is never really an age you can watch a parent die.

'When will Pappa wake up?'

'Soon, *beta*, soon.' I had no other reply to give. She held on to my hand with the tenacity of one who had nothing else to hold on to.

An accident, they said. A crash at full speed. He had been racing home to me. Not to Sukanya. To me. I held on to that thought, it consoled me and wracked me with guilt.

I looked around the brightly lit cabin we were in, sterile and unwelcoming, trying to grab meaning from the words coming out of the doctor's mouth. Words. Words. Words. All tumbling into a stream of meaninglessness. The white light hit the eyes hard, the plastic bucket chairs meant to hurry you off them, a table cluttered with files, papers and paraphernalia, filing cabinets, this was the clutter of a room that was meant to be functional and not welcoming. Did the well-meaning intensivist know what happened to those who receded into the deepest recesses of their consciousness? How they withdrew there to protect themselves from unbearable pain and trauma? How some of them detached and hovered in the limbo? How they needed to summon all the strength they never knew they had if they had to break free from the Grey to return? Would it change him if he knew of the Grey, that those he kept alive with tubes in throats and stomachs were still undecided, hovering above their bodies, waiting, watching, deciding, some choosing to go, others choosing to stay? Was it my place to tell Sukanya that there was no grey above Aman, he wasn't amongst those waiting and watching, that he wasn't undecided, waiting for his body to heal enough before rejoining it? He had gone, his time was done. The connection had snapped. What was here, encased in tubes and wires was but an empty shell. Do I tell her that sometimes empty shells of bodies bereft of their souls were sought out by those hungry to be in corporeal form again, that the one who came back if we didn't stop life support now might not be Aman? But whoever or whatever it was, it would have Aman's memories, be Aman, or pretend to be him in order to survive in a world that couldn't explain shells and bodies and the disembodied ones that populated them, eager to touch, feel, taste again, coasting along on residual brain memory which helped them pretend to be who they were not. For what they didn't remember, there was memory loss, traumatic brain injury did that, and it gave them an iron-clad reason to not be who they were. I couldn't tell them that, not the doctor, not Sukanya, no one would understand. I could.

After all, I was one of them.

Meanwhile, we waited. On guard outside the ICU for the first few days till we were allowed inside. We circled each other warily, with no words to exchange, neither acrimony, nor solace. The day it happened, the skies had poured nonstop all through the day and showed no signs of letting up through the night. The city, as always, was drowning. He had been returning from a day's official trip to Pune through the thumping rain, a wall of water slamming against his headlights. An out-of-control truck on the other side of the expressway was all it took, crashing through the barrier, flipping over, slamming into his car, both careening to the edge of the road, and his car slipping down the side of the slope, turning, turning, turning until air stopped and ground began, to crumple like paper. His driver dead on the spot, the passenger with a faint pulse the medics could detect, and head injuries, brought into the nearest hospital comatose, then rushed to this one in the city. The call had gone to Sukanya naturally. She had called and told me, a kindness I was grateful for. She had held my hand quietly as I collapsed outside the ICU, flailing in agony, a grief too raw for words.

'He's going to be fine,' she told me, her face grim with a belief I didn't have. I knew he had gone. She didn't. This was the moment I had been living in dread of all these years, it had come too soon.

We had come to terms with the fact that we had equal claim on the man lying inside, she with her children flanking her, two supports taller than her, me with Myra knee-high next to me, and in my womb the one who wouldn't even know his father.

Here we were, sitting side by side, Sukanya and me, opposite the intensive care specialist as he explained the situation. Persistent vegetative state. Minimally conscious. Lack of blood flow, lack of oxygen, trauma injury. Reticular Activating System. Brainstem. I heard the words being thrown at us through a fog. They didn't make sense to me. Nothing did. The possibilities we needed to be prepared for. Likely progression to brain death. And this came gently. Permission to remove him from life support if that was diagnosed. A decision to be taken depending on the results of tests to be conducted.

'You need to be prepared for the eventuality,' he said, his voice gentle.

Sukanya looked tired, yet impeccable. Hair blow-dried, nails polished, pale pink lipstick on pursed lips, mascara opening up her eyes. A soft beige silk shirt over tan linen trousers, her feet shod in intricately embroidered hand-made mule slip-ons. It was a dressed-up dressed-down look with thought and effort put into it. It was protection, I realised, an assertion that everything was going to be okay, that Aman would be fine, that life would go on as it had. He would wake up and go home, and life would be as it was. I admired her for that stoicism. Next to her I was a mess: crinkled t-shirt, creased jeans, hair an uncombed mess, home slippers. She would be older than me now, at least by five years. Or was it eight years? Her expression when she looked at me was undecipherable, no judgement, no animosity. An acceptance difficult for me to accept.

I was more than a mistress and a keep, I told myself. We had a child together and now, yet unknown to him, we were having another. It wasn't supposed to happen, one child is what we had agreed upon, and this one, still a mass of cells inside me, was greed, a forgetting that had become a being. I should have known. She had told me – hadn't she? – that I would outlive them all. The man I loved, the children I gave birth to. I should have realised then that there would have been more than one.

'Thank you, doctor,' Sukanya said, her voice calm and composed. I couldn't trust myself to speak. Only shrieks of agony may emerge; there's too much pain that comes with the fear of losing the one you love, pain that the body cannot contain and must release for fear it will make you explode. 'Let me think this over and discuss it with Ana.'

We stepped out of the cabin and to the plastic bucket seats in a row that were meant for relatives to wait in. Uncomfortable and practical, they reiterated that they were just temporary waiting spots, until the loved one recovered or passed away.

She called her children and handed them some money. 'Go to

the cafeteria, eat something, take Myra with you.' They went off, the promise of sandwiches and cake a temptation that temporarily mitigated the anxiety of a parent in the ICU, on life support. All the children looked uncannily like each other, the straight lines of their eyebrows, the set firmness of their jaws, the square determination of their faces. Myra tempered her inheritance from her father with my eyes, my skin and my hair, the hand-me-downs I got from Maa. What were we all anyway but an accumulation of hand-me-downs, our faces, our bodies, our DNA, our hopes, our fears, our dreams, our nightmares.

'What should we do? What should we do?' she said over and over again when the children had gone away, the two older ones holding the younger one between them by her hands, already protective of her, the half-sister they had met for the first time today. Did they know of her existence, of her mother's existence, of the fact that their father had a life apart from them? 'What should I do?' she asked again, shifting to the singular, a subtle shift, a taking of responsibility she was loathe to share. There was no answer I could give. She sat back and sighed, then took out a pack of cigarettes automatically, then looked around her and put it back. Her hands were shaking, a tremor that was not physiological. I realised all of me was trembling, my body, my mind, my thoughts. The fear of confronting what I had lost already at that moment of the car crashing into the barrier and tumbling down the slope, making all of me tremble without pause, without respite. Death wasn't factored into plans for life. But it stalked us every single moment, from the moment we were born to the moment it finally staked its claim on us. It won most times. Sometimes we pulled back. And at others, we stayed stuck in the grey, the infinite, eternal grey.

'What would you do if you were in my place? Would you want him gone?' she asked. There was no answer one could give, so one replied with a question.

'Do you want him to be like this for the rest of his life, incapable of taking a single breath on his own? You know he would hate that.'

'You know I hated you in the beginning?' she said, without looking at me, her eyes fixed at a point on the wall in front of us, awash in white fluorescent light, sterile and neutral as the rest of the waiting room. The smell of disinfectant clogged up my nostrils, a familiar fragrance, disinfectant mingled with pain, human suffering and grief, one that had demarcated my childhood into before and after. Hospital smell.

'I don't hate you anymore. You love him and he loves you. When you had your daughter… He now has a family with you.'

'He loves you and the children very much, he would never hurt you. Myra, well, she was not planned. It just happened, and I insisted I would go through with the pregnancy.'

'He loved me and he hurt me,' she acknowledged with no hesitation. 'And now our love is… different.' He'd said as much. That between them was a unique friendship.

'I can't let him go.' Her voice was soft, very soft. 'I have no one but him.'

Neither did I. We were both adrift, and he had tethered himself to us, waifs in a world that forgot our existence.

'I don't know why you seem so familiar. We've never met before, but I feel like I know you.'

'We've never met before,' I replied. 'Aman was very particular we don't meet.'

She smiled a quick brittle smile. 'I can imagine. I wasn't very… together in those days. I can understand why he needed you.'

'Honestly, I didn't think you would be so understanding.'

'I didn't think I would understand either. But there comes a point in a marriage where you can either understand or you can go your different ways and I was not ready for the latter.'

There was a silence. One that hung apologetically in the air between us, like the presence and the absence of the man who connected us.

She spoke. 'You're beautiful. But you know that.'

'So are you,' I replied.

She snorted in disbelief. 'I was never beautiful. I just ensured I'm well-groomed so folks find me presentable. My mother was beautiful. Like you. A natural beauty. Aman adored her. She would have been devastated to see him like this.'

His parents had both passed away in the past couple of years. His sister was in Vancouver, and had been informed. She would not be able to travel for the funeral, she had replied. He isn't dead yet, Sukanya had messaged back, furious. And then blocked the number.

'How does one take such a decision?' Her eyes were red-rimmed, a tear strolled down her cheek, followed by another. 'How does one know if one took the right decision?' She opened her handbag, took out a tissue and dabbed her face. 'My father killed himself when I was eight,' she said. 'I don't want my children to grow up without a father. Aman saved me. If he hadn't been there, I would have gone mad.'

I sighed. I knew. Her father. My father. We had lived parallel lives, along different tracks of time. My craziness hers. Our saviour the same. We had come to him at different stages in our lives and stayed, unable to extricate ourselves from a connection that the fates had cruelly woven.

'What would you do?' she asked. I kept silent. It wasn't a decision we could take for each other. The children returned, Myra ecstatic at being with her older siblings, siblings she knew about but never met before, the ice-cream she had eaten on the front of her t-shirt, the hand she slipped into mine sticky.

'Has Pappa woken up?' she asked. The possibility of him never waking from sleep hadn't even crossed her mind. People slept and woke up, she knew that. She was still unacquainted with death and its permanency.

'Not yet,' I replied. 'He will soon.'

She nodded, stray curls escaping from the scrunchie. It was the only thing she'd taken from me, the ringlets. The rest was all Aman, a female version of him in miniature; I could see him as a child in her face. And the one growing within me, would he look like me or like Aman, would he pick and choose bits and pieces of both of us, mashing us up into a combination that was uniquely his? Aman's eyes, my lips, his forehead, my ears, his patience, my temper, all burgeoning within him, the cells that made him up still dividing and differentiating themselves into bone, flesh, tissue, organ and spirit.

Sukanya stood up. She bent to Myra and stroked her hair, a gesture tender in its appropriation. 'She looks like him, so much like him.' Without malice, without rancour, a simple statement of a fact.

Her expression hardened. 'I can't let him go. What if there was a possibility of him coming back and I took it away by deciding to take him off life support?'

'What if,' I replied gently, 'he came back but was incapable of functioning on his own? Won't he resent us then for hesitating to end it while we could?'

There were no easy answers, there would never be. These were moments where we, puny humans, were given the chance to play God. To take decisions to end lives, lives we had no power to bestow. Playing God was not something humans did well, we were best at playing human. Over-reaching ourselves only led to tragedy.

'Let's discuss it tomorrow.'

She nodded. 'Tomorrow.' She rose and we stood awkwardly, me holding Myra's hand, she nodding at Esha and Mann, telling them to go on to the car. It was then, at that strange intersection between resignation and grief, that she put her arm around me. It wasn't a giving of solace or seeking of it, it was just the sisterhood of mourning.

We went our opposite ways to our homes in opposite directions, homes that had connected us to each other by a tenuous bond, a person, who was now connected to things that helped his body breathe, eat, live, while his soul wandered in the place where those who have ended go. I had returned. I had not returned. It was the luck of the draw, there was no telling what could happen. I'd read about a woman who came back after almost three decades of being in a coma. How had she wandered three decades in the Greyness to return to the world of the living had always puzzled me. The little time I'd spent in the Greyness had made it exhausting for me to reorient myself to the gravity and noises that living on the surface of the planet brought. Returning from three decades in the Greyness of limbo would have been like a rebirth.

The first thing I noticed about Sukanya the next day was that she was dishevelled. Not much, but just that tiny bit for me to notice that something was off. Somewhere, in the ethers above, unseen to us, Chandrayaan-2 was separating from its orbiter, preparing for its landing on the moon. Here, the one I had been a satellite of, had already separated from us while we held on to the shell in the vacuous hope that he would return. Spacecraft returned, re-established radio communication that was lost sometimes, there was always hope. They landed into oceans, risking burning up in the atmosphere on re-entry. The unmanned probes wandering the expanse of the distant solar system, beaming back images of the outer planets, the rings of Jupiter, the moons of Saturn, their trajectory taking them on and on, eventually to exit the heliosphere and traverse the interstellar. It took them decades. It took me seconds, but I couldn't find Aman anywhere I travelled. He was not in the grey. Sukanya wouldn't accept that, I couldn't blame her, it was something I would be hard-pressed to accept too.

Her hair was not blow dried, and today it frizzed out, embracing the humidity of the city. She wore a Jaipur block print cotton salwar kameez that seemed to have been pulled on hastily, and her eyes were ringed with wakefulness and dreadful nightmares when she pushed the oversized sunglasses from the bridge of her nose to the crown of her head. She sat next to me on the little divan meant for helpers or kin who stay the night. We sat in silence looking at Aman, trying to locate the man we both loved in what lay on the bed, the man before the road and the rain took him as sacrifice.

'I've made up my mind,' she said. 'I'm keeping him on life support.'

'How long can you afford it?'

The questions that were prosaic needed to be asked. I couldn't afford it. Now I could barely afford my own living expenses without Aman to support me. The consultancy projects I took on were scattered, I had to get back to fulltime work now. I had Myra to think of, and the one growing within me, yet waiting for life to enter him, to sink into his cells, to make him a person from a blob of cells. Living was tougher. Dying was easier.

'There is enough I can liquidate.'

I had no rights to any of the assets she could speak about liquidating. I did not ask. But Myra did, the child within me did. The rancour would begin now if I spoke. I didn't. We would manage with what I could manage. There was Maa's flat we could move back into and save on the rent I could no longer afford. There was some jewellery I could sell. I had a consultancy offer I had been planning to take up when the universe had sprung this pregnancy on me. I could take it up nonetheless, work through the pregnancy, it was possible. I would do it. I would do my grieving through work. Acceptance is the biggest hurdle, once I was past it, I would pick up the pieces of myself and glue them all together. I'd done it before. With Pappa. With Maa. I was used to being left behind. I had left them behind and then returned.

'Do you think that is wise?

'I must take that chance.'

I sighed. 'Rethink it,' I said as gently as I could. 'Perhaps he's not around to wake up. Perhaps there is no chance of his emerging. Maybe we should listen to what they say.'

She tightened her lips into a thin line, I could see where the years had nibbled away at the epidermal support and carved out feathery lines along their periphery. She hadn't, like her contemporaries, opted for fillers and treatments to plump them up and for that I had a grudging respect.

'What kind of a person would I be if I didn't give him a chance to live?' Her voice broke and caught on the jagged edge of an emotion I could well identify with. It was choking me too. 'He's the only person I have in my life. I have no one, no parents, a brother who is living far away. Relatives who haven't been a part of my life for years. What will I do with him gone?'

A brother? Sukanya had a brother? None of us had a brother.

'I didn't know you had a brother,' I said. 'Aman never mentioned him.'

'He's much younger than me, almost like my own son. He was born when I was a teenager,' She paused and smiled. 'His birth was a scandal. My mother had been widowed for years when he was born.'

I looked at her in consternation. She continued. 'She was quite a character, my mother. She had an affair with a much younger man after my father died. I suspect he wasn't the first, but he was the first I knew about, because I had a crush on him before I realised she was already sleeping with him. She wanted to keep the baby. One child she wanted, she said, from a beautiful man. She wasn't interested in the baggage of marriage to have a child.'

I nodded. I understood. We both had mothers who weren't cast from the mould they made regular mothers from. Mine had been unloving and rejecting, I had been born out of a love that had not been sanctioned by marriage. Hers had wanted a child without a husband. Both had been mothers who defied the norms of what motherhood meant in the tightly restricted spaces women had in a society men had defined the borders of.

'We moved homes when she got pregnant. She told everyone she had lost her husband, she just neglected to mention he had died many years earlier.' She laughed. It was a brittle laugh, one that was now amused by how many rules her mother had broken to be the woman she wanted to be.

'Did he know, the father of the baby?'

'No, he went off to Dubai, to work in an electronics showroom as a salesman. That's the last I heard of him.'

'Does your brother know?'

She shook her head to indicate a negative. There had been no point. Both of them were flesh and blood embodiments of their mother's little rebellions, a snook cocked at social norms that would seek to police her desires and her lusts.

'Where is he now? Does he know about Aman's accident?'

'I haven't told him how serious it is. He's midterm at his management course in Brussels. He will drop everything without a thought and come here, and I can't do that,' She smiled. 'I resented him when he was born. I only had my mother, and she transferred all her love to him. But it was impossible to dislike him. He looked like his father. And I had loved his father, you know, with all the devotion of a first crush. When Maa died, I brought him up like my own son. I was married by then, Aman was very supportive.'

I kept quiet.

'Aman was very fond of him.' She stopped, put her hand to her lips, holding her mouth shut, an instinctive reflex action. Her eyes filled up, tears spilled down first one cheek and then down the other. 'Why am I speaking of him in the past tense? He's here, he's not yet gone.'

'Let him go, Sue.'

'No one has called me Sue in years, not after Maa died.' She smiled. 'It is strange. To hear it now from your lips.'

'Let him go, Sue.'

She sat up straight, the weight of whatever she had been grappling with flying off her shoulders.

'I can't let him go. He's the only person who loved me. Loves me. Which is why I forgave everything, let him have you, because he didn't love me less by loving you.'

I understood; Aman's heart had grown to encompass us both, and in a strange way, he had grown out of his love for her, but he still loved her. She was me, I was her. And he had sensed it, somehow, in some rudimentary way, he had connected with me because I reminded him of her, although we were very different to look at.

I took her hand, the hand of the yet to develop, plain-looking, heartbroken sixteen year old I'd seen all those years ago, standing on the landing of her stairway, poised to slit the tyres of a motorcycle and realising that her life, as she knew it, was about to shift again with this decision her mother had taken in a moment of lust.

'Let him go, Sue,' I said, feeling her despair mingle with mine, creating a darkness that flooded us both. 'He is already gone. It is just his body here.'

'I don't want life support stopped. I will not sign the papers.'

She looked at me, the faintest of recollections flooding her eyes, a drop of ink in a bowl of water, spreading in an instant. I was the same as she had seen me all those years ago, I had barely gone there a day ago.

'Perhaps he's just waiting for you to let him go.' My voice was kind. 'You must let him go.'

'You said that to me before. It was you, wasn't it? How is it possible? All those years ago. I thought it was a hallucination or my imagination playing up.' She looked at me. 'You disappeared in a second.'

I nodded. There was a long silence in the room, punctuated by the beeping monitors.

'You told me to let him go back then. I'd forgotten all about it. How did you know this would happen? How did you find me all those years ago? How have you not changed?'

'I can't explain it, not now. Now is not the time.'

She looked at me, the hurt and confusion in her eyes the same as it was all those years ago. 'Ana, who are you? Why do I feel I know you?'

'We are alternate versions of who we could be. Alternate selves. It was no wonder Aman and I crossed paths and were together. He found you in me again. And me in you. We are both the same.'

'How did you find me?'

'I just knew how to. I can't explain it. We're all connected.'

'How did you know this would happen?'

'One of us told me.'

She shook her head. 'I can't understand any of it.'

She wouldn't, I knew. No one could understand any of it. I had tried to tell them, but it only got me strange looks and disbelief, a quiet edging away that was self-preservation.

'I don't understand all that you're telling me. But I'm not stopping life support.' She stood up and walked out.

The only sound in the cold, sterile room was the beeping of the monitors in rhythm with the gurgle of the tubes going into the body of the man I had loved, the one man who had loved me like no one in the world had, not in this world, not in that. And the rushing sound in my ears as I felt the world around me spin and crash as I knew what I had to do, what I must do to prevent another hungry walk-in hunting for a host from slipping into him. I knew what could happen, after all, I was living that nightmare. I had quietly slipped into this body when I found it vacant and now all of me, all the versions of me, were trying to make things right for the one stuck where she couldn't come back to her body. It wasn't enough penance, we couldn't undo what we had done wrong, we couldn't find the one we had shifted. I moved stealthily to the monitors and quietly switched off the things that beeped and pumped air into him. When the lines went flat I slipped out of the room through the mirror over the washbasin in the corner.

No permissions were asked, none were needed. Nothing could now take over his body. He was free now.

19

What Lay Beyond

'Memory believes before knowing remembers. Believes longer than recollects, longer than knowing even wonders.'
—William Faulkner, *Light in August*

THE MIRROR HADN'T RIPPLED IN A WHILE. I HAD STOPPED looking through. In the new house I now lived in, the house still to become home, the mirror stared at me unblinkingly and I stared back at it, looking at my reflection in the here and now, no one beckoning from within. It had been months now. I looked at mirrors and saw myself reflected within as it should be in a normal universe with regular people. Me, with the face I had now got accustomed to, the face that was mine and yet not mine, the face I had grown into, the body I had ruthlessly claimed for my own. What did they call creatures like me? Monsters? Demons? Revenants? I was none of those, I was just a terrified young girl who didn't want to be stuck in the Greyness forever and had clawed my way out, hurling myself into the only vacant body I found in a multiverse of me. I was an unwelcome squatter that this body tried to throw out over and over but failed to, because the true owner was now stuck in the Greyness and couldn't find her way in. That's why I travelled. That's why I kept crossing.

Would glass slowly reach out again, sucking me in languidly, almost like uninterested in making the effort, whisking me into their vortex in the blink of an eye? Perhaps quicker. Microseconds. Milliseconds. Nanoseconds. Units of time so microscopic that a name for them had yet to be coined. The neutrinos of time. Planck time. Yoctoseconds. Zeptoseconds. Picoseconds. Units I could not even comprehend or measure.

I slept well here. I couldn't hear Maa here; I wasn't in the room while she tossed and turned and moaned and screamed with pain. At times, in that house, when I was in the bathroom, I had been able to hear my mother gasping for breath from outside, from the room where she lay dying, her body ravaged by illness, her mind delusional with the pain. I hadn't gone back to the house once I'd locked it up. I hadn't thought about whether I wanted to put it up for sale. No broker had the key, which lay in a box, in the locker that held my other precious papers. I had no idea what would happen should I make a stray visit back home to check whether all was well, whether the dampness had spread across the kitchen ceiling, whether the windows had gaps through which pigeons entered and created a nuisance of themselves. I hadn't dared visit, I had no courage. It had been left behind, I told myself, the back and forthing, and now I could focus on getting on with my life.

When it finally happened, it happened all at once, like all important things do, without warning, without time for preparation, on a fine day when I was sitting at my desk fitting together focus group discussions from Tier 2 towns across the country, trying to get a coherent and concise picture of whether women from these towns preferred fragrance of mogra, rose or sandalwood in their bathing soaps. Mogra was seen as wanton, associated as it was with women of easy virtue and practised seductiveness, sandalwood pious, and rose romantic. Right now, rose was winning. It was apparent as to why it was trumping its competition, a no-brainer, I thought. Perhaps it reminded the women of the bygone days when young swains tucked roses into their lustrous locks, before pregnancy and childbirth ruined both the locks and the romance. Sandalwood was associated with religion and ritual and home temples, and then, cremation pyres. It wasn't romantic or desirable, I should have disregarded it, but almost like a reversal of fortunes in a tight race, sandalwood began gaining a lead, a surprise dark horse. Sandalwood was taking over the charts as I looked on, the results tabulating themselves at the press of a key and then my laptop flickered for a moment and then went blank, a blank that was a strange opacity I had never seen before, thick, swirling, reflective. I could see Nayna within, standing in a strange room, looking taller and older than she was when I last saw her. The lights above me dimmed. I waited, taking a deep breath, looking at my other self smiling at me, her hair tied into a careless ponytail, eyes wide and grey, her face that of a girl in the first flush of youth. It had been a long while. Months. Years. She smiled back at me, her crooked incisor a stab of imperfection in her otherwise almost perfect reflection. My nazar batu, that's what Maa had called it. Keep something a little askew and imperfect about yourself, she would say whenever I spoke of getting it straightened or pulled out. Too much perfection singles you out for jealousy. Stay imperfect, stay safe. I had paid heed. She put out a hand and I reached out. The next moment she was in my room, looking down at me.

'Ana,' she said. 'I've been searching for you.' She looked around. 'This is not that house.'

'No,' I replied, 'This is another house. How are you, Nayna?'

She must have been fourteen or fifteen at the most. The years had made her glorious, a beauty so radiant it was almost blinding.

'I'm okay. Crow said crossing made me invulnerable. Nothing

can harm me anymore. I can't be cut, I can't bleed, I can't get hurt. I only can't breathe sometimes because I need more space. I get suffocated in small spaces. Doctor said it is asthma so Pappa took a transfer to Shimla.'

'That is the new house I saw you in?'

She nodded. 'Ana, I wanted to ask you something. Can you take me back to my Maa and Pappa. This Maa and Pappa are very nice, but they're not mine. This was not my life. These are not my parents.'

'I took you away from what would have been a very traumatic experience, Nayna. I didn't want you to live through that. I honestly don't know how to take you back into that time and universe.'

'Can I stay here with you then? This new Maa suffocates me, she doesn't let me be alone, she's always following me everywhere. My other Maa just let me be. I don't want to go back, Ana.'

I froze. Could I keep her here with me – what would happen to the universe if I plucked her out of the time she had filled and keep her here with me? Dare I try? Would she stay with me, in a world that was decades ahead of the time she was from?

'I don't know, Nayna, if I can keep you with me forever. Won't your parents be upset when they find you gone? And I don't know how this works, whether you and I can coexist on the same plane of time for an indefinite period of time.'

She began to sob. 'Why must I live like this? I want to stay here, with you.'

Had I done her a wrong by putting her into another life, one where her parents loved her, one where she had come to no harm, where her father hadn't decided to end his life, where her mother doted on her and they lived in this idyllic little home in the mountains? It was the life I'd hoped for myself and had never had the fortune to have. She had it, and she didn't want it.

'I need to show you who you could have been if I had left you where you were. After that you decide whether you want to go back in time to where I took you from. But we can't co-exist here,' I told her.

'Show me,' she said. And so I did. It took us a moment, a long moment, where time held itself back and took us where the world had forgotten we existed, in a distant corner of a distant time, a room dusty with neglect, a body graven with disuse, lying on a bed, skeletal. She stared at us, unseeing. I felt the horror emanating from Nayna, who shrank from who she beheld. She fled back through the same pathway through which she had arrived, willing the portals to part, the reflection to ripple, to liquify, to swirl into concentric swirls of light that pulled her in, placing her back where she had been standing not a moment ago. She willed it, an ability to control her crossings that I did not have and envied her for. As the mirror solidified again and I fell back, I saw her in the reflection, forlorn, accusation writ large in her eyes, just as her mother, my mother stepped into the room. She'd been gone for perhaps a second, a microsecond in her time. An hour or two in mine. She was not happy, that I knew. But she was safe and she was loved. Perhaps that was human destiny for all of us, to never be happy no matter what the circumstances the fates place us in.

Saachi dropped by one evening with food and wine, wine she didn't touch but kept pouring for me, even more rotund now that she was getting further along in her pregnancy. The baby would kick soon now, she told me. She knew it would be a boy, she felt it in her bones. Her mother, my Lovely maasi, would come down to Mumbai soon, to stay with her for the delivery and till she could manage the baby on her own. My mother wouldn't have done the same, I knew. I managed you on my own, she would have told me. You manage your child on your own. I would manage my children on my own when I had them, I would have them and lose them, lose all the ones I loved. It was the scariest part of loving people, being left behind, being alone, unloved. I missed Maa, I missed Aman, I missed the babies yet to be born to me, I missed their baby smells, their gurgles, their fingers clutching mine, their arms rushing to grab me as I entered, their eyes seeking me out in a crowd. Had I been that way with Maa, I wondered, even though she didn't love me quite in the same way I had wanted to be loved. Her love was acid and steel, corrosive and unbending. I missed the sharpness of her tongue, the reluctant love and the acerbic statements she flung at me. There was comfort in the resentment someone who should have loved you the most in the world felt for you. It meant they were not indifferent towards you. The worst pain would be to know that you didn't matter to them.

After Saachi left that night, I saw Maa wherever I should have been seeing myself, in the mirrors, in the window panes, in the switched off television set. Perhaps I was at the age she was when she was most vivid in my memory, because I was her now, watching me, smiling her mocking half smile, contemplative and contemptuous at the same time, forever judging, forever weighing me up and finding me inadequate. I didn't know where I ended and Maa began. I looked on at her looking at me, sensing the room around me begin to dissolve as the screen grew watery, the ripples circling concentric, spilling beyond the screen, pinpricks of light intensifying until they became whirls and circled her, sucking me in, breaking me up into bits and pieces until she was just a collection of fragments, then molecules, and then just speckles of light as I became neither matter nor anti-matter, just a thought, a form, a blink, a shift in energy capable of traversing space time, like crossing the road and opening the door into another home, the same as yours, a reflection of yours, inverted in layout, opposite your home, and entered, unsure of what or whom you would find within, whether you or you reversed. I stepped through the whirls and found myself sitting across a table, waiting for me.

'How have you been, Ana?'

The room was unfamiliar, I had never been here, not so far, at least in this life, in this time.

'I've been well, or well as I can be under the circumstances. How have you been, Maa?'

'I've been dead. It's been peaceful. Why have you come here? Did you die too?'

'No, not yet.'

She smiled.

'Don't die yet. You have time. But what am I saying,' she laughed, stroking my head with a cold, clammy hand, a gesture she never did when alive. 'You are already dead.'

When I woke up, the day had passed into night, the electricity had come back on, and the light from the laptop illuminated the room, casting vaguely threatening shadows on the wall, shadows that moved even as the objects that cast them stayed still. And in my hand, a broken bit from a string of mogras, fragrant and cloying, the buds browning along the edges of each individual petal, the decay of time already setting in, decay that marked this world and its perishability, not the world it came from.

20

Who Are You, Ana?

'...Our life is not our life, merely the story we have told about our life. Told to others, but—mainly—to ourselves.'
—Julian Barnes, *The Sense of an Ending*

'MY NAME IS ANA AND I AM THIRTY-TWO YEARS OLD.'

'My name is Ana and I am twenty-eight years old.'

'My name is Ana and I am eighteen years old.'

The man sitting in front of her stopped doodling on what seemed like a parchment made of light and looked up. There was no expression on his face, he could have been carved out of marble. Or stone. Or a material that kept him mobile yet immobile, not a material she was familiar with. He was not flesh and blood. He was of no colour but made in the form of man, or rather, what would be considered a man when men had all but changed from what we knew them as. He was, she realised, a construct, solid but not solid, arranged in a form she could identify with. There was nothing mobile about him now, not his hands that a minute ago were scribbling frantically on a device which looked like a thin paper lit up by an unseen source. Not his head which had kept nodding in a facsimile of what might be constituted as empathy and attentiveness as she spoke. Not his body which had turned and swayed in the swivel chair he occupied, a chair that hovered in the air, untethered to either floor or ceiling, movement they might consider natural, but which kept distracting her from what she wanted to say so that she ended up repeating the same sentence for an entire hour and then lapsed into silence.

Another man, if she could call him that, or perhaps another person would be more accurate a term, stepped into what could only be called a room because there was no other word she knew that could begin to define it. It was where they were, an enclosed space that seemed to have no beginning, no end. It expanded when he entered and shrank when he exited. It could wrap itself tight around her when she slept and grew enough to let her pace back and forth when she was agitated. It was not a room, it was a cocoon, a cocoon she realised that aligned itself with her moods, changed colour with her thoughts and feelings, and was designed to keep her in what was now considered the ultimate comfort, and confined. This was a prison cell. She was being held prisoner.

The two began speaking, an exchange of intonations and sounds, undecipherable to her, and she knew they were discussing her, even though the language they used was unlike any language she had ever heard earlier. This wasn't a language from her time, or within her ken, this was language that had now formed after aeons of humankind as she had lived it, the language of humankind that had made their home in the stars. She was, she realised, a thing, a subject of research, a specimen to be dissected.

'Tell me where I am,' she said. They looked at her, their faces expressionless masks.

The man who had stepped in when the other had stopped listening to her came up to her, the floor rose up behind him and became a low stool. He sat down across her, at eye level. His eyes orbs of brilliant blue with streaks of gold within, no differentiation of iris or pupil, his skin translucent and the veins running beneath in a blue riverine map, unfamiliar branchings and estuaries, a waterway where blood was no longer the red she was familiar with, with skin that had lost the protection of melanin, a transparency that was unsettling, because it revealed what lay beneath. It was synthetic, she realised, a covering over the bare working of what constituted the body. He was a construct too, an organic and inorganic construct. An ultimate cyborg.

He spoke to her and now she could understand what he said. His language didn't change, but her understanding of it changed in a manner she could not explain.

'Tell us who you are.'

'I already have.'

'Why are you here, how did you come here, who sent you here?'

Here. She didn't know where here was or when. She couldn't remember how she had reached here, memory had become a wall of blankness that she tried to hammer at ineffectually with determined thoughts. All she could remember was that she had shifted as she always did while sitting at her laptop, and fallen through the screen. There was blankness, acute blankness. And then waking up in this place with no walls and the shifting windows that looked out to nothing but more darkness, a darkness so acute that not even a distant star disturbed it. The room was enough to contain her, it moved with her should she stretch out or double up. It was enough. That was all one needed, enough space to contain one, whether a room, a closet or a coffin. But was there enough space to contain her? Was space enough to contain her? She wasn't sure anymore.

There was no mirror in the room and no reflective surface. She wouldn't be able to get back, she realised, she was confined here unless she found one. The walls, if they could be called that, fluid and mutable as they were, lit up when she was awake and dimmed as she drifted into sleep. Vents in the corners of the room let in gases that put her to sleep and woke her up at regular times, maintaining the room at an even, pleasant temperature. The bed rose out of the floor seamlessly and the mattress was a softness she had never felt before, softness she sank into when she lay down and became firmness when she sat up, rearranging itself into back-supportive seating. Food came through a space in the wall that opened up, a mishmash of what would provide her with adequate nutrition but offered no joy of taste. It was functional, filling and comfortable, the closest equivalent she could think of was the mashed potatoes with butter, salt and pepper that Maa offered her at times to keep her hunger pangs sated. Or the freshly rolled rotis, puffed on the flame, smeared with ghee and sprinkled with sugar, a quick snack that was a carb high for an active child. A liquid accompanied it, but it was not water as she knew it. It quenched her thirst in a few sips; she guessed it was limited, precious. A cubicle at the far end of the room was where she went to relieve herself, the body functioned normally even in this strange place when she didn't; they extricated the waste out of her, a matter-of-fact process where they immobilised her and did what they had to. There was breathing, eating, drinking, excretion to be taken care of. Were there cameras here too in the cubicle where she went to rid herself of the by-products of her metabolism, she wondered at first and then she didn't really care. There was no privacy anyway when she was here, locked up with red eyes following her around the room as she walked, trying to orient herself in this strange ovoid that allowed her to walk all around it defying the dictates of gravity, where the floor and the ceiling merged into a whole, where you could stand anywhere and have your feet tethered to the surface, where nothing allowed you to orient yourself to a sense of earth. Where you were free from gravity but unmoored from yourself.

When she'd first emerged from the blankness, she'd found herself lying on a bed, her wrists and ankles attached by what seemed to be silken cords, silk that was metallic in strength. It took her a moment to realise she was being restrained from moving. How long had she been out she did not know. Time as she understood it was no longer relevant, the solar day she knew was not the day here.

'Why am I in restraints?' she had said aloud the first time she emerged from the blackness of an induced unconsciousness.

'You were violent,' replied a disembodied voice, mechanical, robotic. Someone was watching her from somewhere beyond the room. Perhaps what she thought were windows were actually a one-way glass opening to an observation room where someone was monitoring her. Who was monitoring her? The voice was genderless, the accent unfamiliar and painfully precise, like someone had learnt to speak the language from an app.

'You're lying,' she had replied.

'Would you like to see yourself when we found you?' the voice replied, with a hint of a smirk that made it almost human and not as robotic as she had imagined it to be. What she'd taken for a partition transformed itself into a full-length screen. She appeared on it, her eyes darting from side to side, her hair dishevelled, her clothes torn and muddied. Two persons tried to hold her down as the third attempted to touch her bare skin with a small cylindrical rod. She flung one of the two against the wall and bit the other on the arm; strangely enough, neither reacted with any pain or surprise. Other personnel came into the room and quickly overpowered her, tapping her on the arm with a tube that had her fall unconscious immediately.

That was then, this was now. The translucent man sitting opposite her smiled, if it could be called a smile. There was no joy in the movement of the facial muscles, it seemed like a testing out of movements, in keeping with a log book of what constituted acceptable behaviour to befriend a strange creature. Aeons ago, human explorers landing on unexplored continents would have smiled thus at the mistrustful residents, had they come face to face. These smiles had not augured well for the local residents, soon reduced to the conquered. The smile was not friendly, it was threatening.

Beneath the transparent face, muscles constricted and expanded, a synchronistic dance that made movement possible. Thankfully, his body was covered with a garment the likes of which she had never seen before. It was fluid and moved with his body, almost like a second skin. It changed colours, and was of a material she would be hard-pressed to describe if she was asked. Was this person the post human of the theories that were bandied around during her time?

'Who are you?'

'I am Javen. The Keeper. I am responsible for you.'

He bowed courteously from the neck. She tried to imitate the action but her body, she realised, had lost the economy of motion that being tied to gravity brought. Now she moved despite herself and stayed put when she needed to move.

'What does a Keeper do?'

'Think of me as the person in charge of law and order in a territory. A police chief back in your era.'

There was a certain dignity to him, one that defied positions and authority.

'Can I see more footage of myself when I was brought in?'

'No.'

'I need to know why I was brought here and why I am being kept here.'

She sounded shrill. Somewhere a device beeped, telling those monitoring her about elevated heart rate. The construct in the form of a man who had been asking her about herself moved in with a flat silver rod in his hand, its hand.

'Do you want us to use that?' the translucent man asked, a sigh in his voice, human emotion programmed into him.

She looked at it, noticing how threatening it was even though it was barely the width of her hand and the breadth of her finger.

'What is it?'

'It will render you unconscious if we perceive that your parameters have gone beyond normal, it could be what you consider painful.

I suggest you do what your kind did in the past to bring down heart rates, take a deep breath or two, and calm yourself down.'

It was the last thing she felt like doing, so she did what she did feel like doing: she screamed. It felt good to scream when one was being told to calm down, an island of defiance in an ocean of helplessness.

She noticed the guards at the door, who had come in with this man who called himself the Keeper, immediately put their hands to their waists where little protuberances indicated the presence of something that would come in handy if she seemed dangerous. They took a step forward, but he held up a hand. They fell back to their stations, waiting at either side of the door, their faces impassive, eyes fixed at a point in the distance, unseeing yet seeing. Was Javen a first name or a family name? How had social norms altered from her time, how were people made now, did they reproduce in laboratories, with vats of liquid serving as wombs, grown to adulthood in pods? What all did she need to learn and unlearn to survive in this time?

'Which year is this?' she asked warily.

'Which year do you think this is?'

'2010.'

He smiled, twisting his face again in what was a contortion of tissue and muscle over bone, their movements a mesmerising orchestration. He savoured the year in his mind and then spoke it with a tinge of disbelief.

'2010?'

'Okay, you tell me, what year is this and where am I?'

'We are in 3096 in your time. Solar years of the planet. We measure time differently now. Your bone age isn't more than twenty-five. You are unaltered. Original. Pure carbon-based, organic. That's rare in our times. You are, what we would call, an ancient human. We will never be able to get another prime specimen like you.'

She couldn't understand what it was saying. Original. Carbon. Unaltered. 3096. Ancient.

'What is this place?'

'It is a sanatorium. This is the observation room.'

'Why am I here?'

'You were found unconscious in a deserted building at ground level. You grew violent when apprehended.' He paused. 'We are studying you, to gain an understanding of ancient humans. From before we changed.'

She looked around. Something had gone wrong the last time she travelled; she had emerged where she wasn't supposed to. When she wasn't supposed to.

'I am not a threat to anyone or anything. I'm just... me.' She looked down at her hands as she said this. Her hands were different, the nails cut to the quick by an indifferent hand, the nail polish she remembered having applied after a careful filing had been removed, her nails now bare. Her rings were gone. She used to wear two, one a pearl set in gold that her mother wore, and another an exquisite Columbian emerald surrounded by diamonds that Aman had gifted her, a claim of sorts, on her person without the official documentation required for the same, the only extravagance she allowed or could afford on her body. She put her hand to her neck. Her chain and pendant were gone too, the thin gold chain that hung right to where her breasts met and parted.

'Your decorative precious metals are safe with us.'

Something made her put her hands to her face, her skin was different. It was smoother, younger. She was a different person from who she last was from when she could remember. Bone age 25 he had said. She hadn't been 25 in 2010. Or had she?

'You said this was 3096?' she asked hesitantly. 'Am I in Mumbai?'

'There is no Mumbai anymore, there is no India anymore, there are no ancient countries anymore. The old boundaries have been done away with. The world had just survived the pandemic, followed by a global upheaval of rioting and violence. Then came the turning. Catastrophic climate events across the world. The earth shaking itself, trying to rid itself of you humans. The earth shifted and the earthquakes began across the globe, huge eruptions from the volcanoes, fissures across the surface. Lava flowed over cities and fields, levelling land and people. The entire surface disintegrated or became unliveable. Land collapsed into sea as the polar ice caps dissolved. We are a civilisation of refugees from earth now. Most of us moved away. A few of us though are stationed here, in this outpost to monitor the mother planet.'

'Moved where?'

'To other settlements within this solar group, some still planned outside, but within this part of the galaxy. We are in the sky, Skyzone 242 to be precise. There are thousands of Skyzones around the planet that have been created for a select few of the population to live. A planetary consortium of Skyzones orbiting the remnant earth. The surface has few survivor pockets. Below the surface in caves, tunnels and underground cities are the underlings. The surface is unliveable now.' The voice paused. Then continued, 'You were found on the surface. It is a miracle you survived.'

Her face registered her disbelief. He stood up and waited, as if he was to receive his instructions.

'I have no memory of it, of the surface, of anything.'

'You had passed out. You were lucky a scanner spotted your thermal heat and you could be retrieved instantly.'

A hologram projection played out a visual of her lying on what seemed like parched earth. Winds whipped up a storm around her, obscuring her from direct sight. She had been wearing jeans and a t-shirt, what she had on when the electricity went out as she had been working on her laptop. A team of persons alighted from what seemed to be an airborne ambulance and beamed her into it. Her skin was blue, she was unmoving.

'Did I die?'

'We put you in stasis until you had recovered enough to be revived.'

'Stasis?'

'Hibernation? Like the bears did back on earth during your time, in the winter season. Unfortunately, we have neither real bears nor caves for them to hibernate in now. We do have the specimens of most of the creatures though, to be cloned in bulk when the interplanetary bases are ready. You were in stasis for six months. We have people in stasis for years, with orders to be revived when we had relocated to the bases they had paid for, Terra Vulcan, or the moons. Some have opted to be maintained in cryptobiosis until our kind manages to go interstellar, adapted from a microorganism called the tardigrades from your time. Desiccated humans, to be reanimated by re-introducing water to their systems. Kept in sealed vats, with their vitals monitored remotely.'

Nothing he said made sense. 'Are you even human?' There was no other way to ask it.

'I am, what can I say, what humans now are. We have changed.'

'Are there no humans anymore?'

'Not as you know them, but this is what we are now. Post humans, I think the term was, or superhumans. Cyborgs? Post humans? Your time called us a lot of different terms. We just are. Evolved humans. Like the humans of your time evolved from the apes. It took them millennia. It took us centuries. The human you are is a very different creature from your original ancestor, similarly we are different from you, but we are all descendants of the same tree of species. Of course,' he paused, 'We'd almost reached what your time called Singularity a couple of years earlier before the turning of the earth, that made things easier. We merged into the AI systems we had created, we became the transhumans your time had been talking about and then moved on to become what we are now, what you would call the Post humans. I disembodied many years ago and chose to have my consciousness uploaded to the cloud, and this is my current body suit. I chose this one today because it would seem familiar to you as a human, our other body suit designs could have disoriented you. Not everything is binary symmetry as you are used to. We can change as long as we are connected to the cloud. The cloud runs everything now.'

'The cloud?'

'You had the cloud back in 2010 but it was very nascent a concept. Now it is everything. One might say, it is what your time called God. A supreme intelligence that runs beyond all attempts to control it. We started it, it has taken over now. It controls everything. And makes sure everyone and everything is interconnected. Hive mind, you called it in your time. It was only a concept then, it is reality now.'

'And we're in Skyzone 242 right now, you say. And that the surface is where the rest of humanity exists?'

'Yes, would you like to look out?'

She nodded. He gestured at what had looked like solid walls and they changed to transparent sheets, showing her a blinding vista of stars and space.

'We are at a safe orbital height above the surface. You are beyond the clouds, far beyond. In fact, we now live on these floating platforms orbiting the earth at specific spots above the surface. We still use the seas to siphon the water we need after desalinating it, mud occasionally for our gardens, but beyond that we don't really need the Earth, except as a parking spot.'

She got up wordlessly and moved to the walls and looked out. There was nothing around except darkness dotted with speckles of light. The same speckles that now dotted her mid-section were outside of her, outside this wall of transparency that she could not see but could touch. A faint glow circled the Earth, the lines of a distant rotunda of a horizon demarcated where humans still existed perhaps, in whatever version they were.

A bit of the wall slid open and a man walked in, he was impossibly perfect. A manifestation of male beauty, perhaps modelled on Michelangelo's David. He wore a pair of old-style trousers and a shirt. Javen gestured.

'Meet Monak. He's a synth. We tried to costume him to something you are more familiar with based on our research about your time. He will be your companion for the time you are here. We believe the ancient humans found solitude burdensome.'

Monak looked deep into her eyes and she fell in love. If it were possible to fall in love with something that was an object, like falling in love with a doll or a robot. A Synth. Synthetic as the word perhaps was originally in her time.

'Why do you need Synths?'

'They perform functions needed for human touch and companionship.'

'Human touch?'

'Massages, hugs, sexual intercourse. We have them in all variants. Male, female, male-female, indeterminate, whatever the requirement.'

'Basically, they're sex dolls, aren't they?

Monak looked at her with a start at this, a reflex action which almost made her believe he was hurt. There was an easy familiarity to him, she felt she knew him, almost like she had met him somewhere, in another life.

'We're not sex dolls,' he said. 'We are companions to those who still need touch and togetherness. They are but a handful, and we preserve them as relics, cater to all their needs. They are worshipped as ancestors. For them, we come without the baggage of emotion. The new humans don't need physical companionship anymore. They are synched up in the ultramind. The physical nature of the demands of skin touch can be satiated in the mind.'

She reached out her hand and touched his face. He was beautiful indeed, and her hand felt skin under it, warm and soft, alive. Javen nodded and she turned to him in puzzlement.

'We humans finally made synths in our likeness. We finally played God.'

She blinked.

'It began back in your time,' he said, 'You created a creature called Sophia and bestowed her with all the intelligence and human capabilities you could then transfer. We kept improving on that technology until this point when the real and the synth are indistinguishable. The only thing that separates the two is the lived experience. Synths can be reprogrammed to have any memory or skill we need them to have. As for the rest, they are a better version of humans and we can customise them, even feed in a consciousness from a deleted human.'

'A deleted human?'

He nodded.

She looked out at the blackness speckled with light from long dead stars that came through the vast vacuum that divided the space and time between them.

'I am dreaming, right?'

'If that's what you want to believe.'

'Why can't I remember anything?'

'Tell me what you can remember.'

She looked at the chaos of the night sky unfurling beyond her. 'I am Ana. The year is 2010. I live in Mumbai. I am a researcher. I travel between space and time. I am not the only one among all my selves who can do this. I travel back and forth but I always reach one of my different selves when I do. This is the first time I've reached somewhere where I am not there, where one of my selves is not here. I don't know how I reached here though. I'm sure a version of me is on the surface or somewhere here, if that is where I reached.'

'How do you do this travelling between space and time?'

'It is difficult for me to explain. I just go through.'

'Through what?'

'A reflection. Then I drop through the Nothingness.'

'Nothingness?' he repeated.

She nodded. 'When the time is right, I can move through reflections. The world I am in dissolves and I fall through it.'

'You were asking for Nayna. Who is Nayna? Is she part of the Crusters?'

'What are the Crusters?'

'The people who live within the Crust of the Earth or within the Earth. The ones who don't have enough credit or aren't important enough to live on the platform cities. They're mainly outlawed.'

'No, I don't know if she is.'

The man sighed, his perfect face scrunching into what he thought conveyed pre-determinate concern.

'Is she deleted?'

'What is deleted?'

'Pushed off the platform to land on the earth's surface. Needless to say, it will be a swift and painless death. You might prefer that to being put into laboratory where they will use you as a specimen. I suspect though that they *will* use you as a specimen. They will extract all they can from you and keep you alive until they can extract no more. Then they will off-platform you or if they don't want to waste you, they will recycle you for your organic material.'

In the time she came from, capital punishment was a hood and a noose and a falling into nothingness. Or the electric chair in some countries. In yet others, it was the needle, the syringe and a cocktail of chemicals guaranteed to put you into the sleep of the dead. Life had been cheap then, yet deaths were limited. More lives had been lost in the valour of war and patriotism than in the termination through law. Before her time there was the sword and beheadings, a skill that came from much practice. A revolution in a country called France had made it easier, it dropped a sharp blade onto a precise point on the neck held in a stock. The guillotine, the only cure for grey hair man had yet invented, as a writer had once said. Yet other countries stoned offenders to death, a grim bloodthirstiness that allowed the crowd their collective cathartic release. Now all they had to do was to throw you off. Much like walking the plank that the seafarers of yore decreed as their death sentences. Mankind always had an approved way to kill those they did not want walking amongst them.

She had always been terrified of heights, of falling, she had lived her life having nightmares of falling. Her father had jumped, he had insisted she jump after him. She'd never been able to look down from heights. The falling now was real. One fell from the skies to the earth's surface from a height that guaranteed that you died before you spattered the ground. She'd always been falling, all her life, all her lives. One more fall shouldn't scare her.

It would take a few minutes to hit the surface. She didn't know it yet, the temperature outside at that height would be much below zero, enough to freeze her. There would be minimal oxygen at this height, lower air pressure, she would pass out. It would be a blessing; she wouldn't feel the terror as the earth rushed up at her. The few seconds would be too quick and too long – a paradox only those who had experienced it would understand. She would come back to consciousness after around a minute of freefall only to see the ground rushing up at her. Gravity would hasten her fall, 32 feet every second. She would slam into the surface, bones shattered and spine crumpled, brain fluid leaking from her punctured ear drums. Then she would land dead on the surface, broken, feeling no pain.

This was not how she had envisaged death.

'Tell us about this Nayna you are searching for.'

'She is me. But in a different time and universe.'

'Explain further.'

'I don't know how to.'

'Why are you searching for her?'

'I owe it to her to change her life. I pushed her out of hers and into mine. My life had a terrible fate written in it. I'm trying to right a wrong I committed. I'm sure she's here somewhere, else I wouldn't be here. I only come to times and universes where she is there. And I change it around. Her life. It is my penance.'

'Have you been successful?'

'I don't know. I have no idea of whether I have been successful.'

'We can suction out your memories and screen them but it is a very painful process and I do not want to put you through that. Telling me might be easier. Perhaps I could also help you go back to where you came from.'

She laughed. 'No one can help me go back. I just go. Even I can't make myself go. If I could, do you think I would have been here for so long.'

'You were unresponsive for months. You had suffered some brain trauma from your previous journey. I will take your leave now. Monak will be here, he has been assigned to you as your caretaker. He will provide you healing and solace.'

She did not need healing and solace. She wanted to go back, back to where Aman was, where a regular life awaited her.

'I'm tired,' she said. 'I want to sleep. You have to help me find Nayna when I wake up.'

Javen nodded and left. Monak sat on a couch that appeared from the floor when he began descending towards it, almost anticipating his need for a seat.

'Would you like me to give you a massage?' Monak asked, running a hand softly over her head.

'No,' she smiled. 'I just want to sleep.' He sat back and rested himself against the wall, watching her with eyes that were so dark she could see the stars dance within.

She stretched herself. The seat by the wall elongated itself into a bed and on it a sleeping bag. She understood she was to put herself into it and close it over her. It would weigh her down into sleep without sedatives, a warm embrace of softness, a hug manufactured in a world bereft of humans to administer them.

She stretched herself out and closed the bag over her head. It was warm and heavy embracing her like a pair of arms would. They had weighted blankets in her time, to offer such solace. She closed her eyes, the room went dim. She drifted off into darkness, a darkness so overwhelming and absolute that she didn't know where she was or when she was. She opened her eyes with a sudden sensation of the molecules around her shifting. Monak hovered above her in the air, centimetres away from her, not touching her. His eyes were dark and glowing in the dimness of the room. He was within the sleeping bag with her, she did not know how. The sleeping bag enclosed them both.

'You were not supposed to come here. Go back.'

'Why did I come here?'

'To stop me from jumping. But you are too late. I already jumped a few years ago, rather they off-platformed me. They repurposed my consciousness into this synth. A male synth as you see me now. I can become female or genderless if required. Go back when you can, and while he's still alive, before you lose him too.'

'How can I? There's nothing here to move through.'

'Look into my eyes.'

His eyes were mirrors, reflecting her, one in each, a dark silhouette in each, the binary perfection of his symmetry multiplying her into two. She shifted in her reflection, those black pools of concentric nothingness pulling her in, waiting for her to will herself to shift, through time, through space, using her alter self as the medium.

'What are you waiting for. Move through. Quick.'

She took a deep breath and looked into his eyes again, the mirror blackness of both poised directly above her where he hovered within centimetres of her, so close she could smell the sterile odour of his synthetic skin where the sensual aromas he had been layered with had disintegrated, seeing herself within two selves reflected, one in each, knowing this would smash her into atoms and molecules that would then scatter across the multiverses, possibly never to come together again, and then there was nothing except the light rushing past her, through her, within her, into her, turning her inside out into nothing but light and dust. And as she moved through, an explosion where there once was a person, all that remained were specks of blue light floating in interminable, unseeing pulsating darkness, split into two parts of herself spinning into the void, each separate part seeking a time and universe to return to.

21

Where Do You Go To (My Lovely)?

'My yesterdays walk with me. They keep step, they are gray faces that peer over my shoulder.'

—William Golding

IT WASN'T EASY BEING IN LOVE WITH A WOMAN WHO CAME AND went as she pleased and offered no explanation for it. His wife knew about her. It would have been difficult not to. A woman knows when another woman has touched her man. It is a betrayal that goes beyond the sensory. The feel of another woman on your man's body is tangible. Her smell wafts off his breath, her touch is residual on his skin. Her presence lingers in her absence. His eyes look at you and don't register you, you are incidental to his perception. You throw tantrums trying to elicit a response from him, any response would be preferable to the indifference. He spends time with you grudgingly, allocating precious minutes, hours that he would rather spend with her. Sukanya had accepted defeat at the hands of a woman she hadn't even met, it was a battle she had abandoned before getting on to the battlefield.

Aman always needed a broken project to fix, that was his fatal flaw. She knew it. After all, she had been his first project to fix, the first broken person to be remade into whole. It was inevitable he would move on once he had managed to glue her together with pills and therapy, back into functionality. It was a small price to pay, to indulge him his indiscretions always. He came back to her when he was done with playing knight in shining armour. In the beginning she had thought it would be the same with Ana. Some months of a dalliance, before the charm wore off. It had been years now, not the few months of a dalliance the others were. Ana had taken him away from her. It was an unequal battle Sue hadn't been able to fight. Or hadn't wanted to. Either way, he was grateful that she let him be.

It was never love, their marriage had been first one of pity and then convenience. She had slit her wrists while at management school, and he'd been the one who rushed her to the hospital, stayed with her while she healed and taken her through the procession of counselling sessions, the therapists. By then, it was too late to get out of what could only become a long-term relationship, marriage inevitable once they both graduated. The sex was perfunctory, there was always that sense of incompleteness. He didn't lust after her, he pitied her. Pity did not make for satisfying orgasms. When she got pregnant, they decided she would be the trailing spouse in the partnership. If she had any ambitions for herself, she had quickly let them loose into the ethers of domesticity, focusing on being the perfect mother, the perfect wife. The perfect facade began cracking after around ten years of marriage. She slipped right back into the depression he had painstakingly helped her emerge from. Now he was too busy to pull her out of it again.

He'd fallen right into the trope, the overworked corporate slave with the trophy wife he was no longer in love with, the teen kids disinterested in the midlife crisis their father was going through, and the mistress on the side. There was marriage and children, two boxes he'd ticked off unquestioningly. Until that niggling something surfaced when he hit middle age.

'Couldn't it have been a sports car or an electric guitar?' Sukanya had said, when he'd first told her about Ana. 'Did you have to find yourself yet another stray for your midlife crisis? You will grow out of it, if not her, it will be someone else. And once you've got her out of your system, you'll be fine.'

Now, four years later, she wasn't so sure. Nor was he.

'Tell me when you tire of her,' Sukanya had told him. 'I'll know you'll be on the lookout to replace her soon. I know you. I'm your wife.'

He would never tire of her. Sukanya had always been practical about his philandering, but this one wasn't a fling. It wasn't an affair. It was love. He just needed to figure out how to keep her in his life permanently. And Sukanya. Because he loved her too, but not in that way that made him want her incessantly. Both of them.

'It's not like that,' he'd muttered feebly, incapable of articulating the hold she had over him, which wasn't one of lust. Love was a different beast. It was insanity to fall in love in one's middle age, it was insanity to fall in love with a woman who was teetering on the brink of insanity and all he could do was watch her fall, spiralling deeper and deeper into the tenuous worlds in her head she went into and emerged from, a little diminished each time she went into her states of emptiness. He'd watched her go blank and disoriented, freeze still for a minute or two, and then come back vacant and unable to hold herself up. Was it something in her brain, he wondered, some tumour, a chemical imbalance that made her get these strange seizures.

Ana was not a woman one got out of one's system, he had wanted to tell Sukanya. She was a woman who burrowed deep under one's skin and found her way into a vein, and travelled straight into your heart, where she lodged herself, a constant ache, a discordant heartbeat, a murmur that would eventually grow to a sigh and a gasp and a collapse. He didn't know that yet. He didn't know that love and heartbreak were real and that it could happen to a man as old as him. It worried him, her increasing strangeness. The constant haunted expression on her face, her weight loss, her insistence on never removing the stomach fastener, the things she spoke about that made no sense, about going back to meet herself, going forward to meet herself, about him abandoning her and going into the next plane of existence.

He had booked the appointment with the therapist, but she hadn't gone. He'd paid up for the blocked time without complaint. When she did this thrice in a row, they had squabbled. He told her it was not about the money but about her accepting that she needed help. They had been studiedly cold with each other for a few days and then she relented.

'But come with me,' she pleaded with him. 'I'm terrified of going on my own.'

He agreed. There was always fear the first time round, it would get easier with successive sessions. It had been the same with Sukanya. Now she managed her schedule and her sessions on her own, as well as her medications. So it would be with Ana. What would he do if she came back to as close to normal as she could be? Would he no longer find her interesting as it happened with Sukanya?

Ana had been living in the new apartment for almost six months now, slowly, imperceptibly finding it fitting itself around her, the odd corners becoming accepting of her angles and prickliness, rounding themselves to comfort her, wrapping her with warmth. A grudging acceptance spaces gave those who chose to occupy them. Some spaces were hostile, turned you into wrecks of your former selves. Others took you in, soothed you, settled you into peaceful dreams, woke you up to joy and anticipation every morning. Spaces took to people as much as people took to spaces.

He accompanied her as promised to her therapy sessions and

waited outside in the car until she was done. The clinic was located in an old art deco place built pre-Independence in the heart of South Mumbai, with its rounded balustrades of a stairway sweeping up, terrazzo flooring, and the clinic like a comfortable home of a dear aunt, with bric-à-brac, tapestries, stuffed horsehair couches and crocheted antimacassars on them. He had never been inside, but Sukanya had described it to him once, most amused that in this age of chrome and marble, clinics could still be antediluvian in their decor.

He was worried about Ana. The last time she had disappeared for over a day, she'd returned without the jewellery she always wore and had no explanation as to whether she had misplaced it or been robbed, or where she had disappeared to. She was drawn and her eyes sunken like she hadn't eaten for months, whittled down to half her previous self. The gaps in her memory and what she was willing to tell him was worrying. She wasn't concealing things from him, she swore to him, but she just couldn't recall what was happening with her and this strange obsession with keeping her midriff bound and closed, insisting that it was damaged, when there was absolutely nothing wrong with it, except perhaps a predisposition towards becoming so skeletal as to have the ribs show. She had holes in her body, she insisted, and yet, when he peeled off the waistband when she was deep in sleep her torso was as it should be. If anything, she was wasting away, refusing to eat food enough for her frame, not for the vanity of staying within the confines of what they called fashionably thin, but because she just didn't feel hunger. Come to think of it, he couldn't remember the last time he had seen her eat in his presence, or drink anything, even water. That was an illness too, he knew, perhaps the counselling would help. He would call the therapist and speak with her later, but not in Ana's presence.

He had already spoken to the therapist. That she insisted on being fully dressed at all times, saying she never knew when she would be taken to another time. Her personal hygiene was iffy, she bathed rarely, she hadn't gone to the salon for months, her limbs were hairy. How does it matter, she said. She had earlier been meticulous about her personal hygiene. This sliding into self-neglect was what scared him. She rarely spoke and if she did she spoke into the air, speaking to a point behind his shoulders. She had always been self-contained in a way that frightened him, her eyes dark pools of expressionlessness. Now she was even more so. Sex, when it did happen, was detached and mechanical. She was now prone to making random conversation in the middle of sex. This he had not told the therapist. It was embarrassing.

'If I die, make sure you cremate me immediately, no need to wait for anyone to come to pay their respects,' she said once as he thrust into her. 'Make sure my body is ended. I don't want any other taking my body over.'

It startled him, deflating him.

'Surely Saachi... your aunt...'

'No one cares. And I don't care about them.'

These days, of course, she had withdrawn so deep into herself that he could no longer touch her without feeling he was invading her.

She emerged from the clinic and climbed into the car, drawing her arms around herself. Her arms, he noted, were stick thin. She was shivering, even though the sun was out and it was a warm day. He turned the air conditioning down.

'How did it go?' he asked.

'It was okay,' she replied, pulling her feet up on to the seat and curling herself into a ball. That was all she was willing to divulge of how her session went. It would take time, he knew, there was too much to be resolved all at once. She dropped off to sleep in the seat, undisturbed by the traffic honking and bumps in the road. She slept the sleep of one who had travelled great distances and was exhausted by the journey.

He drove her home as she slept on the seat, delicate as a

sparrow's hatchling, her hair having escaped the rough bun she had confined it into. She breathed heavily as she slept, soft snores emanating from her. When they reached home he woke her up with a touch on her arm. She jumped up startled, looking around in panicked confusion.

'Which time am I?'

'We're home, put your slippers on.'

'We're home?'

Her voice was uncertain, her gaze disoriented. The pale purple smudges hollowed out under her eyes seemed to have intensified. They looked like bruises, a fist to an eye, then to the other. Faded remnants of violence. She put out a wrist to the dashboard as she scrambled around trying to locate the slippers she had kicked off earlier. Her wrist was knobby bone, her hand so pale he could see the blue-green veins travelling from the inner crock of her elbow to her wrist. He could see also on her wrist, still angry and red, the jagged scar of a gash that had long healed over and had never been spoken of since. There was a similar scar on the other wrist. There were scars that were physical, ones he could see and trace with his fingers. What defeated him were the scars within her, ones he could not reach, and try to erase. He held her hand and took her up through the lobby, into the elevator, while she kept looking around in a state of confusion, almost as if she didn't recognise the place she had been living in for the past many months.

'Has the doctor prescribed any new medication?'

'I don't know,' she replied. He sighed. He didn't even know if she took the pills he had bought.

He dropped her right up to the house. She seemed unwell, shaky. She was cold, preternaturally cold to the touch. He held her hand as he steered her into the house. She sagged against the door jamb, her eyes blank and expressionless.

'Why are you so cold? Your hands are like ice. I have to get back to the office, but call me if you feel sick. Perhaps we need to check your haemoglobin levels, get some blood tests done. And eat something for god's sake. I'm ordering some food for you, it will reach in half an hour.'

She nodded, still shivering a bit.

'I'll call you later, eat something, go to sleep,' he said, feeling his phone vibrate with an incoming message. He looked down to check it, and then looked up again, while pulling the door shut. She stood in the middle of the room, her feet planted firmly like she was trying to root herself into the floor, to prevent being pulled out. Her eyes, when she looked at him were black smudges, no white showed at all. He shivered, little realising he'd seen something she'd never ever let him see before, someone she'd never let him see before. She smiled at him, a suddenly radiant smile almost as if she had just registered his presence, a smile that was otherworldly. For a flash of a second he imagined he saw something else behind her, a shadow that shifted. Then immediate darkness, followed by a sound that felt like the earth was splitting apart, followed by a silence so complete he could hear his heart thudding. He blinked, and it was gone, the door was shut and he was just imagining things, the day was bright, the sun was shining outside, the lift pinged as it arrived on the floor he was on, somewhere a telephone rang, someone in the flat across the passageway began a loud and angry conversation, cars honked at the gate and a child called out to a friend.

As he got into the car, he dialled the therapist. There was a familiarity that allowed him to do so, he was already informally in contact with her to manage Sukanya's medications. Sukanya was easier, all she had now were crippling anxiety attacks that she had slowly learnt to take control of. The therapy had helped, years of it. Talking, recreating the situations that triggered the panic, learning how to respond to them, and now on maintenance visits to monitor the medication and her state of mind, she was much better. Ana, he had suspected already, would be different, very different.

'I'm glad you called,' the therapist told him. 'We will need to have a proper conversation about this. I'm afraid, Aman, this is much more serious than you could have ever imagined, much more than social anxiety and depression.'

He felt his heart sink to his toes. She continued, 'It isn't advisable for her to live unsupervised anymore.'

22

And in the Beginning is the End

'There is no real ending. It's just the place where you stop the story.'

—Frank Herbert

THE MORNING WAS IRRITATINGLY BRIGHT. SHE COULD SENSE that from her bed. The bed with its regulation white painted steel rod guards on either side to keep a patient from falling off. No chance of her falling off, she couldn't move, she had been immobile for over a decade now, or was it two? The curtains were drawn across, gaudily patterned vivid red cabbage roses printed on a cheap fabric, possibly bought in bulk by the contractor who had thought them cheerful additions to the gloom of the institution. Or possibly they were so ugly that they were offered at a throwaway price.

She wouldn't mind the ugliness of the curtains, and even if she did, she would not complain. The visitors who came occasionally to check on her and make their reports wouldn't care too. The ones who entered the room on a regular basis did their tasks with the formality of the professionally trained, aseptic and mechanical. But those curtains... were too determinedly ugly and cheerful when they had no right to be. She was not supposed to have been able to see them. But she had.

She could feel the seasons change, the nights now chilly for these tropical latitudes. This was a sanatorium in a hill station in the Western Ghats, a few hours away from Mumbai. The building was old, built of black stone, the summers were hot and winters were cold in the rooms. No one had considered that she might need something warmer, a quilt perhaps, or a blanket, brown and rough as most institutions supplied to their residents. The thin cotton sheet that covered her was functional for modesty, the body beneath long withered to be bothered about any sense of propriety. She didn't feel sensation, she was inured to heat and cold they thought. They had poked her with pins, tested her with heat and cold, shone lights into her eyes, spoken with her, played music to her. She had been unresponsive. Permanently vegetative. Permission to withdraw life support had been requested for years ago. It had been denied. Who was it who had decided that she needed to live, no one knew, when her own mother had decided she needed to die. Lack of oxygen to the brain, supply cut off. A pillow over her face, smothering her. Mother's love. Mothers could nurture. Mothers could also kill.

There was movement in the room, the morning nurse had arrived; she recognised the heavy footsteps, the whine of the trolley's wheels with the basin and towels with which she would be sponge cleaned. The nurse would enter the room, pause, look around and then go to the window to draw the curtains open, those horrible shiny floral curtains with the bright red and pink roses splotched like blood stains. This was Maa now. Not her real Maa, of course, but close enough. She had cared for her longer than her real Maa ever had. She would sponge her, change her diaper, change the sheets if it was bed sheet change day, check her tubes, the wires that hooked her up to the systems that monitored her, beeping with a soothing regularity.

Her real Maa had killed herself after trying to kill her. Maa had failed to kill her but had managed to take enough of the pills to kill herself, so here she was a vegetable lying on a bed, fed through tubes, living in a flesh sack that did not respond to her commands. It had been a double blow. First her father, then her mother. To live a life enclosed in a body that was an unresponsive cage because two attempts to kill her had failed. Both by her very own parents.

She knew about the first, she didn't know about the second. By the second attempt she was already a cripple, p ysed waist down, fast asleep with the dosage administered to kill her. Maa had calculated wrong. The pills had merely knocked her out. Then the pillow had cut off oxygen to her brain, a misplaced attempt to smother her. But not enough to kill her. She had lain unaware, for hours, beside the body of her mother.

She was the girl who refused to die. That's what they called her, her photographs making headlines across the newspapers for days, as the reading public lapped up the vicarious horror of a young girl now condemned to live out her life in a permanently vegetative paraplegic state.

'It's a bright day today,' Maa said, this Maa, as she gently sponged Nayna clean.

'It was a bright day the day I tried to kill you,' Maa said, the other Maa, who wouldn't leave her even though she was dead. She sat on the divan in the room or floated near the ceiling when she visited, which wasn't too often these days. Maa was forgetting her too.

This Maa smelt of talcum powder and soap. She sponged her out with an antiseptic soap solution that smelt sharp. It wasn't a perfunctory sponging with the haste of getting the job done, it was a duty performed with care and affection, love perhaps, a love that she could not lavish on her own, far as she was from home. The damp towel was warm and soothing, just like she preferred it, and it smelt of strong disinfectant. Unbidden, a memory flashed through Nayna's mind of Maa cleaning a scrape on the knee with Dettol, her own eyes filling up with tears as the disinfectant stung Nayna and she squealed with pain. Maa was such a softie, she could never bear pain, either her own, or another's. How she had ever managed to give birth, Nayna wondered. Nayna hadn't given birth though. She wouldn't know how painful it actually was. She would never know. The rape had been painful enough to need hospitalisation until she had healed. Pappa had jumped from the shame of not being able to protect her. Shame that wasn't his. Wasn't hers. Shame she did not understand. She had jumped too, there had been pain but no death. Maa had died, after trying to kill Nayna. She wondered if Maa and Pappa had met in the Greyness.

Right now, the person on the bed was someone she had not wanted to grow into. But there it was, the creature that was her. The skeletal face, with the unnatural pallor of the skin, unexposed to the warmth of the sun's rays, smooth and blanched, stretched taut over the facial bones. Her hair was close to the scalp, a growing out from the perfunctory shaving that made her completely bald every few months. It made for easy manageability. Maa would oil and wash her long waist-length hair twice a week, making her dry it in the sun, then tie it in two tight plaits for school. She would close her eyes when Maa combed her hair, yanking it hard, pulling at the roots, wincing from the pain.

At this moment, her eyes were closed not from pain, for she didn't feel any. At others they were open. Unresponsive both when closed and open. The doctor came twice a week to check her, open her eyelids to check her reactions to the light of a thin torch he shone into her pupils. Her eyes were grey, her hair was black, her skin was white. She remembered that from the last she had looked at herself in the mirror, her features so sharply perfect they could have been chiselled by a master sculptor. She would grow up to be a beauty like her mother, they had said. She would become a model, a film actress, a beauty queen. Maa had discouraged such talk. 'She's going to be a doctor. She has the brains. Why should she get into that terrible world where she will only be valued for her beauty?'

She had never understood what was terrible about that world then, she barely understood it now. But she knew that sometimes, when the ward was dark, the lights were dimmed and the night was deep, a ward boy would slither into the room, squeeze her shrivelled breasts, suck on them and then masturbate onto her. She would lie there, eyes shut, or open, unresponsive. Sometimes, she detached and hovered over him, whispering secrets he thought no one knew into his ear in words of ice and rain. He would stop with a start, look around, his erection deflated and ridiculous in its flaccidity, before slinking out of the room swiftly, looking to check if his intrusion had been detected. In a time before CCTVs, watchmen dozed and night nurses napped behind counters, hoping the bells summoning them didn't ring. The third time he came into her room in the dark of the night, pushing her hospital gown up, wrenching her pipes and catheter out of her and clambering on to the bed, she detached and sat on his head, an icy cold fog that pierced his brain and discombobulated his memories. He screamed and fled in terror, almost tripping over the landing, his diminished penis flapping as he ran, falling, picking himself up, falling again. Lights came on, voices were raised, much brouhaha happened. The night nurses rushed into her room and found her, legs splayed open, shrivelled vagina on full display, clean shaven as it was always maintained, pre-pubertal always. Like time had frozen for her at the instant of her fall. She lay there, as she always did, like a stone. The only proof that she still existed within that skeletal frame was the beating of her heart, the pulsing of her blood in her veins and arteries, thick, red, warm, alive. She had persisted. After all, she was the girl who refused to die.

'Jump, Nayna.'

'Jump, Ana.'

'Jump, Sue.'

She had jumped. She hadn't. Sometimes she wondered if she had. Or she hadn't. It all blurred into the other, the moment, the climbing up, the jumping off towards the man lying splayed on the ground below, the drawing back and twisting the curtains to the balcony in an unspeakable terror, knowing that she had betrayed him, she hadn't followed him as he had instructed her to. She had followed him. She wondered who she was. Was she the one who lay here, broken, a rag doll? Or was she the one who had gone on to live her life, the one who came to visit her occasionally and held her hand when she did, wracked with guilt?

'Ana,' he had said, 'Would you come with me to a special place?'

She had nodded, her eyes wide and curious. Where was this special place she asked him. 'Up beyond the clouds,' he replied.

'Do we have to go by aeroplane?'

He laughed and shook his head. There were beads of sweat on his forehead, she remembered; it had struck her as incongruous then because it wasn't warm at all, it was the monsoon, it was raining outside, the house was cold and damp from the incessantness of it all, the greyness of the sky, the pelting of the rain, the fetid sweet stench of rotting garbage from the uncleared bin outside the gate mingling with the sharp acridity of the marshland gases drifting in from beyond the compound wall on the other side.

'No, I have a shorter route, a quicker and cheaper route. But don't tell your mother, okay? It will be our secret.'

She nodded excitedly. Her father adored her. He adored her all the more because she was the exact replica of her mother, from her delicately sharp features to her grey eyes and her masses of black waves, bequeathed to them by an errant gene of a coloniser who had tumbled into their bloodstream before these things were spoken about. He loved her in a fierce way that he couldn't explain but she sensed it was because her mother would not allow herself to be loved by him as unconditionally. She could never understand why her mother despised her father. Not even the barest pretence of affection or tolerance. Just a deep-seated loathing that percolated down to the marrow and vibrated in the home, a loathing that dampened the walls, the furniture, the mood and flattened everything.

The whispers she would hear afterwards, after it happened.

'It was the shame, he couldn't bear it.'

'Poor Mandira, to lose a husband and then the daughter. As good as dead.'

Her mother had tried to care for her. It was impossible to take care of a child who could not move, without financial support or a family around her. Relatives stepped away when they realised that they might be called upon for help, leaving Mandira to fend for herself and her daughter. When she decided to kill both of them Nayna knew. She knew the dose of pills she was being given to swallow was more than her usual medication. She swallowed nonetheless, she was an obedient girl, she listened to her mother, she always did.

When Mandira gave her the pills and then put the pillow over her face, she too had hoped for death. She hadn't protested, not in the least. Maa was doing it for the best, this was no way to live, there was no way they could survive in this world. And Mandira had taken the pills after she thought Nayna was quite dead. But Nayna wasn't. She was the girl who would not die. These were not Nayna's memories, these were her memories, the other one's. The one who visited, wracked with guilt. Nayna had been too young to have memories, a toddler, brushing her teeth at the mirror.

She lived in the hospital, where she became the orphan the nurses took to their hearts. She became their cause, the collective daughter of the nursing staff, the daughter the matron had never had, the younger sister the ward nurse, Bessy, had left behind in a village in Kerala who had run off and got married to an unsuitable man, the cousin the lab attendant had played with in her childhood in Bihar, who had died by suicide after being raped by the strongmen of the village. Everyone saw in her someone they had lost, someone precious to them.

They checked her every day, monitored her vitals, fed her intravenously, cleaned her, kept her free from bedsores, moved her joints and muscles to keep them exercised and mobile, brushed her teeth, changed her catheter and diaper. They put the television set on to channels that played songs continuously, sat and chatted with her, told her their stories and secrets that they knew she would not be able to repeat to anyone. She was well looked after.

The sun had climbed higher into the sky outside, bleaching it white. Feeble warmth crept into the room. If she could see, she would have seen the dappling of watery sunlight through the leaves of the mango tree outside the barred window. The matron came later to check on her. She was kind, the matron. She would stroke her head, check her vitals, make a daily report and send it off each week. To whom, she did not know.

The clock on the wall ticked on, in a strange slowed-down way, while at times it accelerated inexplicably, the ticking. The silence amplified the ticking, making it ominous at times, comforting at others. Time moved on footsteps that were playful, then hurried, scampered, dragged, and skulked as the mood took it. She hadn't lost track of time, time had lost track of her.

The voices around her had gone silent, there were ringing footsteps coming down the corridor, entering the room, echoes of unfamiliar voices bouncing off tiled, sterile walls. She chose not to respond to anything. Not to sounds, not to voices, not to heat, not to cold, not to pain, not to hunger, not to thirst. Perhaps if she wanted to, she could have, back then. When she had first stepped into the Greyness of this limbo, perhaps she could have dragged herself out if she tried. Now she had forgotten how to, after all these years, these decades. Too much time had passed. Too many lives had been lived out in the interim.

Her jump hadn't killed her, but it had snapped her spine.

Her father had landed on concrete. He had died on impact. The pillow hadn't killed her, it had cut off her oxygen for a long while to her brain. Skin and bone. Fed intravenously. Breathing through a pipe. Muscles atrophied, body emaciated, eyes sunken, she was still glorious. A skeleton yes. But a glorious one. Within her, the light still shone, a light that continued to keep the world fascinated with her.

She detached from within herself to see who the footsteps belonged to. She could detach at will now, it had taken her years of practice, after all, she did have all the time in the world to practice after she had been snatched from her time and her body and attached to this one. The one who had been attached to this body now lived in hers. Had grown up in hers. All she had done was sneeze and flown out of her body. It had been a switch she had not agreed to.

She was visited often by strangers, after all, she was a case study. There were four people in the room. One was an older lady, with frizzy white hair held off her face with a cloth scrunchie. She held a file in her hand and was taking careful notes as she checked the room and the surroundings.

The second was a young man, the one with the whiny, petulant voice, crisp in a sky-blue shirt and carefully pressed trousers. There was someone doing the work for him. A laundry. A parent at home. A wife. He did not have the air of someone who managed himself.

The third person in the room was a young woman, dressed in a block-printed salwar kameez. She ran her hand nervously through her hair as she spoke. Her voice was quick and light, her eyes stayed focused on the bed and the person within it, and her hand lingered on the side of the bed, in indecision as to whether she should dare to touch the person lying on the bed or whether she should keep a distance. She was compassionate, this one, she could sense it.

'Well, that should be quite enough for this report back to

the trustees,' said the older lady. 'This is one case they always ask about in detail. She is the inexplicable one.'

The man scuffed a shoe on the gleaming tiles and cleared his throat hesitantly, 'As I said, she makes for great optics and PR for them.'

'No,' said the older lady, shaking her head so violently that her frizzy white mane bobbed up and down. 'Someone on the board is personally invested in this case. We don't know who it is though. Anyway, let's discuss the report in the conference room, my legs have done enough standing for the day.' She winced as she turned around, walking slowly out of the room. The other two followed her, speaking in low whispers.

She watched them move out and continued to hover above the bed, taking in the entire room from her vantage point. There was one more person in the room, in the corner, against the window. Ana. She was here. Standing so absolutely still she might have been a statue. She said nothing; she was waiting for the others to clear out from the room. She had changed, her face softer, older; the fiercely angry beauty of her early twenties had been tempered down with a calm that she had not had before. Her hair still tumbled down to her waist in an unruly mess, like the chaos of dark water cascading down a hillside. Her eyes a grey that was steel, ice, pewter, mercury, all at once. No one in the room noticed her beauty, because no one noticed her, their backs were towards her. She waited a while till they were out of the room, then drew a quick breath and moved towards the bed.

She put her hand on Nayna's head and stroked it. The newly formed curls were soft to the touch. She was her. In another time, another life, in this body.

'How have you been?' she asked. Her voice was low and soft, like she didn't want to be overheard by anyone. The rounds were done with for the morning, and the next round would happen in the afternoon. No one would come this way for many hours now, this room at the distant end of the corridor, where nothing existed but this reminder that life continued even when the body was broken beyond repair. The mirror that had brought her here, still rippling over the small washbasin at the other end of the room, the path within swirling and unclear, the portal waiting for her to return and then to close over.

'There are many, too many. I can't change everyone's path. I shouldn't have, I regret my decision every day of my life. I was scared, I was selfish.'

She hovered over Ana, feeding off her love and warmth, looking down on Ana and herself, seeing her eyes move beneath the closed lids as her brain responded weakly to Ana's voice.

'You know what you need to do,' she told her, in the way one can tell another part of oneself. 'It will set the wrong right, free me, free you. It will never stop otherwise, you will keep shifting, keep falling through time.'

'I don't have the courage,' Ana replied, her voice hushed and awash with the guilt that had never really left her, which had followed her for the decades since she had done the unspeakable. The room was silent, only the whirring of the fan punctuated the outside noises from the gardens that surrounded the sanatorium; birds peeped into the room from the window and then quickly returned themselves back to the outside, wary of the unearthliness transpiring within the room.

There would be release, Ana realised, and not just for Nayna. Perhaps it was time to do it, to end it all. She walked over to the spare bed at the other end of the room, the bed meant for the accompanying relative of a patient to sleep in. This one was always empty. She picked up the pillow, stared at it like it was something she was unfamiliar with, not a regular everyday item of use, flattened by age and lack of use. No one had stayed the night to watch over Nayna ever, this pillow merely decorative. Now finally, it had purpose, it would serve its task. Then she walked back to the bed, looked at the creature lying within, of no use or purpose to anyone or anything, not even herself. She stroked her head, the tears welling up in her eyes and then spilling down her cheeks. Then she unhooked her from all the tubes and wires monitoring her, and neatened her up. When she put the pillow on her face and bore down with all her strength, there was nothing, no gasp, no struggle, no response. She hadn't expected any. The only thing that pressed down on her in that tiny, airless room, sterile with the smell of disinfectant, was the weight of release, a weight that stayed with her through her journey back into her time. Nayna lay on the bed, her eyes open, lifeless, her body the way it always was, but the essence no longer tethered to it. Nayna would go back to life in the body that Ana had snatched from her when she had been a child. Ana was free now to float away into the blackness of eternity where there was nothing, no time, no pain, no life, no death

The mirror above the wash basin had stopped rippling, it would never ripple again, what needed to pass had passed through, never to return.

Months later, in another room, within the glass chrome facade of the newly built wing of another institution, Ana lay with her eyes closed. Aman held her hand. 'When do you think she will come out of it?' he asked the doctor standing next to him.

'The closest I can explain is like she has gone into hibernation. You know, how bears go into a long, deep sleep through the winter months. I have never seen a case like this. If it is hibernation, she's defied all we know of medical science, our own modern Rip Van Winkle, have you heard about him?'

He had read about him, a man who slept for twenty years and missed an entire revolution. How many years would Ana sleep? Hibernation was different, he knew, it was just a matter of months. Creatures somehow knew how to slow down their metabolism in the cold months. It kept them alive in the months when food was scarce and foraging was impossible because of the cold and snow. Low body temperature, minimal heart rate and dropping the metabolic rate by almost 99 percent. Barely alive. But humans didn't hibernate. There was no known case of such a thing. Humans evolved in the tropical and subtropical climates, their bodies didn't adapt to winter and by the time they migrated to the zones where ice and snow swept the skies, they had discovered fire and furs to keep them warm. Humans had yet not figured out how to drop their temperatures at will, how to regulate their metabolism. Except for murmurs of ascetics in remote caves in the Himalayas, said to look like they were young men when they were, in fact, hundreds of years old, human beings were yet to figure out how their metabolism could be controlled at will. Ana would come out of it, he told himself, she was just sleeping. She had been ill and tired and perennially exhausted, her body had shut itself down.

'I will wait. She will come out of it.' She would come out of it, he knew, and he would wait. Sukanya had agreed to a divorce, it seemed pointless continuing a marriage with a man who was living to care for another woman.

She had been found in what seemed like a dead faint in her bedroom. The mirror, which had been unrippled in this new house, was smashed, the debris and the shards surrounded her, like an intricate performative installation. He had picked her up, uncaring of the splinters drawing blood where they pierced skin, and rushed her to the nearest hospital.

Days, weeks were now a couple of months. There was nothing to be done but wait for her to emerge from the deep stasis she was in with only the low, faint beeping of her heart on the monitor asserting she was still alive. She lay immobile, unresponsive, locked within the body she had now been slammed back into, her own body, one that was now alien to her. She had been attached to one that remained immobile for far too long. And so she lay on the bed, reacquainting herself with her now grown-up body, its limbs and its abilities alien to her, having withdrawn deep within herself because now that was the only way she knew to be, the only way she had been all these years, poring over the memories of this new body, taking her time deciding whether she indeed wanted to emerge from the hidden recesses of its consciousness and live out the life that had been denied to her.

Acknowledgements

And just like that, it is time for the thank yous. If you've reached this part of the book, you've persisted through it and for that, thank you, my dear reader, for sticking with me through this journey, where we're all confronting what it means to know that the only thing that is certain is that nothing at all is certain.

I would be remiss if I didn't begin by thanking Rashmi Menon, my absolutely wonderful editor at Amaryllis. Rashmi has been the powerhouse behind my three previous books with Amaryllis, *The Face at the Window, Missing, Presumed Dead* and *More Things in Heaven and Earth,* and now with *All Those Who Wander*. It is a journey and a friendship that began when I hesitantly sent out the manuscript of *The Face at the Window* to her, after a kind introduction by the very gracious Rupa Gulab. Rashmi is an editor I have worked with four times and will keep returning to over and over again if she will have my books, because she has believed in my writing, in a way nobody has, championed it, and encouraged me. I am truly blessed to have her as my editor at Amaryllis. And I am more blessed to have her as a dear friend.

The second thank you is to Shinie Antony. Because Shinie is Shinie, and Shinie gave me, in her gentle, calm and precise manner, the much-needed confidence about my writing that I had tucked away in the trunk of my aspirations, telling myself that perhaps, I am not good enough, not worthy enough.

To the wonderful team at Amaryllis, Vikas Rakheja, Manoj Kulkarni, Ankita Menghwani. Thank you for this book, and all the previous ones, for the trust, the respect and the faith in my work.

Mishta Roy of Drawater, who I trust to give my books the most exquisite covers ever, you've surpassed yourself with this one, Mishta.

To my lovely family, my mother, my mother-in-law, my sisters-in-law, thank you for being supportive of my writing, of letting me be as antisocial as I please and to get my writing done. To Krish, for being my bouncing board when I ideate, and coming up with the strange and unusual insights that only a teen can bring to the table, and the plot holes I didn't quite spot. You are the purpose and the meaning to all I do. And finally, thank you to Kirit, in every universe I inhabit, in whatever version of myself, I will always be seeking you. Thank god you don't read any of my books.